About the Author

Shiralee Willett grew up on a farm in Queensland and she has always loved reading, so to be able to show her book to the world is like a dream come true.

Forgotten Heir

Shiralee Willett

Forgotten Heir

Olympia Publishers
London

www.olympiapublishers.com
OLYMPIA PAPERBACK EDITION

Copyright © Shiralee Willett 2023

The right of Shiralee Willett to be identified as author of
this work has been asserted in accordance with sections 77 and 78 of
the Copyright, Designs and Patents Act 1988.

All Rights Reserved

No reproduction, copy or transmission of this publication
may be made without written permission.
No paragraph of this publication may be reproduced,
copied or transmitted save with the written permission of the publisher,
or in accordance with the provisions
of the Copyright Act 1956 (as amended).

Any person who commits any unauthorised act in relation to
this publication may be liable to criminal
prosecution and civil claims for damage.

A CIP catalogue record for this title is
available from the British Library.

ISBN: 978-1-80439-177-8

This is a work of fiction.
Names, characters, places and incidents originate from the writer's
imagination. Any resemblance to actual persons, living or dead, is
purely coincidental.

First Published in 2023

Olympia Publishers
Tallis House
2 Tallis Street
London
EC4Y 0AB

Printed in Great Britain

Dedication

To Kylie, this is for you. You are a mother who deserves so much more but for now, this is what I can give you. Thank you for always being there for me.

Acknowledgements

To Jess, my sister, for giving me the courage to write this book. To my grandmother for being with me for the entire process. To Matilda, for always being so invested in the idea.

CHAPTER 1

Crimson leaves of huge trees with twisted trunks gleam and rustle with the first frost of the morning. Their bark permanently stained with the deep red of an ancient battle long ago between the gods, which is why the Blood Wood Forest is avoided by many of the village people of Fallen Crest. Not even seasoned hunters dare venture too deep into the forest, but unfortunately for me, this is not the case. Winter has quickly descended and with it the animals have moved deeper into the forest, looking for soft tufts of lasting Autumn grasses. My bow begins to dig into my back where it is crushed against a boulder, and every time I move, the string twangs as it drags across the jagged edges of the rock. I try to keep still as the sound makes me think of a violin with only one cord playing the same drowsy tune. It is no easy feat, though, as I've been sitting here letting my legs go numb since the first flicker of fading starlight. Waiting for what I hope will be a small deer or a family of rabbits that can at least feed me and my family for a few weeks. If I don't bring home a reasonable kill, my family will most likely eat me instead, although they might think better of it since I'm the one that keeps them fed. My family, like many of the village folk, are vultures, feeding on the weak and defenceless and leaving nothing behind but the scraps that even wild dogs won't touch.

Even though it's only been a few weeks since my last kill, I am already looking malnourished. My cheeks are hollow, my hair is dull, and my body is thin and brittle. My threadbare clothing hangs loosely around my frame and I look more like a milk crate then a young woman, but at least that keeps away any of the lowly scum the town calls men. I once lived in a time where I didn't have to worry about catching a meal or the dramas of peasant boys looking for a tussle in the hay to satisfy their 'manly needs'. My family was wealthy and came from generations of traders and merchants. We used to live in a manor not far from town, but my kind and loving mother died ten years ago when I was eight and left my father to sour and gamble our wealth away. Although I can't give him all the credit, he did remarry a horrid woman with two children who helped spend the last of our fortune on silks and balls fit for a queen.

The snapping of a twig breaks the spell cast over me and I pull my bow into position, locking in an arrow at the same time. The gods must be on my side as a small young buck creeps around the icy clearing, nudging the snow with his nose. The buck's antlers are small and barely protrude through its thick winter coat. The coat in question is shiny and holds summer health, it's painted with the fading white freckles of his youth, which means his meat will be tender. My mouth waters at the fact. He doesn't notice me crouched behind the boulder as it's taller than me by a head and almost twice as round. The buck foolishly drops his guard, letting his nose bury deeper into the snow, his elegant ears twitch, but his eyes close slightly as he chews on a submerged bramble bush. I remember when I was twelve, killing my first rabbit and sitting near its dead body, watching steam rise from it while crying for the life I took. It was then that I realised that I must detach myself from my feelings when hunting. Over time, I got used to the feeling of blood running though my fingers and the heavy weight that never leaves me. I shiver as the snow I've been collecting on my coat begins to melt onto my already frozen skin. Flakes of snow drift down from the surrounding trees, giving the area a fairy-tale feel.

A shiver that has nothing to do with the cold caresses down my back, it feels as if I'm being watched and hunted instead of the deer in front of me. I shake the feeling off. Many village ladies like to gossip and spread rumours to benefit their thirst for drama. It's one of the many reasons I couldn't bring myself to sit with them like my stepsisters do. Stories over time become more myth than truth, but one story that has never changed and will never change, as if they fear it will rain havoc down upon the liar, is that of the unforgiving and cruel Fae. Fae are immortal and can lure innocent humans to their death, or worse, keep them as their slaves in their pristine manors, making them drunk on Faerie wine and poisoning them with the sweet juices of their fruit. Throughout my early learning at school, the teachers warned us about them and told us to never trust our human senses when around the Fae and the human borders of their land, Thyithran. Legends have it that there are six courts within Thyithran and that they are ruled by their most powerful lords, which seems ridiculous to me as who needs six leaders in such a small land? My attention snaps back to the buck as he perks up and shifts nervously on his feet, but he's not looking at me, he is instead staring at the bush to my left. I try and shake the eerie feeling and aim my bow and arrow for the killing shot. My hands shake slightly, and I steady them. Just as I'm about to release my string, a blur of white blocks my vision, which to most people would be normal considering its snowing, but in place of snow falling to the ground, it's a large white wolf the size of a small horse. Its massive paws land silently on the ground in front of the startled buck before its sharp teeth clamp around the deer's neck. A gurgling sound akin to a choking child escapes the deer before it goes limp in the wolf's mouth. This beast is too large to be a native wolf and too graceful to have come from the human side of the border. I still myself from behind the boulder and watch as the beast drags the deer deeper into the forest, leaving a trail of blood in its path. Out of stupidity, or something similar, I edge around the rock and slink into the darkening forest, following the tracks of the wolf. I need this kill and can't have the wolf tearing apart the buck. My steps are light, and I watch for roots or rocks that could trip me. I walk for what could be no more than ten minutes before a flash of white makes me pause. The beast is nudging the buck with its large head. The buck's body shifts under the weight of the wolf and the sight turns my stomach slightly. Before I lose my nerve, I pull an arrow from my sling and put it in place. I have never used this arrow before, since it's of pure iron, one of the only things able to kill a Fae apart from crushed mandrake mushroom. Its intricate design shimmers in the growing light of dawn and I pull my courage from it. I look up and find the wolf is no longer playing with the lifeless deer but is staring at me from where I'm crouching behind a bush. My heart lurches and I find myself standing to get ready to run, but the low growling stops me in my tracks. The wolf is crouched on its haunches, getting ready to strike, it's massive teeth gleaming in the morning light, and before I have time to think, I draw back my bow string and aim for the soft tissue of the wolf's unnaturally blue eyes. I release my string and watch in slow motion as the arrow hits its target and the beast falls to the ground with an ear-piercing howl. The wolf's now still body lets off a soft glow, almost as if the sun itself is mourning the loss. As I creep closer with another utterly useless wood arrow notched, I begin to see its coat shimmering in a way that makes it look as if there has been a thread of sliver stitched in swirls throughout its fur. I grab my knife from my belt and kneel before its massive head. Its pelt would probably sell for a few pennies in the town's market tomorrow, so I begin to skin it and pray to anyone that may be listening that I didn't just skin a Faerie.

After an hour of trudging through knee-deep snow with the buck slung over my shoulder and the wolf's pelt around my hips, the village comes into view. Its dark and meek buildings leech the surrounding light from the sun and leaves everything looking sad and desperate. I hate this place more than what is healthy to hate something. It reminds me of my family's downfall and the suffering I've had to endure because of my father and his wife. The snow on the ground thins and turns into mud from where all the people walk, it's as if we are living in a human pig sty. The potent smell of flattened mud and offal makes me crinkle my nose. My family's hut, if you could even call it that, is separated from the rest of the town's buildings. Its one window gleams in the morning sun and I approach it carefully, hoping that it's still too early for my stepsisters to be awake. The door of the hut is hidden amongst weeds and dead rose bushes, the handle is rusted and barely takes the weight of people opening it. I close my eyes and slowly open the door, trying to avoid the squeak of the rusty hinges. To my dismay, the door groans and shudders as it gets caught on the uneven floor. I silently curse myself for not fixing it sooner. Coughing comes from one of two bedrooms we have, and I stifle a moan. There's no use trying to be quiet any more, so I shuffle into the main room and dump the buck onto the pathetic excuse of a table, which is just a few milk crates stacked on top of each other with an old door nailed to the top, and make my way to the chair opposite the chimney. The wolf's pelt is a heavy weight around my waist, and I gently place it on the chair without sparing a glance at it. My sisters laugh and giggle and I turn around. They are sure to have noticed the large pelt and would be planning ways to make me give them the money from it. Laura, the eldest out of us three, leans against the opening to our bedroom and snorts in a strangely lady-like way. Her dark brown hair is tied back from her face in a braid, and she somehow makes the rags that we call clothes look presentable. She would be pretty if she didn't constantly wear a sneer on her face, like she wasn't the one who was poor and living in a hut.

"I thought I heard a rat sneaking around somewhere. Have you brought back something to eat?"

It never ceased to amaze me how she made everything sound like an insult. I don't know where they got the idea that calling me a rat would offend me, but even I can admit it is one of the tamer names I've been called.

"Wouldn't you like to know," I mumble as I grab a knife from the bench to start carving up the buck. "I thought you would be in town trying to weasel your way into Ben Havey's pants."

I smirk to myself at the look on her face and turn back to the deer.

"I wouldn't be so smart if I were you, Keilee. I'm not the one covered in mud and smelling like death."

I snort and point the handle of the knife at her.

"Well, why don't you carve up the buck while I go and clean myself?"

I knew what the answer would be before she has a chance to open her mouth. It is always the same, I have the responsibility of killing the animals and then skinning it and carving it up, along with every other chore in the house.

"I'm not touching that. It's your job, not mine."

She turns her nose up at me and stalks into the bedroom,

where Isabella will be waiting for the news of my kill and anything else that would be worthy of gossip. Isabella was the prettiest out of all of us. She is the middle child, and she has a face that could turn heads. Her hair is identical to Laura's, but she has the deepest hazel eyes I've ever seen. Many people are fooled by her beauty and are blinded to the monster that hides beneath her skin. Isabella's laugh bounces off the walls and I roll my eyes. Soon I will be forced to venture into town with them and made to give them part of my earnings from the wolf's pelt. Laura will most likely complain about not having enough for a new coat and Isabella will want a new dress, all things which they don't need. Whereas I need new boots to hunt with and yet I will be the selfish one. I will be the one spending our money on silly things. Once I'm finished with the buck and wipe my knife clean, my father and his wife come out of their room and walk to the table. Alice's blonde hair swings from the force of snapping her head towards me from where I'm standing near the fireplace, trying to escape to my room in peace. I am tired and my patience is running very thin.

"Haven't you been to town already? We need the money for your father's treatment."

I almost laugh at that; my father's treatment consists of rum and whiskey. Alice makes excuses and says he needs it for his bad back, but in reality, she is just scared to say no to him.

"I was going to wait until tomorrow, so the pelts have time to dry."

I clench my hands into fists waiting for her reply. I should know by now not to question her as it always backfires on me. My father's eyes widen once he spots the wolf's pelt still draped across the chair near the chimney.

"Where did you get that? Did you steal it, you little thief?"

His tone is slurred and his words are broken, as if he can't concentrate on stringing a sentence together without some difficulty. It wasn't even midday, and he was already drunk. I resist the urge to ignore him, but that would only land me with a bruised cheek, or the three mountain lions standing behind him would pounce and injure me with more than drunken swings. My sisters and Alice smile at me coyly from behind him, waiting for me to dig my grave and lie in it.

"I didn't steal it. I killed a wolf in the forest when I was hunting and I thought it's pelt would make us some extra money."

My father scoffs as if he doesn't believe me. My nails are beginning to dig into my palm from where my hands are still clenched.

"I… I don't want anyone knocking at my door complaining that someone stole…" my father closes his eyes and rubs a hand over his enraged face. "From them. And if they do, I won't hesitate to hand you over.'"

I didn't doubt his words, he would rather face starvation then have to suffer the consequences of defending me.

"Well, its lucky that I didn't steal it then, isn't it?"

Alice's face drops into a scowl and she moves forward from her position next to Laura. My sisters' smiles widen, and they look like hawks who have just found a mouse playing in the grass.

"Don't talk to your father like that. He is doing what's right for his family, and he doesn't want some low life daughter to bring disgrace to his household."

I fight hard to keep still and not lunge at Isabella, who is pulling a face behind my father's back. I grit my teeth and try to keep my growing anger from my voice as I reply.

"Sorry, Father, I promise you that I did not steal anything, I will go to town tomorrow and cash in the pelts."

My horrid stepmother takes a seat next to him and places a hand over his. My father shakes his head and grunts something that I suppose is a dismissal. I unclench my hands and slink off to my room to change out of my hunting clothes. Life wasn't supposed to be fair and easy, but it also wasn't supposed to be cruel and miserable. I once dreamed of a life where I could live freely and have enough money to buy books that could take me to a different world. But now I would be lucky to have enough freedom to own my own blank journal.

Chapter 2

The sun rose slowly, its golden rays casting a soft yellow light on the hut, but by then I was already folding the buck and wolf pelts into my bag. Laura and Isabella were still sleeping, and as much as I wanted to leave them here, the repercussions wouldn't be worth it, so I creep up to the small bed we share. And by we, I mean my sisters sleep on the bed and me on the floor. Laura is on her stomach with her head facing away from me, so I carefully grab my boots from the floor and slam them onto the bedframe, causing both girls to jump and grab for each other. I turn away looking innocent while they both glare at me and throw a pillow, which I catch with one hand.

"Now, that's not very lady-like is it, you two? Hurry up and get changed. I'm leaving for town in ten minutes."

Isabella makes a vulgar gesture and I scoff at the notion.

"Why can't we leave later in the day when the sun is actually awake?" Isabella's voice is masked with sleep and Laura looks as if she is sleeping upright.

"Money doesn't wait for the sun to rise properly, or for people who whine, so I suggest you get a move on."

Both girls look irritated but get up without further comment, which in my book is a good start to the day.

It is more than ten minutes before we start to head to town along the worn, muddy tracks. My hands are frozen and numb from where the cold winter wind seeps through my gloves. I am several paces in front of my sisters as they try and fail to avoid getting mud on the long skirts of their dresses. It is barely six in the morning and the village is already alight with people carrying baskets of food and clothing. Children duck and weave between people walking and I'm almost tempted to stick my foot out and trip them. Their joy angers me, as they are carefree while I'm stuck baby-sitting my older sisters. Market day is always busy and was the time for thieves to hunt and beggars to beg. Many of the wealthier townsfolk dwell around the stalls of jewellery and clothing, trying to ignore the constant pestering of the scroungers to give them a few pennies. Even though I am poor, I would never beg. Something about the act would bring a weakness to me that I wouldn't be used to. Relying on peoples' kindness was a waste of time. They would sooner rather see the gods awaken than give people money. Bells from my left sound and I stifle a groan. It wasn't the loud echoing rings of the hall tower; it was the soft and insufferable jingling of the Holy Marchers. Their deep blue coats and gold trimmed hoods sway in the bitter winter wind, their voices echo the songs of the Fae culture. The Holy Marchers worshipped the Fae as if they were gods and preached of their kindness and loyalty to humans. The sight of people walking hurriedly past the marchers holding out a string of bluebell flowers almost makes me laugh. Bluebells are supposed to ward off any enchantments that could have caused the marchers' obsession with the Fae.

I thought it was pointless and that the marchers were just idiots who were ignorant and blind not to see the suffering we all endure because of the Fae. The ancient battle of the gods was proof enough. The story goes that the gods ruled over the world in peace and the Fae and humans lived beside each other in harmony, but then the Fae started to think they were better, with their extended life and unnatural powers, and they started resisting the rule of the gods. This led the gods to choose sides and the battle went down, with Malki, ruler of Earth and Sea, along with Danti, ruler of Light and Day, standing with the humans and defending them while Dekota, ruler of Dark and Night, and Pacarny, ruler of War and Peace, sided with the Fae. In the end, the gods formed a treaty of sorts and made each side sign it, stating the end of the war. After this, the gods went to sleep and haven't awoken since. Isabella snaps me out of my daydream when we approach the marchers, who were trying to stop innocent bystanders.

"I don't know why they do this every month, it's not like anyone listens to their rubbish anyway."

For once, I didn't disagree with her. A tall man, looking to be in his early twenties, glides up to us and holds out his hands, muttering under his breath. His eyes are glazed and I wonder what mushrooms he has eaten; his voice is hushed, and it sounds like a chant to some extent.

"Follow us and pray to the mighty Fae and in return you shall receive all the happiness you could wish for."

I don't repress my laughter this time and I resent how much it sounds like Laura's.

"No, thanks. I would rather dance with the God of Death then follow you into loving the Fae like silly school children."

I would have thought that was a pretty subtle hint that we weren't interested, but the marcher seemed only more determined.

"Many have doubts about this way of life, but I can assure you we have never known love like this that the Fae have shown us."

This time it was Laura who laughs at him, "I think you've

got your facts wrong, now if you'll excuse me and my sister, we have places to be that don't concern talking to stupid children."

Laura hooks her arm around Isabella's, and they walk past the marcher without a backwards glance. I quickly follow suit, ducking and weaving between merchants and beggars, making my way to the town square. My stepsisters are nowhere in sight, but would no doubt come running at the sound of money in my pouch, much like bees drawn to the nectar of spring flowers. I scan the crowd for any potential buyers, hoping there will be a good flow of newcomers. The old and frequent buyers often underpaid you and became tired very quickly. I lower my eyes when I see Mack, a buyer from a neighbouring town. He is cheap and often scams you out of the money he owes. My eyes are drawn to a short man with a long, salt and pepper beard, sitting atop an old wagon that looks worse for wear. One of the wheels is uneven and the wooden planks surrounding the outside are hanging on by a few wayward nails. He strikes me as the type of man who would wait for you to approach him instead of him hunting you. His clothes are of black silk and shimmer when he moves. It reminds me of a raven flying under the midday sun. He has black ink running up his forearms before fading at his elbows, this is often the symbol of someone who has served the King and Queen for a few years. It wasn't his clothes, though, that struck me as someone with a lot of money to offer but the way he tracks me in the crowd, like a fox tracking a rabbit. I bow my head and shuffle past my usual buyers towards the man on the wagon. As I step up to him, he smiles, and it strikes me as similar to a cat playing with their food. His teeth are white but uneven and his eyes hold a bleakness to them that comes from years of fighting and killing. I know because I see the same look in my own. I lift my eyes to his and supress a flinch. Something about him puts me at unease. His eyes drift from mine to scan over the bag strapped over my shoulder.

"What's your name, Missy?" his voice is etched with gravel and shows nothing about what he is feeling.

Giving a name is dangerous. Once someone knows your name, they can use it against you. But it would also be rude to ignore, so I reply honestly.

"My name is Keilee, sir.'"

He nods and opens his palm, gesturing towards my bag, his eyes hungry. I unstrap it and pull the buck's pelt out first, then deliberately pull the wolf's out slower and almost hesitantly. It seems to do the trick because the man is now tapping his leg impatiently, eyeing the pelts. I hand them over so he can see the quality of them. I hold my breath, waiting for him to place his verdict.

"This is a beautiful pelt, where did you stumble across it?"

He was running a hand over the wolf's pelt and it shimmers in the morning light, the delicate grey whorls catching in the light.

"I killed a wolf in the forest where I was hunting for the deer," I was hesitant to answer because of my father's reaction.

"You ought to be careful when hunting in the Blood Wood, it can be a dangerous place even for the most skilled hunters."

My eyes widen, I never stated the forest in which I was hunting. There were many forests around the town.

"Thank you, sir, but I'm fine. I know how to hunt."

He nods and a small smile tugs at the corner of his mouth, "I never said you couldn't, Missy, but even the bravest of men have fears of that forest and rightfully so."

My curiosity get the better of me and I am burning to know what he knows of the forest. He must see this on my face because he continues.

"The Blood Wood Forest used to be green instead of red. Did you know this, Missy?"

I nod, many people said that the forest was once beautiful, full of life and mystery, and that the Battle of the Gods stained the trees crimson.

"It is said that the forest is home to the mighty Hugan, God of Death. He is said to be sleeping under the roots of the tallest Blood tree. The Fae and humans once worshipped him when we lived beside each other, but once the war started, many forgot he existed and soon he was nothing more than myth."

An unfamiliar feeling pulls at me, and I lean forward to grasp his now quiet words. Letting curiosity get the better of me.

"How can the God of Death be sleeping under the ground we walk on? Shouldn't he be sleeping with the other gods?"

The man laughs and shakes his head.

"He cannot sleep with the other gods because he is trapped in the Blood Forest by the God of Life, Jakarn. Legend has it only the heir of Hugan can wake him and let him rest with the other gods, but there has been no heir and so he continues to sleep. This is why I warn you of the forest. It can be a beautiful place but also deadly."

I stare at him in disbelief, part of me thinks he is old and crazy, but a larger part of me wants to know more.

"Is the heir to Hugan supposed to be human or Fae?"

I don't know how he would have the answer to such a question when he said that there has been no heir, but I try anyway.

"They are both and neither. Only the heir knows this, and since they don't yet exist, we will not know."

I nod and the man taps his hand on the wolf pelt still on his lap. He then pulls a large money bag from his wagon and hands it to me. There is more money in the pouch then what the pelts are worth, and I vigorously shake my head. I don't need charity, especially from a man like him.

"I can't take all this, it's too much."

The selfish part of me wants to keep the bag as it's more money than I have ever carried on my person.

The man waves my protests away, "I have no use for it. This wolf's pelt will keep me warm for many winters to come and plus you listened to my rambling, which many don't, so have it. You need it more than I do."

He chuckles, his eyes bright, and I guess he's spotted my sisters lurking around the market trying to guess if I have found a buyer yet. I thank the man and weave back out to the road we had come to town on and find my sisters waiting for me with hungry expressions. Laura looks at my money bag, which now clangs against my thigh. Here we go again.

"Here, take this and go buy the things you need. I'll meet you at home when you're done," I grab a handful of gold coins and pass them to each of my sisters.

Their eyes widen and I know that they will most likely spend it on useless items instead of something useful. Isabella eyes me sceptically.

"How come you get to take the money bag? How do we know you won't share?"

I ignore her and swallow the retort that it was my pelt that I sold and flex my fingers.

"I guess you don't, you'll just have to trust me. And anyway, it's not like I'll get to keep any of it with your mother's sticky fingers."

Laura huffs, turns on her heel, and starts marching back into the town square with Isabella in tow, but not before Isabella scowls and attempts to shove me. Laughing, I skirt around the Holy Marchers and make the quiet walk home.

The hut's roof comes into view over the slight rise that's covered in fresh snow, and I slow my steps. I wish I could just come home and my father and his wife would be gone for a while, so I can rest my heavy legs and tired mind. As the hut looms closer, I can hear voices in the kitchen. My father's voice is low and unsteady as usual and Alice's voice is meek and uncertain. I open the door and it again gets caught on the uneven floor. Cursing under my breath, I shove it with my shoulder. My father's back is to me, leaning on the hearth, and Alice is sweeping up something he has knocked off the kitchen table. I wince as he stumbles away from the hearth and takes a seat at the table. Once she has finished sweeping the floor, Alice turns to me with a glare, like it was my fault my father has been angry and is drunk. Both sets of eyes snap to the money bag I was trying to conceal behind my leg. My father lifts a shaking hand and points at the bag.

"G… give me the bag, Keilee. Don't try and steal from me, as leader and owner of this house, all profits are owed to me."

I shudder internally. He is really drunk and is struggling to string words together.

"I will give you the bag once you've sobered up but until then I will keep it."

It probably wasn't the best response I could give, but I didn't want him making his way to town and gambling away the money before we've had a chance to spend it on things we needed.

"Don't talk to me like that, you little bitch. I'm your father and you will respect me like you should."

I don't try to hide my anger and take a step towards him.

Alice flinches away from me and I feel something rush through my veins. She is next to my father, with a protective hand on his shoulder.

"Now, Keilee, give your father the money and go chop some more wood,' Alice's voice shakes, and I almost felt sorry for her, but my anger is too palpable.

"You need to stop this, Father; we can't keep living like this, with you sulking in the house while we try to get by."

My words are surprisingly steady and even. My father stands with such force that his chair tumbles to the floor. I am astonished he doesn't fall to the floor with it. Right now, I don't see a man standing before me but an angry drunk with a heart so black it challenges the darkness of Dekota. Before I can move away, his hand comes flying to my face and a second later my face feels as if I have crashed into the solid wall of our house. My vison blots with black before I shake my head to clear my head. Alice stands stock still in the corner of the room in shock. I can see the evil glint of delight in her eyes at my pain. My face stings as I smile up at my father, now rocking back on his heels, his eyes are wide, and I almost say I can see remorse cross his face before he falls back into the remaining chair at the table.

"Next time you'll think better of arguing back to me, won't you, Keilee?"

I laugh a hollow sound with no joy. There will be no next time if I could help it. I had to get away from here, away from him and his violence, and away from Alice and her vipers. A vicious smile pulls at my lips.

"Done with your temper tantrum?" the words spill from my mouth before I can catch them.

My father goes to stand again but I bare my teeth at him, "Sit, don't you dare move from that spot."

Something in my eyes must make him freeze because he listens and swallows thickly.

"I don't know how Mother could stand you."

With that parting comment, I make my way to the door and grab the axe leaning against the wall.

Chapter 3

By the time I make my way back to the hut, my arms are aching, and my back is crippled. Sweat beads on my forehead despite the cold winter evening, I feel as if I've run a mile. Darkness has started to blanket the ground, opening the sky to allow the stars to peek through, and I struggle to see the holes in the path leading to the front door. I can hear Isabella and Laura laughing in front of the fire and guess they are discussing the things they bought with the money I gave them. I step into the house and edge along the wall to our shared bedroom. My father and Alice are nowhere to be seen and I assume they have turned in for the night. Both girls near the fire seem oblivious to the fight that broke out earlier that day. My cheek is tender, and I presume there is a blue-black bruise spread wide on my jaw. Laura looks up from the cloak she is running through her fingers. The soft pink silk slithers against itself and lands in a delicate pile in front of her.

"Where have you been? Nice make-up choice by the way."

My hand automatically flies to my bruised cheek, and I sneer at her.

"I was chopping wood, if you must know, and now I'm going to bed if you don't object."

I mock a bow and make to go to the bedroom, but not before Isabella stops me.

"You'll have to learn to keep your mouth shut one day, and by the looks of it, you didn't succeed today."

Her face is turned up in a scowl and I resist the urge to throw the axe at her. One day the tides will turn, and I will be the one sneering at her while she suffers, but for now, I walk to our bedroom without them stopping me this time.

The bedroom is small and dark, due to no windows, and the bed is large enough for the two girls sitting by the fire to share, but I make my way to the pile of blankets on the floor near the wall between this and my father's room. I have a scarce number of belongings, which include my mother's leather journal and my necklace she gifted me before she died. Its gold chain is visible even in the dull lighting. I clench it in my fist and start changing into one of the only pairs of clothes I have. The dark black of my tunic hugs my slim form and does little to block out the cold, but it's more comfortable than my hunting clothes. The necklace in my hand is cold as it bites into my palm. It's shaped as a Dahlia flower and, in the centre of the flower there is a shining opal found in the river rocks of Fallen Crest. I cherish it and sometimes can feel my mother's presence in the flower. I slip the chain around my neck and tuck it under my tunic, already feeling at ease with it around my neck. The necklace, along with the journal, is the only things my father and Alice didn't sell of my mother's, and I will keep it that way. He may have forgotten her, but I never will. Slowly, as I stare at the ceiling, sleep creeps up on me and drags me under into the pits of black nothings.

A loud bang rips me from my sleep and I bolt upright. Dust is swirling in the air and my sisters jump at the sound of another bang. I grab my hunting knife from beside me and tuck it under my tunic. Isabella is whimpering and it is one of the most pathetic sounds I've heard.

"What is that noise? Keilee, go check what it is."

I sigh and stand up, keeping close to the wall as I make my

way to the opening of our bedroom. Laura makes to hide under the bed and bangs into the wall, causing more dust to swirl and a dull thud to echo around the room. I bring my fingers to my lips to silence her.

"If you don't shut up, I will kill you before whatever is out there does. Sit on the bed with Isabella and don't move until I come back. Understood?"

For once, there is no argument and they both nod their heads. They would gladly let me go out there and die if it meant they would be safe.

I slip around the corner and crouch behind the kitchen table. From where I'm crouched, I can see the front door hanging off one of its hinges, swinging sadly. My breath catches as I see what's standing in the doorway. It looks to be a massive dog, the size of a deer. The colour of its coat is chestnut, and when the creature swings its head to smell the air, flashes of red blink in its coat, making it look like flames flickering there. If only I could get to my bow and arrow, which is leaning against the hearth. The dog tentatively steps into the hut and I'm amazed it hasn't seen or smelt me yet. I clench my knife harder in my hand and try to crawl to the other side of the table. Just when I'm about stand, its massive head snaps to me, but my father comes into the kitchen, swaying where he's standing. It's in this moment that I wonder if he is ever sober. Alice is close behind him with a chair leg in her hands, as if it could protect her from the massive beast in front of her, whose jaws open slightly at the potential food standing before it. Laura and Isabella come out of their room at the sound of their mother's gasp, and I want to slap them. Instead, I drag a hand across my face. I'm still hidden behind the table and decide to stand up and face the creature since that seems to be the plan around here. Its massive head swings towards me again and it sniffs the air once more, but now it's snarling. Goosebumps ripple along my skin and I see uncanny intelligence within its blue eyes. I angle my knife at it, and it crouches slightly. Just as I think it's going to pounce, a whistle cuts through the night and the dog steps aside to reveal a tall man bathed in shadows, only illuminating his sharp green eyes. My breath catches and something in my chest whispers to me. Nobody has spoken and the room begins to feel too small. We are caged animals, with the only exit blocked by a monster and its master. The figure steps past the dog and waves his hand to the room.

"What? Don't I get a welcome into your lovely..." he pauses, and I can practically smell his sneer as he glances around the room. "House, or is that too much to ask for from humans?"

I freeze and can feel everyone in the room do so as well. He means to say that he's not human, which can only lead to one other explanation, and it's that he's a Fae. My skin turns cold and the white wolf from the forest flashes in my mind, so it wasn't just a wolf but indeed a Fae and is this man here to collect payment for the life I took? The thought makes me visibly shudder and the stranger laughs at us.

"What do you want from us?" Alice's voice shakes and she grabs onto her daughters, holding them close.

I am on the opposite side of the room from them, and the man shakes his head.

"I want many things, and usually I get them, so let's start with redemption."

All eyes, including the man's, snap to me. I straighten my spine and twirl the knife in my hand. My father glares at me and turns towards the stranger. In his drunken state, he probably doesn't connect the dots and just thinks the stranger is someone I crossed in town.

"If she's done anything to you, I will personally see that she's punished. Nobody wants a rat running around in their family."

The words sting and I close my eyes for a few short seconds before focusing on the man again.

"I don't doubt that you would, and even if you did object, you couldn't stand in my way."

My blood goes cold and, for once in my miserable life, I want nothing more than for my father to stand up for me and protect me like a father should, but he just smiles and waves his hand at me.

"Go ahead and do your worst, I won't stop you, especially when she no doubt deserves it."

I swallow thickly. If he wasn't going to fight for me, then I guess I will have to do that myself. Gripping my knife, I step forward and let a cunning smile cross my face.

"What have I done to wrong you? I don't even know you and I think it's a bit rude barging into someone's house in the middle of the night."

Even to my own ears, the argument sounds weak and desperate despite my attempt to sound unaffected by the intrusion.

"What have you done? Is that even a question that needs answering? You killed one of my men in cold blood. Did you really think you would get away with it?"

I don't balk from his hard tone or the way his vibrant green eyes narrow on me like a snake readying to strike.

"I didn't know the wolf was one of your men. I didn't even know that it wasn't just a wolf in the first place."

Once again, he smiles, white teeth flashing, but there was no humour behind it.

"I never thought I would see the day when a human would try to lie to my face. How interesting."

Alice makes a small noise as the large dog sitting patiently at the man's feet crouches down, rising his hackles.

"Now, we can do this the easy way, where you come with me to live in Thyithran without a struggle, or we can do this the bloody way, where you still come to live with me in Thyithran but your family..." he clicks his fingers together. "Perishes. I for one wouldn't wish that upon anyone."

The way his eyes light up tells me otherwise and as much as I hate the people around me, I wouldn't want that to happen to them. So, I swallow my growing panic and step forward. If I leave with him, I can escape on the road. The thought brings little comfort as my eyes drift over the pair.

"Very good choice, although I must say a rather boring one."

The man steps outside and looks over the hut again, "I'll leave you to say goodbye to your family and will meet you out here in five minutes, which is very generous on my part."

Self-righteous bastard. I watch as he sits on the stump next to the road and starts whistling to himself. Whoever this guy is, he's heartless and a smart-arse, which doesn't make for a good combination. I turn to Laura, Isabella, and Alice, who are standing frozen next to the hearth, their expression showing all the fear gathering in the pit of my stomach.

"The rest of the money from the pelt is in the bedroom and the deer should last a few weeks. After that, you'll have to help yourselves out."

I turn on my heel and hurry to the bedroom to grab my mother's journal. I reach for my necklace and squeeze it, drawing a tiny flicker of courage from it. I duck back into the kitchen and chuck the money bag at Laura, who catches it but fumbles. Once

I'm happy that I've done all I can, I walk out the door without a backward glance towards my father and stepfamily.

I step out into the cold air and choke back a sob. I've lasted this long without crying and I wasn't going to start now. The man stops his whistling but keeps his back to me, he raises his right hand and flicks his hand to the right. All of a sudden, I feel heavy. I try to ignore the feeling but it's too thick and I can't resist the tether pulling me into a blissful silence. Before I fall under, I swear I can taste a metallic tang covering my tongue and I feel my mother's journal drop from my hands. Magic.

Chapter 4

I wake with a start and blink rapidly, trying to rid myself of the heavy weight behind my eyes. It's dark and damp and I can't see past the thick cover of trees in front of me. I stretch my legs and begin to shake as the cold attacks my weak body. Nothing makes sense and I'm beginning to think I'm dreaming before a rush of memories about earlier tonight hits me. Oh, Gods. A tremor that has nothing to do with the cold rips through my body. I've been taken to live in the land of the Fae with an insufferable arsehole. I snap my head around and my eyes land on a tall male figure who's bent over a small fire the colour of ocean blue. Hysterical laughter wants to tear out of my body, but I swallow the feeling and instead curl my knees to my chest.

"Oh, good, you're awake, and that's probably the nicest thing someone has ever called me," he pauses as if thinking something over in his head. "Insufferable arsehole has a nice ring to it."

His back is still turned to me, and I cower back into myself. How did he know what I was thinking? Did I say it aloud? Is the magic still affecting me? Let the Gods be in my favour.

"Not very talkative, are we? And I was beginning to get lonely sitting here by myself."

Despite his words, he sounds as if talking to me is the last thing he wants to be doing.

"What do you want from me? Where are you taking me?"

My hands shake, and I curl them under my arms, trying to

keep some warmth in them. The large dog is still sitting by his feet and lets out a low growl when I move my knees tighter to my chest. The man pats the dog on the head and sighs.

"Easy now, Kai, you can calm down and come give me some real company, I'm rather bored talking to her by myself."

I stare at him dumbfounded. He's talking to a dog like it's a human, or in his case, another Fae, and he still hasn't answered my questions or turned to look at me. As I start to wonder if he's all there in the head, the dog shakes its large head and stands. The next moment, there's a blinding light and I have to squint to see. Instead of a dog, there now stands another man, slightly shorter than the other, but still broad-shouldered and well-built. His face is like nothing I've seen before. His eyes are a striking blue, and his hair is a flaming red too deep to be orange. There is no other word to describe him but beautiful. Beautiful and Fae. His high cheekbones and full mouth make me wonder how such a dark creature lies beneath his skin.

"Look, now you've startled her into complete silence and her jaw is touching the ground."

I snap my mouth closed and turn away my gaze.

Kai scoffs,

"Next time you make me stay in that form I will use your leg as a chew toy. I'm not your personal lap dog."

Kai takes a seat next to his companion but angles his body so he is half facing me. He smiles and I flinch at the viciousness of it.

"Now come on, don't be so harsh with me. You make such a good pet, and you are just the cutest when you wag your tail."

Kai shoots him an exasperated look before turning back to me.

"So, this is the human, and might I add human *girl*, that took down our great Tiran? How intriguing."

I feel anger rise at his clear mocking and swing my back to him, which on my part isn't the smartest thing I've ever done, so I turn back. To turn your back to the Fae is to give them your life.

"What do you want from me?" I repeat.

The man whose name I still don't know, and whose face I've yet to see, snarls at me in a way that would be better suited to Kai's dog form.

"I want my friend back, but you killed him, so that's not an option, and now I'm stuck with you until I fix this mess," his tone is tired and angry.

Despite my better self, I can't help but feel slightly guilty.

My voice is bleak when I reply, and I remove all emotion from it, "I'm sorry about your friend, but if I'm to stay with you, I would think I'm entitled to know where I am and what you plan to do with me."

Kai replies, not bothering to remove the sting from his words, "Trust me, if it were up to us, we would dump you and let your body rot in the cold, but we are stuck here with a murderer."

"Can I at least know his name?" I point to the mysterious man and Kai regards me for a moment before turning to face the man next to him.

He whispers something I can't hear, and the man stands from where he's sitting to turn and look at me. The moment his eyes lock with mine, I freeze. If I thought Kai was beautiful, he has nothing on the man before me. His eyes are the most stunning green, his hair is raven black and shimmers with almost a blue sheen when he moves his head, and his lips are the most sensuous thing I have ever seen. His cheekbones and jaw could cut glass and, on anyone else, would look feminine. I blink and look away. Why did Fae have to be so beautiful?

"My name is Alcinder, but many of my friends and a few enemies call me Alc."

I slowly nod my head, still transfixed with his beauty.

"Now that we got that over and done with, can we get a move on? Dawn is coming soon, and I don't really like the inhabitants of this forest and they don't particularly like me either."

I resist the urge to argue with him and tell him that he still hasn't told me what he wants from me, so instead I settle with, "How long have I been sleeping?"

Alcinder's face twists into a predatory smile,

"I would say the better part of two days, and may I say you are heavier than you look."

I gape up at him. Two days? The thought of being unconscious around these two Fae for more than a couple of hours makes my skin tingle, and the fact that Alcinder had to carry me makes me want to scrub my skin raw.

Kai points over to his left and waves his hand at two large horses tethered to a tree. My heart skips. The horses' coats are of pure white and absorb the darkness, turning it to light much the same as a natural lantern. Their eyes are like large, black beetles gleaming against the striking white of their coats and there is only two of them, which means I'm either walking or sharing with someone, and I would rather piss off the Gods then share a mount with the males in front of me.

"Our rides await us and, if we don't get moving now, Isaac will move us himself and I really like my head," Alcinder laughs and shakes his head.

"I'm sure Isaac would be more accommodating since he still owes me for the mix up between him and the High Lord of Winter."

This is the first I've heard about the High Lords, apart from the stories I was told, and my skin itches to know more, but I bite my tongue at the look on Kai's face as he scans the clearing. I strain to see what he's looking at and notice Alcinder is tilting his head with a curious expression on his face.

"Although, with that said, we should definitely head off now. I can hear his men about three miles back along the Narkos river."

Kai makes his way to the shorter of the two horses and swings gracefully onto its back. Alcinder pulls me to my feet and half drags me to the other mount, I dig my heels into the dirt and tug my arm from his grip. There was no way in hell I was riding a Fae's horse by myself let alone with him. Alcinder raises his eyebrow at me and waits for my complaint.

"I'm not hopping on that horse with you. How do I know you won't drop me or let the animal kill me itself?"

Kai sighs into his hand and begins to walk his steed to the treeline.

"Like Kai said earlier, we would have dumped you the moment we crossed the border if we had a choice, but we don't, so you're going to have to suck it up. Understood, Princess?"

I swallow and nod. I do not want to anger him any further than I already have.

"By the way, don't call me 'Princess', my name is Keilee."

Alcinder snorts,

"Whatever you say, Princess."

He grabs my waist and lifts me into the saddle and my heart races at the contact. The same sensation from when I met him pulls at me. One flick of his powerful hands and I would be dead. As he swings up behind me, I try and keep as much space between us and internally curse, hoping the trip will be short and swift.

My muscles scream at me by the time we stop at a small river crossing. The sun casts a soft, golden glow over the trees, their leaves are in various shades of orange and red, making it look like they are constantly burning. The ground under the horses' feet is damp and shines as the sun's rays hit it. I wonder to myself if this land ever experiences dire dry seasons and flooding wet seasons like back home. The breeze is crisp, and I try to pull my tunic sleeves down lower. I must stink and I don't know how Alcinder manages to sit in such close proximity to me. The trip has been silent, and I often drift off into my own thoughts, pondering how my father is getting on without me and if my stepsisters and Alice have spent the rest of the money from the wolf's pelt. Soft gurgling from the stream pulls me from my thoughts and I blink at the soft layer of mist floating in eddies in front of my hands. The surface of the water ripples, as if there are tiny bugs dancing along the top. The water itself is crystal clear and I can see the wavey reflection of the horses as they bend their heads to drink. I need to stretch my legs and get out of the saddle and away from Alc. His hands occasionally brush my sides when he changes course or halts the beast. I struggle to repress the urge to shudder every time. When did my life go from hunting in the woods and fighting with my sisters to riding on the same mount as a Fae and with his friend? And what was more pressing was why wasn't I already dead? I killed their friend and Fae aren't known for their mercy or kindness to humans, so there must be some use to me even if I don't know what that is yet, and the thought turns my stomach.

"How much longer until we get where we are supposed to be going?"

My voice is hoarse form lack of use over the last few hours.

"Not long. After we cross that mountain range, I will be able to transport us to our destination."

His breath tickles my neck and I cringe away from him. My eyes follow where his finger is pointing, and I almost groan at the sight. Massive rocky mountains stand in the near distance and their caps are laced with white. It would be no easy trip.

"Where are we now? And why does it look like it's in the middle of autumn when it's supposed to be winter?"

Kai glances over at Alc and something inaudible passes between them. I feel Alc nod and see Kai's face pull into a small, devious smile.

"We are in the Autumn court and will be heading to the Night court soon. Isaac, the male we were talking about earlier, is the High Lord of Autumn and that little devil over there…" Alc gestures to Kai as he pushes his horse through the shallow water. "Is the High Lord's son, but he was banished when he killed his older brother."

My breath catches and I glance away from Kai, suddenly feeling sick. He killed his own brother? Masculine laughter drifts across the breeze as Alc notices my too-stiff shoulders, the sound vibrating off my back.

"Don't worry, the little prick deserved it, he murdered his sisters."

I didn't know the true feeling of dread until now. What was my life to become if I was surrounded by family murderers?

"All of you are sick and twisted, who murders their own family?"

This time it's Kai's turn to straighten and he snaps his head to me. I recoil, hitting a firm wall of muscle, and I jerk forwards, looking like an idiot all the while.

"I didn't have a choice, and if you think that is twisted and sick, then you won't like many people here. So, I suggest keeping your mouth shut and your weak human opinions to yourself."

Alc continues with his history lesson as if the argument never happened.

"There are six courts of Thyithran, all ruled by a High Lord with a skill set to match their court. They are Winter, Autumn, Spring, Summer, Day, and Night. The courts range in power, with the Night court being the most powerful and Spring being the weakest. But don't be mistaken, all are as deadly as the next. Kai is one of five children of the Autumn court, and when his father dies, his power will transfer to the strongest of the surviving children. This is why most High Lord families often pick off the weak to solidify their chance at ruling over the court. It is ruthless and often gruesome. Having children while being a Fae is almost impossible, so to kill them is one of the worst sins to ever exist."

I keep my face neutral; I would never have guessed the Fae had morals. It seems to be too human for them to waste their time worrying about it.

Our horses pick their way up the uneven path that is starting to narrow. And I run over the piece of history Alc has given me. If I can find a way to get free of him and make my way back to the human lands, I might have a chance of hiding from him. Although my hope is small and pitiful. I wrap my hand around my necklace, still hanging around my neck, and squeeze it. I lurch in the saddle and pat my tunic, trying to look for my mother's journal, my heart stutters as I can't feel it. Please don't let it be left at the hut with my father. I turn in the saddle, the action bringing me closer to Alc, but I didn't care. Not if I didn't have the journal.

"Do you know where my journal is? It's leather bound, and I need it back."

Alc smiles at me, but there is nothing friendly in the action, and reaches into the saddle bag next to him.

"What, this old thing? I thought it could make for an interesting read later."

I snarl at him and try to wrench the book from his hands. He clicks his tongue over his teeth like I'm a disobedient child.

"Not so fast, Princess, you haven't earned it yet."

I grind my teeth together and knock an elbow into his ribs and he barely flinches. I'm about to respond when he clamps a large hand over my mouth and, not for the first time today, my heart lurches. With his Fae sight and hearing, he can sense things I can't, and I wonder if he can hear the tempo of my heart increase. Kai looks over at us and nods his head once, answering some unspoken question. Alc answers aloud, much to my relief. I don't like not knowing what's happening, especially when it involves the Fae.

"A few hundred paces away, back near the stream. We should take the Calipo trail and skirt around the base of the mountain. Hopefully they will think we are taking the easier and quicker route."

"We could, but that would mean another half hour to our already tiresome trip."

"Don't fight me on this, Kai. We don't have the time or the luxury and plus Isaac will think we took the easy way up and through rather than around."

Kai looks like he wants to argue but the look Alc throws his way stamps out his reply and his mouth opens and closes like a fish trying to find water. The horses' pace picks up until we are galloping through the red and orange forest, the stream growing further away with every pound of the powerful hoofbeats. As the forest flashes past, I swear I can see figures moving around us, but as I look at them more closely, it turns out to be nothing more than drifts of shadows. My teacher's words echo around in my head.

"Never trust your human senses around the Fae and human border, I cannot stress this enough, young ones."

By the time the mountain peaks become more than solid walls of rock, the sun is crawling towards the earth, blurring the start and finish of the once bright blue sky. Light-blue fades into various shades of purple, pink, and gold, the sun itself an orange orb sinking lower by the minute. Kai pulls his horse to a stop and waits for Alc's mount to fall in step with his. His expression is stony as he looks up at the jagged rock face. I wonder if he misses his family and his fire forests, although I don't miss my family, my home, yes, but my family no. I was never part of them, I was an outsider, used as one would use an arrow. Good until the tip becomes blunt and useless, then thrown away when maintaining it becomes a waste of time. My arm aches for my bow and I miss the strain of pulling back the string and the precision with which the arrow hits its target. That part of my life is over unless I can find a way to escape here, but the chances are very low. I may have a good aim with a bow and arrow, but other than that, I'm completely hopeless and may as well lay in the open with a sign on my back saying 'free food'. I glance back at Kai and find him staring at me. I blink, and he rolls his eyes, the gesture too human for his face.

"I said, do you want to camp out here or continue on until we reach the place we're going?"

I'm surprised that my opinion matters and I look back at Alc, who is slouched behind me waiting for my reply. Alc quickly cuts in as he sees the surprise written on my face.

"We aren't asking because we care about your opinion, we just don't know how strong your human body is and don't feel like lugging around a dead weight."

Again, I feel the weird sensation of being laid bare in front of him. It's like he knows exactly what I'm thinking and that nothing is private around him. I suppress the urge to hit him again. Violence isn't the answer to everything, and I need to be smart about how to extract information from him and Kai. The only way to do that is to get to the unknown destination they keep talking about. Alc chuckles behind me at the shift in my mood, the sound circling us, bouncing off the sharp walls of the mountain. I ignore the protest of my sore limbs and muscles as I answer their question.

"I'm fine to keep moving. The sooner I get off this horse, the better for me and my numb legs. And don't patronise me, I'm not some weak kitten."

Kai laughs darkly,

"Don't worry, nobody would mistake a mountain lion for a kitten no matter the size of their paws."

In a way, it's a compliment and I smile to myself, not letting it show on my face. Kai moves his mount on, and I envy the way they never seem to run out of energy. What I wouldn't give for my pile of blankets on the floor. Alc also urges on our horse and the gentle sway of the horse's pace makes my eyes heavy and sleep is lurking in the corner of my mind.

I lose track of time as the hours tick by. The sky is blanketed in bright stars, all different sizes, and I wonder if someone has had the time to name them all. My mind whirls at the many different constellations splattered against the deep, indigo canvas above me. I never noticed how beautiful the sky was at night. When the gods were awake, did they sit amongst the stars on thrones of glittering starlight watching us as we slept in the safety of our homes with the family we loved? I notice Alc is also staring at the sky, his green eyes reflecting the many lights, and he looks almost human, apart from his unnatural beauty and slightly pointed ears. He said we were eventually going to the night court. Was that his home? Did the night sky remind him of it? I wonder to myself what power the High Lord of the Night court could possess. Would it be the ability to cover something or someone in complete darkness, or would it be something of a more sinister kind, like manipulating shadows and creating nightmares for the sake of it? My imagination plays many different scenarios in my head, and I have to shut them down as they become more twisted and confusing as my body strains with the effort of staying awake and alert. I resort to counting the horses hoofbeats on the hard stone of the winding path around the base of the mountains, which climb high into the sky like they are reaching for something they can't seem to find. Their snow-capped tips like a constant cloud hanging over them. My finger taps in time with the horse's steps and Alc shifts behind me as if I'm beginning to annoy him. He hasn't said a word to me since the last time we stopped, and Kai may as well be a living statue. His back straight and unmoving as he guides his mount through the rough patches of the path. I don't mind the silence and bask in it. The only time I was alone and had quiet back home was when I was hunting, otherwise it was yelling or arguing at the hut with my father. The thought causes me to grab hold of my mother's necklace and I swear I can feel it beat against my palms. I yearn to flip through the pages of the leather-bound journal and feel the presence of her through old paper and splatted ink. I hate Alc all the more for taking it from me and I picture myself stabbing him and taking it back, but I have no iron or any crushed Mandrake mushroom. My finger tapping slows automatically with the slowing of the horse's pace and I snap back to reality.

Kai has pulled his horse to a stop again but this time he dismounts and walks over to a tall pine tree whose leaves have shifted from the colour of golden fire to a green so lovely it matches the colour of Alc's eyes. I was so caught up in my own head, I didn't notice the change of scenery. It was like stepping from one book to another. I glance around and see soft tuffs of grass poking through the ground that is no longer coated in red leaves.

"We are in the Spring court now," Kai answers my unspoken question.

Alc swings a leg over the horse we share and jumps gracefully to the ground, turning to reach his hands out to grab me. I glare at him and follow his actions, landing on the ground with a thud and the grace to rival that of a mountain troll, but at least I'm standing. Alc smirks at me and turns to head over to Kai. The horses stare at Alc and he spins back around, frowning slightly.

"Willow Whisps, your time here is done."

At first, I blink at him in confusion and a small smile tugs at Kai's mouth as he watches me, then my attention is snagged by the horses as they disappear. Their white coats turn to soft white dandelion fluff and their black eyes shift into small beetles that flutter their tiny wings and fly off into the surrounding darkness. I don't realise how dark it is until the horses are no longer standing with us. I pick my jaw up off the forest floor and turn to Alc, who is now smiling with Kai.

"Ah, you have to love human ignorance."

I glare at Alc and march over to the tree Kai was so interested in earlier, before the disappearing horses. The tree's bark is damp and tiny patterns have been carved into it. I run my fingers over it in wonder and jump back as they start to glow. Alc and Kai step up behind me and Alc flicks his hand. The tree starts to spin, no, not the tree, us. Everything becomes a blur of colour, and it feels like the air from my lungs is being squeezed out. Before I can grasp my bearings, the world stills and the first thing I notice is the sky. The canvas is so black, I wonder how the sun could even begin to pierce it with morning light. The stars are bright and wink at me from above. I swing my head around and my breath whooshes out of my still too tight lungs. A city sprawls out in front of me in the most beautiful colours I have ever seen. Lights of various shades glitter and shine, challenging the stars, but they are in perfect harmony, like a dance between land and sky. I can hear the soft strains of music and laughter even from where I'm standing next to Kai on a balcony of some sorts. I turn and find Alc staring at me with a curious expression. He quickly catches himself and tears his gaze away to speak with Kai.

"We made it in good time, despite the trail we took. I suggest you go rest up. We have things to discuss in the morning and I need you on your best behaviour, especially if the whole gang is going to be here. I don't want a near miss between you and Naomi again."

Despite his harsh words, I can hear a smile in it. Whoever these people are, they are friends not foe. I ponder to myself if the High Lord is one of the people I will likely meet tomorrow. Kai walks into the building without a word to me and disappears from sight. Suddenly, my legs are weak, and I have to lean against the railing to keep myself upright. Sleep is clawing at my brain and my vision blurs. Alc notices and turns to me.

"The same goes for you, I don't need another burden added to the list. I'll get Tilly and Alyssa to get you settled into your rooms."

I nod my head once and he strides for the doors on the balcony, swinging them open with one hand. I'm amazed by what greets me on the other side. A high ceiling room, with couches and bookshelves lining the walls, makes my breath catch. This is no ordinary house, it's made for someone with a lot of money, and even though the furniture is extravagant, it's worn and looks as if it's used quite often. The smell of cinnamon makes my stomach growl. This is a home, not just a place. It reminds me of what my house would have looked like if my mother were still alive. My heart clenches at the thought and the sweet-smelling air turns my stomach to acid. This is the home of a dangerous male and his even worse friends. The only way I could feel at home here is if they were dead and buried, and since I don't have any power against them, I may as well be living in a fancy cage. My sour thoughts are interrupted when two females enter through one of the many doors lining the walls. The taller of the two is slim and her skin glows a soft blue in the light. Thin, dragonfly-like wings protrude from her back and her black hair sways loosely as she walks. She is beautiful, as all Fae are beautiful, and my skin becomes clammy. I'm meant to let her lead me to my sleeping chambers? I would rather find my way there in pitch black then turn my back on her. As she smiles, her teeth gleam white and their pointed edges makes the hairs on my neck stand. The other female is short and round. She reminds me of someone's aunt, who would spoil the children when the parents aren't watching. Her face is pretty, and her hair is a similar colour to mine, except hers is all brown while mine has gold streaks when in the sun from days of hunting in the heat of summer. Her smile is warm, and I feel my muscles relax despite myself.

"Alyssa and Tilly are here to make you comfortable and to help you settle in. They will run you through some of the rules while you stay here and will be at your beck and call," Alc smiles at the females and walks past them, heading through the door they came from, and I wonder where he stays in this massive house.

The tall Fae turns to me and beckons me to follow her with a flick of her hand.

"I'm Alyssa, by the way, and this…" she points to the kind-faced female. "Is Tilly. We are here to help you should you need anything."

I try to smile and feel like it comes out more like a grimace. Alyssa leads me out a door opposite the one Alc left through, and I gape at the massive stairwell in front of me. Its polished wooden steps are covered with a deep red carpet, making me feel like we are in a palace about to see the King and Queen descend. The long hallway has many branches and I lose track of them all as we walk closer to the staircase. If I were to try and escape this building, I would be in for a rough journey. Tilly places a gentle hand on my shoulder and I jump, not realising that I had stopped to admire the architecture. She laughs softly and walks at my side as we ascend. The carpet sinks slightly under my feet, and I wonder what it would feel like to sleep on something so soft. To my surprise, I see no human slaves on our way to my rooms. Nor do I hear any screaming or shouting. In fact, I hear nothing but our soft footsteps and the gentle tick of a grandfather clock at the top of the staircase. Once we arrive at the top, it sections off to the left and right and Alyssa leads me to the left. Tilly trots beside me and claps her hands together, lighting the many torches adorning the walls. It's then that I notice the different paintings hanging on the walls. They are mostly of the night sky in different formats, but my favourite that we walk past is one with the stars winking out into the slow blush of a sunrise. We come to an abrupt stop in front of two white doors carved with small flowers on the trimmings. Its golden handles gleam in the hall light and I marvel at whoever carved the doors with such care. Alyssa pushes open the door and I almost faint where I'm standing. The room before me is gorgeous. The floor is the same dark wood in the hallway and the walls are pearl white. There is a massive chandelier on the roof and the trimmings have the same flowers carved into it as the door. What is most wonderful of all is the bed fit for a queen. Millions of pillows sit against the headboard, and even from where I'm standing, I can see the sheets are of the softest wool. A bathing chamber lays to the left of the bed, along with a walk-in wardrobe. A large writing desk is on the opposite wall, next to a huge hearth with armchairs of deep blue in front of it. I'm still gaping as Tilly walks into the bathing chamber, and I hear water rushing as she fills the bath. Alyssa crosses over to the wardrobe and pulls out a night gown of lilac silk. I would prefer pants as they are easier to run in but bite my tongue as she lays it out on my bed. I nod my thanks and silently relax as the two females leave my room with a reminder that, if I need anything, to just sing out. They didn't go through any rules like Alc said they were going to, but I'm not about to complain. I walk on soft feet to the bathing chamber and sigh to myself at the sight of the large tub sitting in the corner of the room. Swirls of steam rise into the air and I can smell rose petals as I strip from my dirty and stiff clothes. When I was living in the hut, we had a small bucket of water that we heated over the fire where we would scrub ourselves clean. But that wasn't often as you would just get dirty again sleeping, in my case, on the floor. I step into the water and let loose a groan. It's so hot and my muscles relish in it. I sit in the water until my hands and feet wrinkle, then dress and pad my way over to the bed. The sheets wrapping around me like a cocoon, I let sleep pull me under and, just for tonight, let myself wonder what it would be like to live in a place like this permanently. My dreams are filled with rivers of silk and beds of feathers.

Chapter 5

I wake to my curtains being ripped open and for a moment wonder where I am before I remember the events of the last few days. My heart races and I fling myself into a sitting position, taking in Tilly as she ties back the curtains with a piece of cream string.

"Sorry, M'Lady, I didn't mean to startle you. Master Alc had me bring breakfast and to help prepare you for the meeting in an hour."

I snort into my hand; I am no lady, and I don't think I would ever want to be one. I turn to Tilly as she sets my breakfast tray on the writing desk.

"Please, call me Keilee, and thank you for the breakfast."

Tilly nods her head tightly and I have the feeling that she won't stop calling me Lady, so I don't bother to correct her when she asks. "Would you like help in dressing this morning, M'Lady? Or would you like to do that on your own?"

I swallow my reply that I'm not a child and know how to dress myself. She's just doing her job and I have no right to lash out at her.

"I should be able to manage just fine on my own."

I swing my legs off the bed and walk to the wardrobe. I freeze as I see all the dresses lined on the racks. When was the last time I wore a dress? Tilly comes to a stop at my side and smiles up at me.

"A lot to choose from, isn't there? I think this one..." she reaches for a stunning pale blue gown to her left and pulls it from the rack. "Would suit your eyes and hair."

I run the delicate silk through my hands, worried that it will disintegrate beneath my touch.

"It's beautiful, thank you."

Tilly smiles and sets about making my bed while I eat, then go and change into the gown. When I come back out of the bathing chamber, Tilly motions for me to sit in front of a vanity I hadn't noticed last night while she pins half my hair away from my face with little blue bell clips and leaves the rest to fall softly at my shoulders. I take the chance to look at myself in the mirror. I blink at the sight. My eyes are a deep blue, and my nose is pert. I have my mother's high cheek bones and strong jaw, which still has a faint blue and purple mark from where my father hit me; I see nothing of him in my face and I am glad for it. The dress hugs my too-slim form and I wonder what it would look like if I had a healthy body. Tilly pats my arm and I'm ripped away from my thoughts. She catches my eye in the mirror and a frown draws her brows together. I stand quickly and move to the door before I lose my nerve and change into my usual slacks and tunic. My thin slippers slap against the polished floor as I follow Tilly back into the hallway and down the massive staircase we climbed last night. My hands shake and my heart is unsteadily galloping in my chest. Is this the day that I receive my punishment for killing a Faerie? Is that why I'm dressed up, so I can go to my grave with a small bit of dignity? The more I think about it, the more my stomach turns. I'm led through a door to the right of the staircase's base, and we walk in silence through another huge hallway. Doors line the walls and I see more of the art hung on the walls that are similar to the ones on the way to my room. We come to a stop at large white doors a short while later. They are larger than my bedroom doors and I wonder to myself if a giant lived here before Alc did. The doors swing open of their own accord, and I jump back a step. I turn to Tilly in hopes that she can save me but find she is nowhere to be seen. So much for being here to help me if I need it. I try and strangle the growing panic and wipe my sweaty palms on my gown, hoping I don't ruin the soft silk. I can hear soft voices drifting from the room, which all stop when they no doubt sense my arrival. Kai is the first I see as I take a step into the large room. He is draped across an armchair swirling a glass of amber liquid in his hand. Next to him are two females sitting with their backs to me, also holding a glass. A stunning man with pure blonde hair and hazel eyes is standing facing me with his face set in hard lines as he takes me in. A soft glow radiates from him, and I wonder what power he holds. I shiver at his scrutiny. Lastly, I notice Alc's muscular form standing in front of large bay windows displaying the city below him. His handsome form is draped in a black tunic with silver stitching and his pants hug his muscular legs. I mentally slap myself for allowing myself to admire him. Damn Fae and their beauty. Kai salutes me and the girls sitting across from him swivel in their seats as I set my legs into motion and walk over to stand awkwardly in front of them. My panic is consuming me, and if I don't sit down soon, I fear I may faint. Alc turns from the window and takes stock of my appearance in my dress and hair. It sends a jolt through me, and I try to hide the blush creeping across my face. Once he seems satisfied with whatever he sees in me, he gestures to the empty seat next to Kai.

"Tilly sure does work miracles to make a human look presentable," Kai smirks, and I shoot him an annoyed look which he just laughs off.

Alc sits in a large armchair at the front of the group, and I notice the tall blond shift so he stands slightly behind him, like a bodyguard. The two females look in Alc's direction, waiting for him to speak.

"Everyone, I would like you to meet Keilee. She's small but feisty, so I would watch your backs if I were you," Alc smiles and the man behind him frowns deeply. "Keilee, this guard dog behind me is Neron, our spy master, and these two lovely ladies here are Naomi and Ianira."

The one Alc called Naomi waves her hand in a friendly gesture and I smile weakly. Her hair is blonde, like Neron's, and her eyes are a striking blue. She is beautiful and would surely pull anyone in just by her bright smile. My body relaxes a little until I notice Ianira staring at me with a hunger on her face that makes me worry about what she eats. Her hair is jet black and her eyes glow in the soft lighting of the morning sun. They are the colour of a raging fire whose embers float into the sky, falling to ash. I wince internally and she sniffs the air like a wild dog hunting its prey and smiles at me like a Cheshire cat. Alc clears his throat, and everyone swings their heads in his direction. I let loose a breath I didn't know I was holding, no longer holding the room's attention. My hand goes to my neck where I can feel the cool metal of the necklace. I absentmindedly trace the opal in the middle and feel my body relax slightly.

"Now that all the introductions are done, shall we get down to business?"

Neron nods his head, but Naomi interrupts him, her loud voice booming around the room.

"Can't we have a little fun first? It's been too long since we've had a newcomer."

Kai smiles at me and I can't tell if it's for reassurance sake or if he's waiting to see how things will play out. I'm inclined to think it's the latter.

"Yes, I would like that. I want to know how a human brought down Tiran," Ianira's voice is like melted chocolate, and I shudder at the irony that something so sweet belongs to a death trap.

Ianira turns to me and her eyes role over my face, "Go on, girl, tell us how you did it. Was it out of hate? Or just a sport you find entertaining?"

Straightening my back and clasping my hands, I speak,

"I killed him when he went for the buck I was hunting. He was about to lunge at me. I didn't have much choice."

Naomi frowns slightly, the action drawing a crease between her brows, "Ahh, I see now. You killed him out of fear for your own pathetic life. Tell me, what did you use to kill him?"

I try to keep my voice steady as I reply,

"An iron arrow."

The faces around me drop into scowls and I smile to myself. They do fear something. Naomi sits straighter in her seat and her eyes narrow on me.

"Where do you come from? Alc has told us very little of you and I'm curious to know more."

It's such a simple question that it knocks me off balance after the conversation about her friend's death. I stare at her for a moment, noting the way her lips tip up in a small smile like she finds my existence amusing.

"I come from Fallen Crest, just outside the Blood Wood Forest. I lived with my father and his wife and daughters."

Alc shifts in his seat like he wants to say something but Kai cuts across him.

"Tell me, Keilee, is your father always so drunk when he has company, or did we stumble upon him on a bad day?"

My body tenses and I try to lean back into the chair to settle my flinch at the question.

"That was actually a good day and now, if you don't mind, I would like the interrogation to be over with and for you to leave my family out of this."

Naomi's eyes darken, and I swear I catch a glimpse of remorse flashes it's way across her face before its replaced with calm indifference. Ianira looks at me and tilts her head in a searching way.

"You should fear us, girl. While Alc might be tolerant to have a murderer in the house, I'm not, so be careful not to turn your back on me."

My anger rises at the threat, and I can feel a dull pounding in my blood at her words. I wouldn't be in this mess if that damn wolf hadn't been in the clearing that day. I wouldn't have to find a way to escape while getting my mother's diary back.

"That may be true, but you should also be cautious of me. Hunters like their prey with a bit of fight in them," I smile broadly at her and, somewhere in the back of my head, I can feel the faint brush of masculine amusement.

I try and shake it out and turn to look at Alc, sitting in his armchair, tapping a finger on it, to find he's already looking at me. His green eyes piercing me. Ianira turns her nose up at me and also turns her gaze to Alc. He looks around the room and smiles at each of them, with the exception of me, and opens his mouth to speak.

"That was interesting, I think we can all agree. Now, the reason I called this meeting this morning is because the High Lords are getting impatient with us and are waiting for our response to the proposal they sent. I for one don't want another bloodshed, which the letter clearly states will arise."

Alc turns to me and I fight to keep my eyes on his as I hear Kai groan in his seat.

"We will need to be smart about this and somehow prevent war between us and the mortal realm, which will be no easy task. Trying to keep the old dog and his pet in line will prove to be testing to the patience."

Neron nods and I blink in confusion. Why would there be a war between humans and the Fae? For as long as I've been alive, I've never heard talk of war. It may be tense between us, but it would only end in humans being slaughtered without the help of the gods this time. It would be pointless. I assume when he said the old dog and his pet, he meant the King and Queen, and while I've never had much to do with them, I still feel protective over my monarch.

"I can get my guys in there to keep a watch on them if you want. It will give us an insight on what they are planning."

It's the first time I've heard Neron speak, and I'm taken back at how deep his voice is. Alc twists in his seat to glance at him

"Keep the number to a minimum and only send your best men. I will not risk anyone for one small slip up."

The spymaster nods and his jaw tightens. I get the feeling he's not happy with the insinuation that he would ever send anyone less than perfect. Naomi smiles at Neron and I feel more then see him relax. I wonder if there is anything going on between them? From the way Neron's gaze lingers on her even when she's not looking tells me that there is, but when he notices me watching, his face drops into a warning look and I quickly glance away. Alc turns next to Naomi and Ianira, who are both sipping from their glasses, waiting for his request.

"I need you two ladies to hit the books and find anything you can on Hugan and the human monarchs. Keep it strictly between the two of you and report back to me once you find anything."

Naomi frowns as she nods her head,

"We always get stuck with the boring jobs, why can't someone else do it?"

Alc laughs and takes a swig of his amber liquid,

"You do the boring jobs because you are second in command and there is no one I trust more to do the job. And Ianira's extensive knowledge when it comes to the gods will help you, and it doesn't hurt that she scares the librarians. You know how cagey they can be when giving information."

I'm more shocked that Naomi is second in command than I am by the fact that Alc is looking for information on the God of Death.

Naomi smiles and shakes her head softly,

"You have such a way with words, cousin."

At this point, I may as well keep my face frozen in surprise. Lastly, Alc turns to Kai and smiles with a wicked intent in his eyes. Kai straightens and returns the gesture.

"I want you to go to the High Lords and arrange a meeting with them in four weeks' time. Let them pick the meeting spot to quench their thirst for control and tell them that the High Lord of Night has an answer for them."

Kai's smile widens and I look between them, Kai catches my eye and looks back at Alc,

"As you command, my High Lord."

With that, he bows and spins on the spot, disappearing into thin air. I look at Alc with a deadpan expression, trying desperately to hide my dread at the news that I was indeed kidnapped by the High Lord of Night, not just some random Fae. Naomi smiles at me before both her and Ianira leave the room through the door I ventured through earlier. When it's just me,

Neron, and Alc left in the room, Alc looks to Neron and waves his hand in a dismissal.

"Get your men ready and send them out tomorrow."

Neron nods and turns to leave but stops and glares at me. Alc notices his hesitation and smiles at the spymaster.

"It's fine, I can handle her."

Neron doesn't look so sure but listens to his High Lord and leaves the room. I twist my hands together nervously when it's just me and Alc left in the room and try to swallow my panic. Alc turns to me and places his hands on the arms of his chair. He leans forward and leisurely taps his finger on the chair. He seems to be enjoying toying with me and making me uncomfortable. Finally, he stands and comes to a stop directly in front of me. I take my time running my eyes over his fascinating body to try and calm my nerves.

"Come with me."

The demand sends my muscles into a crazed frenzy. I stand slowly on numb legs but lift my head. If I'm going to die, I'm going to do it with my pride intact. My mother's necklace suddenly feels too tight. Have I failed her? I hate that I feel weak and helpless. My mother's kind words float through my minds defences:

'You are strong, my little flower, and remember you are never weak, just slowly blooming. All the best things take time.'

With her words tucked away, I follow Alc through yet another set of doors. I was never going to know this place off by heart. I would be lucky to even get a chance to see the soft bed I slept in again. Alc leads me off to the left and we enter a small, modest study with floor to ceiling bookshelves and deep oak writing desks. The soft yellow light of the chandelier casts a welcoming glow throughout the room. It's not the sort of place someone would be taken to be executed and my heart flutters with relief. Alc turns to face me with a stern expression on his face.

"You are going to learn how to lift your mind defences, I'm sick of hearing your thoughts echoing around in my head."

I tilt my head up at him. So, he can hear my thoughts? Part of me is relieved that I wasn't going crazy, and a larger part is repulsed by him. What did that make him? A mind reader?

"Princess, I'm not a circus clown, I'm a High Lord, the High Lord of Night, which makes me the master of nightmares and dreams, so of course I can enter people's heads."

That must have been him when I felt laughter that didn't belong to me.

"Can't you just block me out with your mighty power? I am just a useless human after all."

Alc looks at me with a thoughtful expression.

"Usually I would be able to do so, but you seem to yell your thoughts out louder than most and I only hear them when you are feeling a strong emotion, like anger, sadness, or fear."

I shift uncomfortably on my feet.

"Now, I'm going to try and enter your mind and I want you to shove me out with all you've got and raise your mental shields. Ready? Three, two, one."

I feel my mind being ripped open for all to see and I stumble back. My head is reeling as I feel rather than see him rifle through my thoughts, bringing forth the memory of when my father hit me with his bottle for spilling it on the floor when I was ten. A brush of anger floats through me and I can't tell if it's his or mine. My body begins to shake with the effort of standing.

Alc says from afar, "Push against me, throw me out."

I try and my breaths come out in quick pants. I picture myself shoving him with all my strength. His grip on my mind falters a bit and I imagine walls of reinforced steel rising and taking off his talon-like fingers, which are digging into my head. I see him flinch and rub his hands together like I actually hurt him. He is smiling and I'm taken back by how much more handsome it makes his face.

"That was good, brutal and aggressive, but good."

The adrenaline is starting to wear off and I need to sit. I walk over to one of the many armchairs and sink into its soft cushions. A dull headache is forming and sweat beads at my forehead.

Alc takes a seat next to me and places his hands in his lap, "I want you to keep practising raising that mental shield, and we will start physical training tomorrow morning. I have a few things I need to do and will see you at dinner to mark your progress."

I look at him and take in his furrowed brow and tight lips. Why was he helping me? What have I done to deserve his help? I killed his friend. And Fae and humans aren't supposed to be friendly towards each other.

"Why are you helping me? I thought you said you would rather dump me then have me as your burden."

His and Kai's words echo through my head.

"Why not? If I'm stuck with you, I might as well make use out of you."

I didn't believe that was the truth, but I didn't get a chance to argue back as he stands abruptly and walks to the door and leaves, but not before turning back to me, "Tilly and Alyssa are around if you need help, and remember to keep working on those shields. I will see you in a few hours, don't disappoint me."

I huff a hollow laugh. Why should I bother not disappointing others when I've already done that to myself? My headache turns from a dull throb to a stabbing every time I move my head, but I work through the pain, drawing from it, raising my shields and dropping them, imagining me slicing off a bit of Alc every time it rises, and when there is nothing left of him, I move on to Kai.

By the time Alyssa comes to collect me to get me ready for dinner, I've chopped my way through Alc three times and Kai two times. My head throbs and a permanent outline of my mental wall is etched behind my eye lids. Alyssa walks me back to my room, grabs a pale-yellow dress from the wardrobe, and drapes it over the chair in front of the writing desk.

"Master Alc would like you to know that he expects you downstairs in half an hour with your mental shields intact."

I nod and grab the dress off the chair.

"Where are we having dinner?"

It seems like such a stupid question, the dining room would be the suitable answer, but I don't know where that is. Alyssa points to the door.

"Down the stairs, third door on the right. Shouldn't be hard to find," Alyssa's iridescent wings flutter slightly and her light-blue skin shimmers.

"Thank you, where's Tilly tonight? I thought she was supposed to come get me this afternoon?"

Alyssa smiles at me, her slightly pointed teeth perfectly straight and white.

"She was but then she was needed down in the kitchens to help get dinner ready, so you're stuck with me, M'Lady."

I laugh and run the soft cotton of the yellow dress through my hands.

"Ok, well thank you for collecting me and picking out the dress."

Alyssa smiles again and leaves the room to let me bathe and

change. Fifteen minutes later, the light cotton gown I'm wearing swings and gently brushes my legs as I move. I tie back my hair with a matching ribbon and leave the room with false bravado. I silently pray to the gods that it will only be Alc, Kai, and me at the dinner. I don't think my nerves could handle another interrogation. I follow Alyssa's direction and find myself standing in front of the dining room doors. I hear soft voices and internally groan. Even from where I'm standing, I can make out the voices of Naomi and Ianira as they laugh at something Kai says. The doors swing open of their own accord. I step into the room and my eyes land on the massive dining room table. Alc is sitting at the head of the table, with Kai flanking his left and Neron flanking his right. Naomi and Ianira are standing off to the side and stare at me as I enter. My heart beats loudly in my chest and I focus on putting one foot in front of the other. I check that my mental shields are up and make my way to the spare seat next to Kai.

"The devil herself has finally decided to join us," Kai grins up at me.

"If I'm the devil, what does that make you? My play toy?"

Kai salutes me and takes a swig from his glass. Alc's brows are pinched, and he regards me with caution. He continues to stare at me, and my hands begin to sweat.

"What? Take a picture, it may last longer."

Coughing starts from beside me and I see Kai wipe his mouth on his sleeve.

"Someone sure has a quick tongue tonight," he glances at Alc. "And here I was thinking we captured a mute with no humour."

Neron looks at me over his glass and I see the faint flicker of amusement before it's replaced with his usual scowl.

Naomi's voice floats over to where we are seated, "Finally, another female who doesn't take Kai's shit."

She smiles brightly as she walks over to sit next to Neron, "We can now level out the playing field, can't we, boys?"

Alc smiles slightly and glances at Ianira, who is the only one left standing, looking for support.

"Don't look at me like that, boy, I play no part in defending your soft feelings."

Alc places a hand over his heart in mock hurt. He doesn't look like a High Lord now. He just looks like a man enjoying the company of his friends. My head hurts at the irony and a feeling I don't want to acknowledge grips my heart.

"I thought we had an alliance, but I can see that I'm mistaken and have been betrayed."

Ianira's lips tug into a small smile and she too takes her seat next to Naomi.

With a twist of Alc's wrist, the table becomes laden with dishes of meat and vegetables of many kinds. The sour smell of lemon dances on the air and my mouth waters. I had missed lunch and my stomach has been protesting ever since. I've never seen so much food in one place before. Even at the markets, food was limited and was restricted to dried meat and freshly harvested vegetables. Before I get a chance to admire the food further, everyone lunges at the plates to start filling their dishes. I'm amazed at the informality of it. From what little I remember of my time living in the manor, we always had people serving us the food and we wouldn't start until the head of the table took the first bite. Alc laughs at something Neron whispers and my heart aches for the close friendship they all seem to share. My eyes roam over the table and I feel out of place around these people. Again, I find myself as an outsider and I hate it. In a way, I was jealous of Isabella and Laura, with the way they made friends so easily. They had beauty and the ability to seem nice when around others. I thought it pointless and a waste of time to pretend to like someone when they could just as easily stab you in the dark when you weren't watching. It's funny that, when I'm surrounded by people, I feel the loneliest I've ever felt. Alc glances at me over his plate of food and I quickly check if my shields are still intact and breathe a gentle sigh of relief. He continues to stare at me, and I place my fork down aggressively.

"Do you have a problem? Is there something wrong with my face?"

It's the second time I've caught him staring and I'm losing the last of my already low patience. Naomi coughs to cover her laugh and Ianira tilts her head curiously. Neron doesn't look at all impressed and stabs his chicken aggressively, as if trying to channel his anger away from me. Kai just leans back in his seat, so I have a clear view of Alc's face. I grip my knife harder in my hand.

"No, I wouldn't say there's anything wrong with your face, I might even go as far to say it's a rather pretty face. What's bothering me is why you are still shouting thoughts at me even when your shields are up."

I blink at this and furrow my brow. Is he messing with me?

"It's rude to be privy to other's thoughts without permission, so stop reading my mind."

Kai snorts and rubs his chest, leaning further into his chair.

"Trust me, I would rather not have to suffer listening to your sad thoughts if I could help it."

The knife I'm holding in my hand becomes heavy and I roll my shoulders. Neron clears his throat and I glance at Naomi and Ianira, who have begun eating again like nothing's happening, it only adds to my sudden anger.

"You're a jackass, did you know that? All you've done since I've met you is throw insults at me and you won't even tell me what I'm doing in this godforsaken place. Is it an apology you want from me? Is that it?" I take a deep breath and continue. "Well, I'm sorry I shot your friend. Maybe he shouldn't have been trying to kill me in the first place. There, happy now?"

All eyes find me and the soft clink of cutlery on dishes cease to exist. Alc roams his eyes over the group before stopping on me.

"You got yourself into this mess, not me. I wasn't the one living with a drunk and his little pets. And need I remind you that you murdered a friend? I don't care for one minute if he was supposedly going to kill you, I care that we are now stuck with you and that you are wearing down my will to let you live."

Naomi glares at Alc and shakes her head slightly.

"As for your apology, you can keep it. I don't want the lies you tell no matter how sugar-coated they are."

The tension in the room is thick enough to cut. Ianira stares at me, and I can feel Kai's gaze as I continue to look at Alc. Neron clears his throat again and I shoot the spymaster a glare, who returns it.

"Ha, I couldn't care less if you don't accept my apology but don't bring my family into this, they have nothing to do with this."

Alc smiles and fire rips through my veins.

"What family? The one that would rather see you die than look after you? If that's what you call family, I really do pity you."

I stand abruptly and swing to face him fully,

"I don't need your pity."

He smiles at me, and I turn abruptly, letting the skirts of my dress swing against my leg as I walk towards the doors of the dining room. I freeze as I hear Alc's laughter bounce through the room. I spin towards him once again, take the knife still clutched in my hand, and throw it as hard as I can at him. I watch as it flies through the air to land directly in front of him, where his hands were clasped together seconds ago. The handle wobbles from the force of the tip being embedded into the solid wood, and his eyes widen. I smile and spin on my heels, leaving the room but not before I hear a low whistle from Kai and Naomi's booming laughter. I make my way up the stairs and collapse on my bed with a groan. This was the worst way the dinner could have gone. I had lost my temper and threw a knife at a Fae, and not just any Fae, but one of the High Lords of Thyithran. The adrenaline is wearing off and in its place is a dread so heavy I feel like I'm sinking through the bed. I get up, change into my sleeping clothes, and wrap myself in the blankets, like a mother's embrace. My eyes drift closed and, right before I drift off, I swear I can hear the soft tap of someone's knuckles on the door.

Chapter 6

The sheets are pulled from my legs, and I groan, slapping beside me to bring them back up to my chest. Laughter sounds and I bolt upright at the sound, finding Alc standing at the end of my bed with fighting leathers in one of his hands and a jewel-handled dagger in the other. I grasp for the sheets and pull them around me.

"What do you think you're doing?' my voice is rough with sleep and doesn't mask my anger very well, flashbacks of last night come into play.

"Training, remember, or did you think you would get out of it because of last night's episode?" he smiles at me, and I huff but climb out of bed and rip the fighting leathers out of his hands.

"You can leave now. I don't need a babysitter."

I turn to head to the bathroom when his voice sounds behind me,

"And how do you think you'll make your way to the training ring without a guide?"

I groan and wave my hand,

"Fine, stay if you want, but don't move from there, I don't trust you."

His laugh is husky and a shiver courses through me at the sound,

"Trust me, the feeling is mutual."

My hand stills on the bathing chamber's door handle and my head whips to his while a wicked smile plays on my mouth.

"What? You don't trust me or yourself?"

Alc waves me away with a small smile spread across his handsome face. I slap myself mentally and make my way into the bathroom. Now is not the time to goad a High Lord. I strip from my sleeping attire and pull on the tight fighting leathers, strapping and tying everything in place, which is no easy task. I feel as if I'm being strapped into a fishing net with the never-ending strings. I glance at myself in the mirror near the door and try to pull the legs of the leathers down a bit. With these clothes, I might as well parade around naked. The shorts barely reach mid-thigh and the top hugs my form like a second skin. I tug on knee-high boots I found in my wardrobe and tie my hair back from my face in a braid. By the time I leave the bathroom, I find Alc lounging on my bed, one leg tapping against the other.

"Finally, I thought you had drowned in the bath water or something."

I shoot him a glare,

"It's not my fault. These leathers are so tight and have so many strings in places I didn't know needed tying off."

Alc runs his eyes down my body and back up again, his eyes darken, and I swallow thickly. He clears his throat and gestures for me to follow him. We walk down the stairs and head straight until we come to large wooden doors that lead outside. My breath catches, it's the first time I've been outside since the night we arrived here. I blink at the growing sun casting early morning shadows across the sight before me. Buildings litter streets of cobblestone, their roofs gleaming in the light. Fae and other creatures mill about, enjoying the crisp morning, I can see from where I'm standing children running around, one carrying a small fluffy creature of some kind. I gape at the gardens lining the street and accidently catch the eye of an old woman bowed with age trimming her rose hedge. She smiles brightly and waves at me, I'm taken back by the everyday gesture and return it with an awkward flourish of my hand. I wonder to myself if they know who I am and that I killed one of them. My chest constricts and the unfamiliar feeling of guilt creeps through me. I turn to Alc, who is waving to people as they pass with a bright smile plastered on his face. Even with his people, he is carefree and open. They don't bow to him or cower away like he is the ruler of them, instead they talk to him like he is a friend. Alc turns to me and his smile drops off his face as if he's ashamed I was witness to his kindness. I clear my throat at the sudden tension between us.

"How come not everyone looks like you?" I gesture to him, and he stiffens.

"Because I am of the high Fae, and others are from the lesser Faeries groups. Only people from the high Fae look like me, with my human features."

I nod, still confused.

"So, your friends in there," I point to the house. "Are high Fae as well, while Alyssa is a lesser Faerie?"

He nods his head and continues to explain it to me.

"Many of the lesser Faeries have animal and insect-like features, hence Alyssa's wings and blue skin. While high Fae have more restricted appearances but can sometimes have one or two animals features, like a tail. Most don't though."

My mind whirls and I look out over the busy street to spot many of the lesser Faerie-kind milling around and a few high Fae mixing with them.

"Isn't it a bit offensive to call them lesser Faerie just because they look different?"

Alc tilts his head towards me, curiosity playing across his features,

"It is and that's why many protest being called something different. The name comes from when we were divided as a different race but has long since become habit to call them this."

I again nod and look down at my feet. I would hate being called lesser just because I look different, and I wonder if Alc is one of the people who believe in changing the name. I change the subject as the silence grows.

"How are we getting to the training rings?"

Alc smiles again and I get a feeling that I'm not going to like his answer.

"We fly."

Before I get to ask how, massive wings spread out from behind him and I jump back. They are beautiful and dark, the colour of molten molasses. I can see thin veins running through the parts where the skin is stretched to cover the fine bone structure. I resist the urge to run my hands across them and clench my hands at my side to stop myself.

"I thought only lesser Faeries had insect-like features?"

Alc glares at me,

"Do these look like insect wings?"

I shake my head; they look like dragon wings.

"I'm the High Lord of Night, we were born to rule amongst the stars."

It makes sense that the King of Night would have wings to fly over his people as they dream but it doesn't make the fact any less scary and magnificent. Alc grabs my hand and tugs me towards him. I freeze when he scoops me up in his arms like I'm no heavier then a sack of feathers. When I realise what he's about to do, I grab onto his leathers and let out a shriek. There was no way I was flying with him holding me. I didn't have a strong enough heart for that kind of fear.

"I not flying with you."

My protests are drowned out as he crouches and shoots to the sky, my scream leaving me in a hollow breath. He straightens out and glides through the early morning. My heart is a raging beast in my chest, and I feel as if I might pass out. I gulp and turn my head into his chest out of fear I might vomit on him. He laughs, the sound vibrating off his chest.

"Now, Princess, don't worry, I'm not going to drop you."

I laugh at that,

"Yeah, right. I don't believe that for one minute."

Alc raises an eyebrow and releases me from his arms. At first, I can't believe he actually dropped me, but then I'm screaming as the ground comes closer with each passing second. Next moment, strong arms close around my body, and I start punching every inch of him I can reach while he's holding me.

"You are such a dick, why would you do that?'

Alc laughs and I aim a punch at his face, which he dodges easily.

"That's what you get for doubting my words, I was never going to let you hit the ground, well not by the end anyway."

I pinch him hard on the arm and wish for the knife I had last night.

"Ow, that hurt, Princess," he rubs his arm while still managing to hold on to me.

"Don't call me Princess. You know my name, so use it," I look up at him and catch him staring at me, his green eyes piercing me.

"Yes, but it's much more fun to see you bite at me for calling you Princess."

I slap him and turn to brave a look over my arms at the sight spread beneath us. The city is turning into farmlands, and I notice hills of yellow and red spread wide. Farmers are tiny dots, like ants scurrying around their nest. The soft hills turn into rugged mountain ranges and soon we are diving down to meet the rocky surface of one of the many ridges. As the ground becomes more than a blur of colour, I notice a small congregation of huts lined up next to each other in ordered chaos. Next to the houses is a large arena filled with sand and fighting warriors sweating under the morning sun's rays. They move with unnatural grace in a deadly dance, the glint of steel clashes together in practiced movements, and I forget that I'm in a High Lord's arms. Alc lands gently on the ground and lets go of me once I find my feet. The fighting in the ring stops and I notice the familiar head of red hair blowing in the wind. Kai waves us over and claps the man he was fighting on the back with one large hand.

"Took you long enough to arrive. Take the scenic route, did we?"

Alc laughs,

"Couldn't pass up the opportunity to show off, is more like it."

I don't doubt his words,

"You mean you liked scaring the living shit out of me and didn't want the fun to end so soon."

Kai laughs, the sound low and deep. I glance at Alc as he takes in his surroundings.

"Where's Higens? I thought he was supposed to be overseeing the training today?"

Kai rubs a hand over the back of his neck and sighs,

"That was supposed to be the plan, but I think he had other ideas that involved his other head."

I wince and pull a face at the implication,

"Okay, way too much information for this early in the

morning."

Kai and Alc grin at each other before Alc's face falls into a serious expression.

"All jokes aside, he has a job and I expect it to be done. Go fetch him for me and tell him I'm not at all impressed."

Kai nods and makes his way through the small crowd that had gathered at the arrival of their High Lord. Males dressed in leathers and armed to the teeth glare at me, and women with small children stare at me like I'm a mare on display.

Alc notices and claps his hands together, "Back to business, everyone."

I sigh internally and thank him silently for his perceptiveness. Kai comes trotting back a minute later with a man that looks to be in his early thirties but, with the Fae's immortal lifespans, it means he could be older than a century. His dirty blonde hair is dishevelled, and he reeks of alcohol, but when he speaks his voice is even and low.

"Sorry, my Lord. I had urgent business to attend to this morning."

Alc glares at him and sees right through his lie,

"Is that so? And does this urgent business involve a pretty young tailor?"

The older man looks at Alc and then me, a smile spreading across his face,

"I could ask the same of you, my Lord."

Alc's face drops into a scowl and the male realises his mistake and takes a step back.

"Don't you assume that I would sink to your low level, Higens. Now, apologise to the lady."

I look at Higens as his face turns sour.

"I am sorry for the insinuation, Lady," his face contradicts his words.

Alc shakes his head and looks over at Kai, who is standing with his arms crossed.

"Get the troops doing survival drills I need the arena this morning for Keilee."

Kai nods and calls over to a woman dressed in full length leathers. She looks fierce, with her hair braided back and keen eyes.

"Move to the west side of the village, we are going through some survival drills."

The woman nods her head and leads a small group into the small town and out of sight. With a wave at us, Kai follows at a steady jog. When it's just me, Alc, and Higens, I shift on my feet, eager to see where the morning will lead. Alc turns on his heels and walks over to the sandy arena. Higens follows and stops at the side of the boundary.

"What do you need my assistance with, my Lord?"

Alc turns back to the male and smiles keenly,

"I need you to be our test dummy this morning. Keilee, here, is very practiced with a bow and I would like to see what we need to improve on first, so I thought we could use you as a target."

Higens' face pales.

"But don't worry, she won't be aiming to hit you. Well, not at first anyway, just depends on how you behave."

Higens shakes his head quickly,

"With all due respect, my Lord, I don't fancy putting my life in danger because of some *human whore*."

Alc nods his head once, the action more frightening than any glare. His eyes sharpen and soft swirls of shadow encase his hands. I take a step back at the calm rage as he stares down Higens, who cowers under the look.

"I said she has exceptionally good aim and now I'm wondering if we should even bother pretending to spare your life. Get in the ring. Now."

The command awakens the fear hiding on Higens' face, but he follows Alc's command, not before mumbling under his breath at me when he passes. I stare after him and Alc places a bow and quiver of arrows into my hand. I welcome the familiar weight and sling the quiver over my shoulder, slowly walking over to a large wooden wall with many arrow holes from previous training. Alc leads Higens to stand in front of the middle of the wall. His large body blocking the whole target except for two small lines on either side of his head. Once Alc is happy with where Higens is standing, he marches over to me.

"I want you to aim for those lines next to his head, get as close as you can without hitting him."

I fiddle with the bow and Alc places a hand over it, "Don't worry if you hit him, he is a waste of air anyway."

He smiles at me, and I pull an arrow from my sling.

"Won't he just move when I shoot the arrow?"

With a shake of his head, he turns to Higens, "We won't move, will we, Higens?"

I see him try to nod his head but then he gives in and answers,

"No, my Lord, I will not move."

Alc turns to me and grins, a mischievous glint in his eyes.

"He's had some persuasion," Alc flicks his hand casually and Higens brings a hand to his face and slaps himself.

I gape up at Alc as he smiles down at me,

"'You're controlling him, aren't you?'

A single nod from him, and I turn my head to look at Higens, locking the arrow I'm holding into place. Higens' eyes widen, and I smile at him, half scared at the sudden viciousness I possess. The other half marvels at the fact that I'm not just some weak human. I pull back the string of the bow and catch, out of the corner of my eye, Alc smiling at me. My hand shakes slightly and I steady it by focusing on the faint black line next to Higens' head. I aim with practised ease and release the arrow with a flick of my hand. The arrow flies through the air and I hold my breath as it lands directly next to his head where the mark is. Before I can lose my nerve, I pull another arrow from my quiver and pull the string back again, aiming for the other side of his face. I let the arrow go and smile as it catches a lock of his hair and pins it to the black mark not even an inch away from his ear. Alc whistles and I see Higens go limp, pulling the arrow out of the wood and releasing the bit of hair that was pinned. Anger like no other I've witnessed crosses his face and he stalks to where Alc and I are standing, but instead of lunging out at his High Lord, he turns to me and spits at my feet.

"You stupid girl, you could have killed me, and for what, to make yourself look less useless?"

The words strike deep but I keep it from showing on my face. Alc stiffens and before I can blink, Higens bows over and screams under the pain of invisible hands punishing him. Alc doesn't so much as blink and lets Higens lay on the sand panting.

"Next time I will not be so forgiving, do you understand?"

Higens barely nods, Alc steps over him and walks towards the weapons rack.

"Get up. Go fill your time with something useful and keep it in your pants. Also remember to never insult her again, otherwise I will be the least of your worries by the time she's done with you," Alc points at me and I can't help but smile slightly.

Whatever game he's playing, it will surely end with me on

the receiving end, but for the moment I play along and follow Alc to come to a stand in front of him.

"Since that's out of the way, shall we get down to business?"

I nod and Alc continues, "Spread your feet shoulder-width apart and straighten your back."

I do as he says, and he nods.

"Think of fighting with your opponent as a dance that's constantly changing. You need to be light on your feet and quick, you can't always rely on brute strength to save your arse. Now, hands up and punch this," he holds up a punching pad and I raise my fist, getting ready to aim.

He shakes his head, "First mistake, you dropped your elbow and presented a weakness to me. Once you drop your elbow when aiming a punch, it gives the opponent an opening to hit you when your balance is off."

I raise my elbow and punch the pad, rocking back on my heels.

"Good, but you need to swing your body into the punch for a better effect, just using your fist and arm won't win you the fight."

I look up at him and grimace,

"Who knew punching was so complicated?"

I aim for the pad again, keeping my elbow up and swinging with my hips. When I connect with the pad, Alc smiles at me and I smile back.

"Better. I want you to keeping hitting this pad, changing between sides, until I can see that it becomes second nature for you. Ready? Go."

And so, we continue like this until the sun is high in the sky and my arms feel like lead. Left then right, over and over, Alc giving me pointers on the way. Sweat beads at my forehead and my leathers cling to my slick and hot skin. When he drops the pad, signalling the end of another round, I sigh and run a hand through my hair, catching the stray pieces that have escaped my braid. I need water and a good long nap. Alc motions for me to follow and leads me over to a water stand I hadn't noticed; he pours me a drink and I gulp down the cool liquid, thinking to myself that nothing has ever tasted so good. I turn when I hear footsteps approaching the training ring and meet Kai's gaze.

"Someone looks like they've been busy," he gestures to my sweaty body. "What did you have her do? Run laps?"

Alc smiles, "Core and punching work, she has good form, but extremely poor balance, and we might need to start with the very basics of footwork."

I glare at him and chuck the cup at his chest; he just laughs and wipes the splash of water off his black tunic.

"You said that I did well, you're only changing your mind now that we have company. Are you scared what others might think of your kindness to a human?"

It's Alc's turn to glare, and I smirk back at him.

"You've wounded me," he places a hand over his heart and Kai rolls his eyes.

"Listen here, you two, we have places to be, and the sun is not going to wait for you to stop your bickering, so come along now," Kai grins at Alc, who makes an obscene gesture, which Kai slaps away like reprimanding a naughty child.

"Don't forget who's in charge here, your head doesn't need to become any bigger than it already is."

Kai flips Alc off and winks at me.

"Keilee, I want you to come with me to the town house where we will work on your mind defences again. And, Kai, Neron has apparently found out from a source what the King and

Queen are planning in the coming days, so I want you to run through it with him and report back to me."

Kai nods and disappears in front of us. Alc turns to me and extends his arms, "Ready to go?"

I nod but my legs turn to jelly, I don't know if my nerves would be able to handle another flight wrapped in his arms. Placing my life in his hands quite literally makes my stomach turn. Before I can voice my concerns, he scoops me up and holds me close to his chest. I breathe in his scent of cedar and leather, and it calms me slightly. I don't know how he manages to be my worst nightmare and still be able to make me feel safe. We fly over the same hills and fields we ventured over in the morning and soon we arrive at the town house. The streets are still crowded, and the activity shows no sign of slowing, I've never liked the company of people much; I find them to be too loud and annoying. But here, I find myself wanting to explore amongst them and hear their stories of this magical land. Alc places me down and we walk through the silent house to the same study as the last time we practised the mental shield. I stand in front of the large hearth and Alc takes a seat in a worn leather chair. He nods to me.

"I'm going to try and enter your mind again, but this time I want you to push me away before I can get too close."

I square my shoulders and roll my neck. My fingers flex and I feel my mental shields, making sure they are solid. Next thing, I feel the phantom brush of talons against my walls and it makes me want to lower them, but I keep them up and stab in the dark at Alc's greedy hands. I feel myself hit something and he recoils back until I can no longer feel him and his talons. Alc smiles and pride floods through me. I'm sure that, if he really tried, he could shatter my wall without a second thought, but I don't let that bring me down.

"Very good. I'm going to try again and this time I'm going to be a bit harsher to test how strong your walls are."

"I'd like to see you try," I tease him and he smirks.

I shiver as his talons brush my shield again but harder this time. A sweat breaks out across my brow as I concentrate on keeping him out. He pushes harder and I feel a crack form in my wall, Alc again pushes and breaks through this time. He rifles through my thoughts like he did the first time, and he brings forward the memory of my mother sitting on my bed, humming as I fall asleep to the sweet melody. Anger surges through my veins at the violation he's committing. I'm laid bare before him; I feel amusement from somewhere far off.

"You are making yourself weak by allowing me to be in here, get rid of me," his words bounce around in my head and I have the strange urge to follow them. So, I do. I walk towards where the voice is coming from. When the dull echo fades completely, I can see a transparent bridge, like one that would join one town to the next. Black mist floats in the air, glittering like crushed starlight, and I run my hand through it, finding that it parts for me. I put a cautious foot on the bridge to find it solid. I begin to walk across it and the mist begins to darken, my heart races and I get the growing instinct to run. But why run when I'm just inside my head? No longer can I hear or see Alc and I wonder if I've managed to push him out and if I'm just wasting time. The black mist suddenly rushes past me and my footing slips on the bridge, but I regain my balance and freeze as the mist forms a large black wall with all the constellations of the night sky engraved into it. I walk closer and place a hand on the wall, my hand looks pale against such a dark surface. I test it by pushing my hand against it to find it falls at my touch, revealing a space much like my own head. But I know this is not my mind I'm in but someone else's. Is Alc showing me what it's like to enter someone's mind and why it's so dangerous? I walk further into the area only to find myself coming face to face with millions of stars floating right in front of me. Out of stupidity, or something equally as dooming, I reach out and touch one of the floating stars. It latches onto my hand, and I try and shake it off only to find it engulfing my arm, I take a step back and collide with the wall that I had removed earlier. As the star consumes me, I fall forward to soon land on my feet again, but I'm not in the star-filled space any more but instead I stand in a field painted crimson by human and Fae bodies laid bare. Their sightless eyes stare at nothing and I can smell death leaking from every pore of their still bodies. I turn and almost vomit as more bodies pile on each other. This is slaughter. A figure in the distance hunches over a body of a Fae male, their shoulders are shaking as a sob tears through them. I feel sick to be surveying such a horrid thing that seems too personal. Curiosity pulls me closer all the while to the hunched figure and I notice dark, silken hair and beautiful green eyes fogged over by a never-ending sleep. My heart stills as I stare down at a dead Alc. I glance over at the figure still bowed over the body and a tremble rips through me. His black hair is tied back at the nape of his neck, the fighting leather hugging his spectacular body. He blinks and stands slowly, his face erasing all emotion. I step back with the sudden change. Alc's green eyes hold something so powerful I have to look away. My gaze lands on the prone figure on the ground, this man, no boy's face is young and free of the stresses of adulthood. His smooth skin is tan, like Alc's, and his ears come to a delicate point at the end. Realisation hits me with the force of a hundred stampeding horses. Alc's brother is who lays on the ground, torn from the world too soon. I turn back to Alc, who is sheathing his sword. My whole body shudders and the instinct to run is pushing at me like I've never felt before. Something pulls at my heart, and I gasp. The High Lord of Night has broken, and nothing will stop him from destroying the world to avenge his brother. I fear for the soul who has to encounter him next. Shadows dance at his fingertips and wrap around his arms like armour, his massive wings spread behind him, and he shoots into the sky, pushing me back with the force of it. Death on swift wings. The land around me fades and takes the bodies with it. I find myself standing in front of the stars again, but instead of touching another one, I run to the wall and find it falls just as easily as it did when I entered. The bridge still stands, and I sprint away from the black mist, my legs burning. Suddenly, I'm falling and I close my eyes to try and stop the impact of hitting the ground. When no pain hits me, I open my eyes to find myself standing in the same place I was before we started the mind training. The hearth's heat sinks into my skin and it's then that I realise I'm shivering with a cold that doesn't have anything to do the with the room temperature. I look away from the fire and straight into eyes so green they challenge the spring fields. Alc stands before me with wide eyes, shock is written into every feature of his face as he begins to back away.

"Wait, what just happened?"

I try to grab onto his tunic but he's too quick. He spins and leaves the room without so much as a backwards glance. My legs choose this moment to fail me, and I sink into the chair Alc had vacated. I sit there staring into the dancing flames until sleep lures me in and pulls me under. I don't know how long I sit there, but by the time my eyes flutter open, sunshine is no longer encasing the room in light, but darkness is instead blinding me, and I have to blink a few times to adjust to my surroundings. The silence is deafening, and I shiver at the drop in temperature now that the fire is no longer warming me. I stand and walk to the door and enter the light-flooded hallway, I look left then right and hear nothing but pressing silence. Racking my brain for the way to my rooms, I don't notice the creeping darkness at the end of the hallway until I'm enclosed in it.

"Shit," my voice echoes through the empty house and fear tries to hound me, but I shove it down. Why are the lights out? I blindly search the walls for any way to light the torches adorning the walls. I try to soften my footsteps on the floor to not alarm anyone nearby, which is useless and I seem to be the only one in the house. A window approaches and I can see the faint glow of moonlight seeping through the open curtains. The city streets are empty, but lights glow softly from houses and I breathe a sigh of relief; I'm not completely alone. After some more stumbling and tripping up the many steps, I find my chambers and practically run over to the lamp and switch it on. Light floods the room and I sit on my bed to stare at the clock ticking away on the wall. The handles show that it's one o'clock in the morning. My stomach protests at missing dinner but I can't bring myself to care. Darkness that has nothing to do with no lights encases me and I'm suddenly back in the small hut watching my father as he swings a hand at me, landing sluggishly on my face. Pain spreads across my cheek but it barely registers as I'm too busy gaping at Alice, Laura, and Isabella as they flaunt the assorted colours of silks on the table.

My voice is stiff and tired as I ask,

"Where did you get those; please don't tell me you used the savings for food on them?"

My twelve-year-old body is aching and the pain in my cheek spreads to my neck.

"Your father said it was all right, so stop fussing. We have plenty of money for food."

Anger rises at Alice's words; did she have any sense? We were poor and losing what little was left of the fortune Father didn't spend on alcohol.

"Are you mad? We don't have enough to pay for salt let alone the finest silk the world has to offer, you're wasting money."

Isabella sneers at me, "Just because you want to live like a commoner doesn't mean we want to."

I rub a hand over my face and ignore the pain it causes. I walk over to the food storer to find it empty and my heart pounds.

"Have you even looked at this? We have nothing left and you thought it smart to spend the money on silk instead of food?"

Alice's eyes narrow on me, and she looks as if she wants to say something, but my father interrupts her.

"Are you questioning my ability to look after this family, Keilee?"

I scoff and turn to face him,

"Only when you're stupid enough to let us starve."

As soon as it leaves my mouth, I regret it. Not because of guilt or love towards him but because I see his fist before it collides with my already aching face. I stumble back and spit blood from my mouth. I glare at him, tears in my eyes, and grab the bow and arrows leaning against the wall. Stalking to the door, I turn and spit at him. It lands at his feet and Alice steps forwards, but I'm already out the door and trudging down the mud track to the Blood Wood Forest. It was my first, and no doubt first of many, hunt and I will never forget the fear I had as I stepped off the trail to hunt the rabbit I spotted. I lost part of myself that day, but I had also gained something, too. I gained the ability to hide my emotions and never let them show to the monster sitting in the hut near the dead village. I snap back to reality and stand from my bed, my leathers digging into me. I bathe and change into my sleepwear; my movements are stiff and my muscles protest. Despite my long nap. as soon as I lie down on my pillow, sleep drags me down and drowns me.

Chapter 7

Weeks pass in a blur and my life becomes like a routine; up early, training with Kai in the arena, then back before noon to work on my mental shields. Apart from my training with Kai, Alyssa and Tilly are the only ones I see milling around the house. I haven't laid eyes on Alc since the incident in the study three weeks ago and I'm beginning to think he's avoiding me. As for the rest of his gang, I haven't heard a peep from them, not that I mind. It means no further interrogation. I don't know how much scrutiny I could take from them. After training with Kai this morning, my legs and core scream at me. I've become good at punching, and we have moved onto balance and footwork, which apparently involves lots of push ups and squats. Alyssa buzzes around the study I'm in looking for only god knows what. I was helping her but, after I got in her way three times, I thought it better if I just sat down and let her find what she needed. I've asked both her and Tilly where Alc is and all I get is, 'He's been called away for important business'. My head throbs after removing and replacing my shield. I blink rapidly to clear the fog in my mind and turn to where Alyssa is standing with a large tome in her hands. It looks like it weighs a tonne. She stalks over to the desk in front of me and slams the book down with more force then necessary.

"Someone seems a bit flustered this afternoon.'

She shoots me a glare,

"You would be too if you were told you had to teach

someone a whole year's worth of history in three days."

I cringe and she pulls a face, "Yes, I'm supposed to show you the ins and outs of a ducks bum in three damn days otherwise it's my head on a silver platter."

"Why all of a sudden? I've been here for over a month with plenty of time to learn this."

She shakes her head at me, expression tight, "Master Alc has received word from the other High Lords of Thyithran and they've decided to have the meeting in three days at the Winter court. He thinks it wise that you know the history and background of each court."

I run a hand through my unbound hair,

"Three days to learn all that? I'm going to be dead by the end of it, and why teach me all this when I won't even be attending the meeting?"

Alyssa chooses this moment to busy herself with flipping through the pages of the old tome. I arch a brow and she sighs.

"I have been informed that you are to attend the meeting with Alc and are to present yourself as his representative of the human realm."

A laugh burst from me, and I have to hold my stomach as it protests at the sudden movement. Me? A representative? He has to be out of his mind.

"He should have selected someone with a bit more knowledge than me. All I'm bound to do is embarrass him, and don't even get me started on how I'll be the only human surrounded by the most powerful Fae in Thyithran."

Alyssa nods, a frown tugging on her lips.

"You have the High Lord of Night's protection, so no harm will come to you if you stay close to him."

Anger flares at her words. Typical of him to get other people to relay a message he could have told me himself.

"And how am I supposed to do that when I haven't even caught a glimpse of him for the last few weeks? He should be the one teaching me this if he wants me to attend this stupid meeting."

Alyssa's frown only deepens,

"That may be true, but his word is law, and I am not one to question him. Now, let's get this over with before I lose all patience."

I nod reluctantly and she flips through the book until she lands on a page with different spring flowers adorning the edge.

"The Spring court is the smallest of the courts and is in between Winter and Day. The High Lord of Spring is Kelby, he is young by our standards and is untested as a leader, but he shows a streak of cruelty, like his father before him, so he is not to be trusted. He can control flora and is able to shift forms to suit his needs," Alyssa points to an outline of a man with straight forward features.

The page no doubt not giving his beauty justice. The man's hair is deep brown with blonde strips running all through it and it hangs past his shoulders in gentle braids. His eyes are a pale blue, which matches the crown sitting on his head, much like the soft waters of the lakes surrounding the Blood Wood. I shiver as he smiles at me from the page, cunning hiding behind the boyish charm written on his face.

Alyssa continues, "He is able to create nature wherever he travels as long as he has some sort of plant near him, no matter its state of life."

"So, the only way to stop him would be to put him in a cell with no plants?"

Alyssa looks at me like I'm stupid, which she's not exactly

wrong about when it comes to High Lords and their limits.

"Not exactly. He draws his power from nature, yes, but even if he's locked away in a cell in the middle of a desert, he could still find the pull of a weed hidden in the sand. It would only give him weak power, of course, but it would not be impossible."

I sit back in my chair and groan, "So, there wouldn't be a way to stop him if he were to turn ugly?"

Alyssa shakes her head at me,

"Even the most venomous snake bites have an antidote, one only needs to find it."

I blink at her, my confusion clear as she rolls her eyes and continues, "The High Lord's weakness is ice, plants don't often survive the cold and it weakens his ability to pull from them, which is why I'm guessing he's not too happy to be having this meeting in the Winter court."

I wonder to myself if they planned this to gang up on the younger High Lord. Alyssa flips to the next page, which reveals a sun shining at the top and I don't have to be a genius to guess that the man standing on the page is the High Lord of the Day court. His strong face is covered with sun-kissed skin and his hair is the colour of the sun itself. Even from the paper, a weak glow radiates from him, and I feel calm just looking at him. His eyes are a deep blue to match the fiercest ocean waters. Alyssa taps the page with a slender blue finger.

"Adian is what the other High Lords call the peacekeeper, which is a bit overrated as he's the one that starts most of the small bickers between them all. He has a sense of humour that most people would find offensive, so I suggest keeping a sharp tongue when around him. But he's wise and the oldest of the High Lords at seven hundred and thirty-five years old."

Alyssa smiles at me as I balk at the number. It shouldn't

come as a surprise to me. I knew that the Fae were immortal, but it still hits hard to learn just how long they can live when I will be lucky to make it to one hundred.

"Adian's weakness is water, believe it or not. He draws his light from the sun, and when it's wet or raining, the sun's power is weaker so he becomes weaker. But he is the oldest for a reason, so I wouldn't be so quick to judge him."

I nod, absorbing as much as I can from the page, my curiosity thriving with the information. Alyssa eyes me curiously, then turns to a piece of paper that wasn't there before and slides it over to me. On it is all the birth days of the High Lords and next to them are their parents' names. The youngest is indeed Kelby, him being only two hundred and thirty years old, which to me seems to be ridiculous as two hundred is two human life spans and is no funny thing.

Alyssa taps a finger over Adian's and Kelby's names,

"Focus on memorising their details today, and tomorrow we will move onto the High Lords of Summer and Autumn, and the day after we will work on Alc and the High Lord of Winter."

"Why do I have to learn about Alc when he is going to be with me the whole time and is the one I know the best?"

Alyssa taps his name and rips the sheet from my hands before I can read his age.

"Master Alc has said that you must learn about *all* the High Lords, including him. So, if you have a problem with it, take it up with him not me."

I glare at her but listen as she runs through more details about the High Lord of Spring and Day. How am I supposed to ask Alc if he's avoiding me like the plague? My stomach aches by the time we finish and all I can see is the outline of flowers and the sun after all the studying. Tilly comes bounding into the study, a smile plastered on her face, breaking the dreary spell over me. Alyssa smiles back and places the tome we were using back on the shelf for tomorrow's use. Tilly turns her grin to me, and I await her words, dreading what has brought such a smile to her face.

"Master Alc has requested a private dinner with you, M'Lady. He wishes me to tell you to be dressed and ready in half an hour."

Alyssa turns to me, her eyebrows raised. My hands begin to sweat, and I worry as to why Alc wants to see me now when the last time we spoke was when I somehow saw a memory of his. Alyssa stands and I notice I'm still staring at Tilly.

"A private dinner with me?"

The words blurt out before I have time to stop them.

Tilly nods,

"Unless my hearing fails me, then yes, that's what he said. Now hurry, we don't have much time."

Tilly trots from the room and I follow, trying to match her quick pace. Once we arrive at my rooms, she runs off to the bathroom to run a bath and I set about picking a dress from the wardrobe. I settle with a dusty pink dress that billows softly in the slight breeze wafting through the open window. Once the bath is ready, Tilly pushes me into it, scrubs me, and plucks me like I'm a chicken being prepared for a feast. Soon I'm dressed and she combs my hair into a braid, wrapping it delicately at the top of my head. She then hands me a ring that matches the colour of the dress and I slip it on my finger, looking at the way it shimmers in the light. Right now, I wish for my trousers and simple blue tunic I've become accustomed to wearing. I glance at the full-length mirror on my way out of the room and freeze at the sight of a once weak and starved girl. Now my body is full of feminine curves, and I tug at the neckline of my dress to hide the sudden cleavage showing. I cross my arms over my chest and Tilly bats them away to straighten my skirts. My hair glows and my face is healthy and has lost the look of constant wariness. I've grown to like the company I keep in the house and would even call the two females my friends. Plus, I'm not dead, so things could be worse. It's dangerous to feel this safe around these people, but I can't help it. I feel as if I could, with time, become used to this way of life. Tilly stops at the doorway to the hallway and waves me through I look back at her, pleading her not to leave me, but she's already gone and I curse her silently. I find my way to the dining room and my stomach rumbles at the smell of freshly cooked food wafting from under the large doors. I open them with the push of my hand and look over to where Alc is draped in his usual immaculate black tunic and pants, standing at the window overlooking the bustling city below. He turns to me as I enter, and I feel his scrutiny from all the way across the room. He clears his throat and gestures to me with a flourish of his hand.

"You look different."

I laugh at his poor attempt at a compliment.

"Thank you, you look nice in your usual black."

Alc smiles at me and I breathe into the stunned silence. My heart is tugging at me, which I ignore.

"Never thought I would hear a compliment to me leave your mouth, but here we are."

I glare at him,

"Don't let it go to your head, I don't think your neck would be able to support it if it got any bigger."

His laughter rumbles through the room and he points to the table.

"Please, take a seat. I feel like I might faint at the weight I have to carry around on top of my neck."

I snort and take a seat near the head of the table, expecting him to take the seat he usually inhabits, but he instead takes the seat directly across from me and I feel small and weak sitting across from him. Alc places his arms on the table and looks like he's fighting for words.

Suddenly, he blurts out,

"I'm sorry for the way I reacted a few weeks ago. It was uncalled for."

I shake my head to make sure I heard right. Alc, the High Lord, was actually apologising to a measly human. Be still my heart.

"As you should be. I tried asking you what was wrong, so you ignore me for three weeks. A bit of an overreaction, if you ask me, don't you think?"

An emotion much like shame flashes across his face.

"I didn't intend to be away for so long. As it so happens, I was called away for urgent business and I needed time to sort out what happened and why you could pass my shield so easily."

I blink at him,

"I thought you let me through, and I accidently went the wrong way in your head, if that makes sense?"

Alc shakes his head,

"I never let you anywhere near my head and yet you walked through like it was nothing. I must say, I'm impressed. But more than anything, I'm curious and I want to know how a human got past my defences when you don't possess any power."

It wasn't an insult, just a statement based on facts. How was a human like me able to get past a High Lord's defences, let alone the High Lord of Night who rules over dreams and nightmares?

"Well, if you didn't let me through, then that must mean that you let your guard down accidentally."

Alc gives me a look and I shut my mouth.

"I don't just let my guard down. Now, tell me how you entered my head, tell me what you saw before you entered and how you got there."

The command doesn't have much room for argument, so I do as he tells me, trying to remember what happened.

"I heard your voice as you said to push you out and I felt a strong urge to follow the sound of your voice," I blush slightly at how ridiculous it sounds aloud, but Alc just nods his head encouragingly. "So, I followed your voice and came across a clear bridge. There was black mist floating around and when I put my hand out to touch it, it parted for me. Then I slipped, and the mist rushed past me, forming a wall with the constellations of the night sky engraved into it."

Alc's eyes narrow but he keeps his mouth shut.

"I reached my hand out and touched the wall and it fell away."

"You mean to say my wall just fell away when you touched it?"

I roll my eyes at him,

"That's what I said, yes. Anyway, after the wall fell, I was surrounded in a space with millions of floating stars.'

His voice is so quiet I have to lean forward to hear it properly.

"Memories," he says, and I nod slowly.

"I touched one of the stars and it latched onto me, engulfing my arm in light. I tried to shake it off, but it wouldn't leave. Next thing I know, I was falling, only to land on my feet again in your memory."

I close my mouth, not wanting to bring up what I saw in his

head. Alc's eyes widen with shock, and he rocks back on his chair like he wants to leave.

"Interesting," he says slowly and cautiously. "I've never heard of someone with that ability before."

I want to slap him. He doesn't make this easy for me. If he doesn't know the answer to this riddle, then how do I have a hope of figuring it out?

"What about you? You're the High Lord of Night, quite literally the King of stars. You walk into people's heads all the time."

Alc smiles at me like I don't understand what he means,

"My power is much like seeing through other people's eyes. I become part of them. I can control them like it's their own conscience doing the work. I don't walk through their minds, I become their minds. I see their desires and their fears, nothing is kept a secret if I walk into their minds. I become them."

I gape at him. My jaw touching the floor.

"Well, if you become them, how come I can feel you in my head? I shouldn't be able to tell the difference, should I?"

He shakes his head,

"You know I'm there because I make you think I'm there inside your head. I could enter your head right now and you would never know. It's much harder to get rid of me when you just think it's your own conscience."

My body shivers and I stare at the man in front of me. He's more powerful than I could fathom and while most of me is terrified, I can't help but be intrigued by him.

"Okay, but maybe your power is developing and you didn't know until now?" the pitch of my voice rises as panic rushes through me.

Alc laughs, forcing out his next words.

"I was born with my power, I think I would know if it changed, and besides, you were the one to penetrate my defences, not the other way around."

He has a point, but a point that I was unwilling to consider.

"You said you walked into my head across a bridge. Was the bridge over anything? Like water?"

I rack my brain to remember the details,

"No, it was just hovering over the black mist. It was like walking through the night sky."

Alc rubs his chin and seems to have come to a conclusion that I have to pry from him.

"What is it?"

"I think you may be able to use other people's abilities to your own advantage, but when you use them, they become stronger and better than the original form. It's exceedingly rare and has only been recorded once, but that was millennium ago."

I start laughing,

"And where do you think I got this power?"

I shift uncomfortably on my chair.

"Your parents may have come from a special lineage of human mages that were thought to have died out many centuries ago. That or your parents aren't actually of your blood."

I stare dumbfounded at him.

"Of course they are my parents. My father may be a drunk and my mother dead, but I'm definitely their child."

Alc regards me with a guarded expression before he responds, "I would like to research further into it before we jump to conclusions. So, on top of your physical training, I want to help you master that mind invasion ability of yours before it lands you in deep trouble."

Just as I'm about to reply, plates of food appear before us. I load my plate and run through what Alc has said. The more I think about it, the more my head spins. I shove it to the back of my mind and start eating. We eat without talking and soon the sound of clinking cutlery fades and a contented silence falls over us. I'm the one to break it as curiosity plagues my thoughts.

"What would it mean if I did have this ability? How can a human have something like that?"

I have heard of human mages before through tales told by the villagers, but the King and Queen banished them long ago when they were thought to be forming an alliance with enemies from afar. Alc takes a sip from his glass before answering.

"It would mean that you are incredibly rare and that you may not be full human. Even if your line was tainted centuries ago, it could still have an effect on you."

I sigh and raise my glass in a toast,

"To tainted lines and mysteries unsolved."

Alc raises his glass and leans forward to clink it against mine. We both take a large swig from the glasses, and I immediately feel sleepy. All the training and studying of the High Lords has drained me. We sit like this late into the night and talk until silence is stretching between us. I yawn and Alc pushes out of his chair.

"All right, bed now, Princess. You have a long week ahead of you."

I stand and sway on my feet slightly. How many glasses had I drank?

"I told you not to call me Princess, I'm far from royalty. I'm more like the handmaid."

Alc smiles, and I marvel at the beauty of it.

"You are very pretty did you know that?" I clamp a hand over my mouth, horrified that it slipped out.

Alc laughs, a sensuous sound that bounces off the walls surrounding us and, strangely, my heart.

"I have been called many things in my life, but pretty? That's new, thank you."

I sigh and concentrate on walking back to my rooms; I stumble on the carpet and Alc places a gentle hand on my back to steady me. As we make our way to my room, I smile to myself. What was supposed to be my dooming has begun to save me in a way.

"Thank you for tonight, despite myself I enjoyed your company for once."

Alc smiles down at me,

"The pleasure's all mine, Princess."

I smile and nod, the doors of my room loom closer and Alc steps away from me. I suddenly miss his warmth.

"Try and get a good sleep, you have lots to learn tomorrow. Goodnight, Princess."

I don't have the energy to tell him not to call me Princess as I slip into my room and fall onto the bed, not bothering to remove my dress as sleep washes over me.

I wake before dawn and dress in my leathers. Tying my hair back from my face, I walk over to my bedside table and halt as I take in the jewel-handled dagger that rests on a piece of folded parchment. It was defiantly not there when I left to change. Its hilt glitters under the chandelier light, large sapphires adorn the centre of the handle, and I turn it over in my hand in love with the way it shines. The blade itself is covered in a leather sheath that has smaller sapphires sprinkled into it. I grab the leather thigh holster and place the dagger into it. Picking up the folded letter that came with the dagger, I walk over to the mirror to admire it. I open the letter and read.

Princess,

I will see you after you have finished your training with Kai and Alyssa, from there we will work and see if we can figure out your ability. You have earned this dagger and I hope you like it. It will come in handy for idiots like Higens. Remember when you strike to strike true and aim for the heart.

Sincerely yours, Alcinder

High Lord of Night.

I stare at the letter and fold it gently into my pocket. My heart light as I walk down the staircase and out the entrance of the front door to find Kai waiting for me, tapping his hand on the steps. I come to a stop next to him and he glances up at me from where he's seated. He notes my dagger attached to my thigh and his eyes widen slightly.

"What's wrong?"

"Nothing. Nice dagger."

I frown down at him, and he smiles up at me.

"Alc gave it to me. Now, can we get moving before the sun sets?"

Kai stands and grabs my hand before we twist into nothing and reappear in the training arena. The air is crisp and is desperately trying to hold onto the last strings of winter. I shiver and start the warm ups that have become routine. As I move, Kai takes a seat on the railing, watching me intently. I swing into the three and two punching set but stop when Kai keeps his gaze locked on me.

"Something entertaining?"

He nods and smirks,

"You've got the body of a woman, not a starving child."

I stop moving and cross my arms over my chest, feeling

suddenly self-conscious.

"Thank you for that bit of information, but I would prefer if you kept your gawking to a minimum."

Kai throws a dirty grin my way,

"Whatever the Lady wishes, or should I be calling you Princess?"

I glare at him and, if looks could kill, he would be dead and buried, but all the same my cheeks heat and I look away.

"It's Keilee, nothing else. I am no lady, and I am most defiantly not royalty."

Kai salutes as usual and picks up the long-bladed dagger sitting next to him and begins to sharpen it. I shake my head and continue my exercises for another twenty minutes. By the time I'm done, I'm sweating and regretting my decision to wear my longer leathers. My arms ache and my feet are numb with the constant movement. Kai twists the sharpened blade in his hand and slowly rises from where he's seated.

"Good, you're getting better with the flow of your movements and your balance is strong enough to start working on sword play, my personal favourite."

Kai walks over to the weapons rack and grabs two wooden swords; they are long and have been well kept, despite the brutes that use them. He walks back and hands me one. They are lighter than I expect, and I swing it around with ease.

"I'm guessing you don't trust me near your limbs with a real one?"

I hold up the sword and point it at him. He rolls his eyes.

"Not when you point it at me like that…" he comes to a stand in front of me. "A sword should be an extension of your arm, they should move as one, and when you wave it around like that you give the opponent many openings to disarm or kill you."

"So, it's like punching, move with my body for better force?"

Kai nods,

"When fighting with a blade, you have to awaken every muscle in your body. The sword does not know friend from foe, so if you're not careful and precise, it will cut you."

I grip the blade tighter and swing it gently in front of me.

"Better, but keep your grip relaxed to a point that you're not choking the handle, like this."

Kai swings his sword and I'm in awe with how it does in fact look like part of him, like a friend greeting him.

"Now do what I just did, and remember, work with the blade, understand it."

I copy him and he smiles.

"I think I'm getting the hang of it slowly."

Kai brings his sword down in a slow arch, attacking a non-existent enemy.

"It will take time, but you know how to wield a knife. It's like that but with a bigger blade and you're not just chopping up a deer."

I smile and reply, "No, I'm bringing down a Fae."

Kai's face breaks into a shit-eating grin and swings towards me and I just block it in time, my arms shaking with the force of the blow. His Fae strength and speed has me on my arse more times than not, and if I thought I was hot before, its nothing compared to now. We spar back and forth for a few hours and it's noon before I can begin to calm my racing heart. Kai is barely panting, and it makes me angry that my human body can't keep up with him without dying in the process. I make my slow way over to the weapons rack and place the sword away. Kai does the same as I walk back and over to the water stand. As I'm filling my glass, I hear the familiar voice of Higens talking to someone as they approach me. I try to look busy and keep my gaze averted but, to my horror, Higens stops next to me and spits out a laugh.

"Look what the cat dragged in, although Kai's a mutt so perhaps dog?"

I glance up at him and fight the urge to recoil at the sinister glint in his eyes. I look to the man standing next to him, he's taller than Higens by at least a head; his face is framed in shoulder length hair, and I can see the faint shadow of stubble across his firm jaw. He would be stunning except for the hideous scar running from the corner of his mouth right through his eye and into his hair line. An eye patch covers the eye with the scar, and I have the strangest urge to look under the patch. His smile is crooked, and it tells me the ugliness of the scar is only matched by what's hiding under his skin.

"Last time I checked that dog could rip you to shreds, and not to mention his companion, who could easily hurt you with a flick of his hand, or do you not remember last time?"

Higens steps forward and I look over to where Kai is arranging the weapons, oblivious to this conversation. Higens notices where my gaze has gone and he smiles, moving in front of me with his friend so I'm completely blocked from view, and it would seem to Kai that they are just getting a drink.

"Oh, I don't forget things easily, little girl, and I most definitely don't take slag from a filthy human whore."

The insult seeps into my skin but I refuse to acknowledge it.

"That's rich coming from someone who had their High Lord tell them to keep it in their pants."

This time the large man steps forward and I almost take a step back.

"You have such a quick mouth. I wonder when it will land

you in trouble."

I think to myself that it already has as I glance at them. Higens reaches forward and grips my jaw, jerking it up so my eyes meet his, and I shiver as repulsion rips through me at the touch.

"Get your hands off me," I shove at him, but his grip remains firm, and the tall man grabs my arm and slams it to my side, sending an ache through it where its fingers grip into my skin.

"Shall we see if the rumours are true? I've had many different sorts in my bed but never a human plaything."

My heart drops and my limbs are weak with fear, but I keep my eyes on him, hyper-aware of his friend moving closer to me. My mind reels and I wish for Kai to come over and help me.

"I said get your hands off me, unless you don't mind losing them."

Higens laughs, the sound turning my stomach. He twists his hand and my jaw aches with the movement. He leans in and I freeze, my hands are still stuck between his friend's grip and I can't reach my dagger. Suddenly, I feel light and I begin to lean towards him like I might faint, then I realise I'm standing surrounded by grey fog. I can't see anything past my own hands. I walk forwards and nearly slam into a wall the same grey as the fog. My heart lurches as I recognise I'm nearly in someone's head, and by the dull grey, I can only guess that it's Higen's head I'm nearby. Before I lose my nerve, I walk through the wall, not even having to touch it for it to fall into small pieces, like crushed glass. Pathetic. The space is dark and cold, sending shivers down my spine. It's not like Alc's mind, which was beautiful and inviting. This place is dead and no stars float around, only the same grey fog. But instead of a thick wall, it drifts in small eddies around the room. I don't bother touching the fog, I don't need to see the twisted things he's done. I walk through the space, not sure what I'm looking for until I come face to face with a row of orbs the colour of the darkest night. They drift slowly towards me before they snap back into their place. As I stare at them, they continue moving then snapping back. My transfixed gaze is broken when sudden anger rushes through me when one of the orbs come too close. I move to my left and sorrow floods me in place of the anger. It hits me hard, and it dawns on me that these are his emotions. A sinister smile spreads across my face as I move through the orbs and stop when I feel the familiar twang of pain. I reach a careful hand out and touch the orb. As soon as I do, pain shoots up my arm, but it's gone as soon as it arrives. Once the orb stills in my hand, it twists and becomes soft. I squeeze it and I feel the distant scream erupt from the host, it shakes the ground I'm standing on. The orb bends at my will as I make Higens pay for his cruelty. I'm often hiding from monsters, but I wonder if I should really be hiding from myself. It's funny how, when you spend enough time around them, you begin to become one yourself. My father's face flashes before me and I squeeze the orb again, placing the orb back as I feel Higens buckle to his knees. I find my way back to the wall, it's easy as the space is open and almost empty. The grey fog still swirls around and I'm careful not to touch any of them as I walk through the wall again. As soon as I'm through, I feel myself falling and land back into the present, with Higens on his knees sobbing. His nose is bleeding, and his arm is at an odd angle. The large man that was with him is gawking at me and begins to back away as I smile at him.

"What? Scared of me now? I was only playing."

He shakes his head, and I can tell from where he's standing that his hands are shaking.

"What are you? May the gods purge you from this land."

I smile and he flinches at me, tripping on the still sobbing Higens.

"What am I? I'm just a human whore."

Higens looks up from where he's sprawled on the ground and stares at me. All I can see is his fear, I can almost taste it. I look him in the eye as I speak.

"Next time someone tells you to get your filthy hands off them, you better listen. And never underestimate me, or a broken arm will be the least of your problems."

Higens shoots me a glare full of hatred,

"You should be the one not to underestimate me, little girl."

I smile and he recoils from me slightly.

"A wolf never backs away from a rat, so don't assume I will either."

Higens climbs to his feet, and I grab the dagger from its sheath, I twirl it around in my hand and don't miss the way he regards it with caution.

"You've seen what I can do with a bow, shall we see what I can do with a dagger?"

Higens makes to move towards me, but strong arms wrap around stopping him,

"I suggest you answer the lady's question," Kai smiles at me from behind Higens and I grin back.

Higens friend is gone and now he has no one to help him out of his grave.

"No, I don't think we need to, M'Lady."

I pout at him,

"That's not very entertaining, but maybe next time I will have better luck at convincing you otherwise. Now, go and find the sewer you crawled out of."

Higens throws me a filthy look but stalks away, limping and wiping at his bleeding nose. His other arm dangling uselessly by his side.

"What was that all about?" concern laces his words and I turn my gaze to Kai.

"They didn't know what no meant, so I had to show them."

A low whistle escapes him, and I laugh.

"Remind me never to cross paths with you."

I grunt and sit down on the railing, my legs feeling heavy.

"As much as I enjoyed the show, we should probably get you to Alyssa for history lessons before Alc skins me alive."

I nod and groan as I stand to take his hand, "Don't lie, you just like to see me suffer; you're not scared of Alc."

Kai huffs a laugh that sounds empty,

"You think so low of me, and it hurts."

I laugh and shove him, knowing my attempt is feeble as he barely moves.

"Don't take things to heart otherwise you will live a noticeably short life."

Kai flicks my nose and I scowl up at him,

"Don't I know that's true, now come on, let's get going."

I nod, and then we are spinning, coming to a stop in front of an angry-faced Alyssa who's iridescent wings twitch with irritation.

"About time you two arrived, I've been waiting for the better part of an hour."

Her face is pulled into a scowl, and I resist the urge to step back. Kai just laughs and pats her on the shoulder.

"Come now, darling, don't be so sullen, lighten up a bit."

I'm surprised Kai doesn't drop dead with the look Alyssa shoots his way.

"Don't darling me. If you think I'm going to be calmed like one of your bedside companions you are sorely mistaken, now go before I kick your arse," her words are betrayed by the small smile spread across her lips.

Kai bows low and leaves the study, not before shooting a wink my way. Alyssa turns to me and ushers me into the same seat as yesterday while she retrieves the tome from the shelf. I lean back in the seat and stretch my legs.

"What time is the meeting tomorrow if we still have to go through four High Lords before then?"

Alyssa turns to me and places the tome on the table.

"All I know is that you'll be leaving tomorrow midday so we will go over the last two High Lords in the morning."

I flip open the book and wait for Alyssa to sit down. She flips past a large number of pages and stops when the familiar shape of sunflowers appears. The page is the colour of pale ocean sand. My heart stills momentarily when it lands on the angel of a man on the page. His skin is dark and was made to withstand the sun's heat, his eyes are a deep hazel, with green flecks throughout them. He has hair a pale blond that is cropped short and is left to dangle in elegant waves.

"May I present to you the High Lord of Summer; Dorian. He is my personal favourite, never a dull moment when he is around," Alyssa's eyes twinkle and I can't help but smile. "He is the trickster and often is the first to throw a punch when things get ugly. He has no self-control when there comes a time to show off, but he has respect for the other High Lords and knows when he's close to the line."

Alyssa takes a breath to continue but I cut across her.

"How old is he? Is he older or younger than Alc?'

I'm shot with an annoyed glare and shut my mouth, waiting

for her to continue.

"He is six hundred and seventy years old and is the second oldest. He has three siblings, and they are triplets. Cassy, Bella, and May. They are five hundred years old, and he will kill anyone who looks at them funny, so I suggest keeping them out of the conversation. His weakness is the cold, much like Kelby, but he draws his energy from the heat of the sun and can't when it's too cold."

It sounds to me like the Winter court is at a massive advantage when it comes to upping the other High Lords.

Alyssa continues, tapping the page impatiently, "The High Lord of Winter and Summer are as close as any High Lords could come to being friends and will band together to hunt their prey if given the chance, so just be careful. Remember, when engaging with them, keep your sharp tongue and don't let your guard down even when you are sleeping, it can be a dangerous place. Now, onto the High Lord of Autumn, which you may have heard of before. His name is Isaac and he is as cunning as they come. He has had a feud with the Night court for centuries because of Kai and Alc's relationship. He will not hesitate to destroy you if given the chance."

I shiver as Alyssa turns the page and I come face to face with a man surrounded by autumn leaves. Hair the colour of fire is in a bun at the top of his head, and he doesn't look a day over thirty. His eyes are the same colour as Kai's but his are hard and cold where Kai's are full of laughter.

I stare at the man and ask Alyssa,

"How old is Isaac and Kai?"

Alyssa shifts uncomfortably in her seat but answers a minute later,

"Isaac is six hundred and fifty and Kai is four hundred and

twelve. Isaac had Kai when he was incredibly young and him and his siblings are close in age. Isaac found his mate when he was young, thus finding it easy to set up a family. I don't know how Coraline can put up with him, but being someone's mate can do funny things to a person."

Mate? My brain ticks over, trying to form any kind of explanation for the word, but comes up empty.

"What's a mate?"

Alyssa looks at me like I'm speaking a different tongue.

"A mate is the most sacred form of love there is for our kind. If you're lucky enough to find your mate, it's like finding a part of yourself. It is stronger than any marriage bond and can only be broken when one of the partners die. And if that happens, the other often becomes a shell of their former self."

It sounds a bit pathetic to me, I couldn't see myself depending on someone so much that, if they were to die, I would become weak and would be better off dead with them. I rub a hand over my face.

"So, having a mate is like being stuck with someone for the rest of your life and not being able to be free unless they die? Is there any way to get out of the bond?"

Her dark wings flutter and she twitches her hand like she wants to hit me.

"The mating bond is not a burden, it's a form of life and is as wonderful as it is deadly. You don't have to accept the bond if you don't want to, but most mates have a love between them that cannot be broken."

I nod slowly,

"Why is it so dangerous then?"

The page in front of me crimples as Alyssa fiddles with it, her hand shaking slightly.

"Because if one of the partners is hurt by another, the mate becomes incredibly violent and it often blinds them with the need to protect and kill. It can be an ugly affair and only the cruellest or stupidest play with another's mate. It's almost as bad as killing our young."

I'm utterly speechless and turn my gaze back to the page before me. I wonder if anyone has tried to hurt Isaac's mate and if they lived to tell the tale.

"Since you know that bit of information, shall we get back to it?"

I nod and she continues, "Isaac's weakness is water as he has fire and can control any flame. I assume you know that flame can't survive with water around?'

Her sarcasm hits a nerve and I glare at her.

She just ignores me, continuing on, "Isaac and Adian have the same weakness, but the High Lord of Day can control it better and can still draw a weak power from his source, whereas Isaac can't unless there is some sort of amber around. The order of the courts are based on the natural order of things, with Day at the bottom, Night at the top, and Summer, Autumn, Winter, and Spring in the middle. As I said earlier, Spring is the smallest of the courts and Night is the largest. All the High Lords must respect the laws each court has in place to protect the peace between them. If the laws are broken by anyone, it will be punished by death. All courts worship the gods and that must be respected when around the temples. I assume the humans also believe in these gods?"

I shake my head. Many of the humans have given up believing in them as they are sleeping and are no use to us, but I always thought that we should still respect them and acknowledge that they once ruled over our lands. Over time, humans have lost the ability to worship Dekota and Pacarny as they didn't favour us in the war with the Fae, which is seen as a betrayal by us. If given the chance, I wonder if the Gods would dare fight for us again or let us sort it out amongst ourselves. I don't blame them for sleeping for the past thousand years. If I was a god, I don't know if I would see anything worth fighting for. All there seems to be is monsters and cowards, and if you aren't one of them, you just hide in the shadows, waiting for the chance to lead a better life on wasted efforts. I long ago lost the ability to decide if I'm the hunter or the hunted. I would like to think I still have my humanity, but the past weeks have tested that.

"We do, but we don't worship them like you do. Many have either forgotten or find it a waste of time to try."

Alyssa shakes her head in disbelief.

"No wonder humans are so sour and hungry for something more. They have wasted their efforts on trying to separate themselves from something that can offer them more then gold."

Irritation at her words dances across my skin and I'm reminded of the Holy Marchers.

"How are we supposed to believe in something that has given us nothing? It's easy for you to make assumptions when you have the advantage."

Alyssa just smiles at me, fuelling my irritation.

"You believe, don't you? And you consider yourself to have nothing. Why waste the effort if you receive nothing from it?"

I consider her words as I answer.

"I believe because, if I don't, I have nothing else to fight for. I believe because I might drown in myself if I don't. Hope is a drug that, despite my better self, I'm addicted to. That's why I believe. I hope that there is a better way to live, I hope that things can change, and I hope that one day I might see the world as a place where people can live, not just survive. But I understand why it's so easy to just forget and let go."

Alyssa eyes are sad as she regards me, and I hate the pity I see there.

"For you to say that and mean it shows that you are stronger than most."

I scoff at her,

"A fool is not strong; a fool is someone who dreams and gets stuck in that reality."

She shakes her head at me, her long hair gleaming under the light,

"Having a dream and holding onto it is not weak, it means you are a fighter and have hopes and ambitions for a better reality."

I nod half-heartedly, if only I could share her view on things, I might see the world as something other than a graveyard waiting to collect more headstones. The clock on the wall chimes and it breaks my trance. Alyssa closes the forgotten tome in front of us and puts it back on the shelf.

"That's enough for today. Alc should be waiting for you in the dining room. If you need anything, Tilly and I will be preparing dinner. Alc's inner circle will be there to discuss the plans for tomorrow, so I suggest dressing nicely. Tilly will meet you in your rooms to help you dress."

I supress a groan and contemplate faking sick to get out of the dinner. I walk silently to the dining room and push open the doors. As Alyssa said, Alc is waiting, tapping his foot on the ground to a rhythm I can't hear. He is dressed in leathers that hug his marvellous body and I have to stare at my feet as my face heats. What's gotten into me? Memories of last night flash before me and I almost smack a hand over my face. How could I have forgotten that I called a High Lord pretty? My face feels like it's on fire and I hear Alc laugh from where he's seated. My mental shields are intact, and I glare at him as I snap.

"What's so funny?"

I try and keep my face neutral as he answers.

"Oh, Princess, you have no idea how much I love seeing you squirm."

A sinister smile spreads across his face and I feel my own drop into a scowl.

"You're such a prick."

His grin widens and I deepen my frown, "That's quite different from what you felt last night."

I stalk towards him until I have to look down at him from where he's sitting.

"Don't think for one second that I don't hate you any less, my mouth often runs unattached to my brain."

Alc huffs a husky laugh as his eyes darken,

"I wouldn't have it any other way, Princess. Life would be too boring if you fell at my feet."

I choke on my laugh as I regard him.

"Only the blind would be dumb enough to fall into a wolf's den," I smirk at him and walk to my seat, plonking down to glare at him.

"You see, I'm told they fall at my feet because they can see, and they like what their eyes have landed on."

"Well then call me blind."

"I wouldn't say you're blind, just smart," he scratches his chin like he's in deep thought. "Although you do have a nerve standing up to a High Lord, so you can't be all about in the head."

I laugh,

"Can't give a complement without an insult to follow close behind, can you?"

Alc nods his head,

"Where would the fun be in that ?"

I wave my hand at him,

"Your fun doesn't align with mine at all."

He wiggles his eyebrows at me

"In some certain activities it might," Alc gives me a meaningful look and I throw a pen at him that I find on the table.

"Pig."

He catches the pen with one hand and smirks at me.

"You always think I imply the worst and I'm wounded by it," he places a hand over his heart, and I can't help the smile that grows on my face.

"I'm deeply sorry, what did you mean by it then?"

Alc grins,

"Oh, I meant what you thought, I just wanted you to know that not all my intensions are ill placed."

I groan into my hands and shake my head,

"You are impossible."

He nods but freezes and his face falls into a serious expression. It's like watching a mask slip into place. I strain my ears to hear what he's heard or seen but find nothing amiss. I open my mouth to speak but he holds up a hand, stopping me. The temperature in the room drops, and when I breathe, my breath comes out in misty swirls. Alc rises from his seat and casually leans against the table, one hand playing with the pen I threw at him and the other tucked behind his back. He looks like a portrait of calm power. His shadows swirl gently around his fingers like friends whispering secrets to him. I press my back into my chair and wish I could disappear like Kai. The atmosphere in the room is thick and I struggle to drag in an even breath.

"I need you to be silent and still, do you understand me?"

I nod my head quickly, wondering what has caused his stiffened mood and for his mask to be slipped on.

"What's going on?"

Alc shakes his head to silence me and I'm about to retort but it gets stuck in my throat as a violent shiver rips through me. Frost starts to coat the table, the wood turning blue. I look at the fruit on the table to find that it's frozen solid. A bitter breeze pulls at my hair and swirls around us, on it floats snowflakes of varied sizes. They twirl and swing to their own dance. I'm mesmerised as they stop in front of Alc, swirling around like a winter snowstorm. The cold bites at me and I have to constantly fight back a shiver, clenching my teeth to stop them chattering. Alc looks unaffected as he stares at the snowflakes, waiting for something to happen.

"Quit showing off, I don't have all day. You've wasted enough of my time with your entry already," his tone is cold enough to match the room and I'm taken back by it.

I have never heard him speak with such authority before and I realise I'm watching him become the High Lord of the Night court. The small storm in front of him dances as if it's laughing and I almost fall off my chair as a deep voice echoes around the room, it's timbre bouncing off the walls, amplifying the voice.

"Now, now, that's no way to welcome a friend. Solitude has not helped your people skills, Alc."

A humourless laugh rips from Alc as he stops twirling the pen in his hand.

"Friends usually give warning before they barge into someone's home."

The storm stops moving, and I can see every tiny snowflake

shining in the light of the room.

"I come with a warning that Isaac and Kelby are trying to form an alliance between themselves, so I suggest you keep your eyes in the back of your head open and alert. Even I do not know the true nature of this meeting that you have set up and I hope that it will bring no ill fate to my court. I respect you and would go as far to say like you, but be rest assured, I will not tolerate the risk of the lives in my home for your scheming."

I shiver as the voice becomes deep with warning.

"I do not take threats lightly and will warn you not to question me and my motives. You know that I have called this meeting to try and stop the bloodshed of our countrymen. Don't think that I won't bite the arm of my feeder to stop a war from killing my people."

Snowflakes begin to swirl again more violently this time and I question if Alc has approached this in the best way. I wouldn't think angering the host of this meeting a good thing.

"We both don't want unnecessary bloodshed and I have already given you my word to help you in this, but don't think I won't change my mind if it doesn't suit me and my people."

I roll my eyes at the two males as they bicker about trivial things. I would think the two High Lords trying to form an alliance amongst themselves would be more concerned with pressing matters than running around each other trying to assert dominance. Alc's warning to keep quiet flashes briefly in my head as I open my mouth to speak.

"Enough of this bickering. I'm going to assume you came here for a reason, not to just speak of your morals, so can we get to the point? I have places to be and don't feel like listening to male pride."

The room stiffens as Alc's green eyes find me, anger flashes through them but is drowned out when booming laughter drifts from the snowstorm.

"What beautiful flower are you hiding from me, Alc?"

Alc glares at me and turns back to the High Lord in front of him. His face falling again into calm indifference.

"Nobody important or of your concern."

The voice grunts and turns his attention to me. I fight the urge to balk at the figure I can't see.

"Well, if you don't bring little miss unimportant to this meeting I will be sorely disappointed in you. We need someone with a little bit of balls. And to answer your question, yes, I do have a point and it is that we need to keep an eye on Isaac and Kelby. I don't like them neither do I trust them. They are up to something and I'm guessing it involves the human King and Queen."

Alc nods, urging him to continue.

"My spies have informed me that both of them have been sending mercenaries to the human realm over the last three months and that they have been preparing forces with more urgency than usual."

Alc nods and speaks,

"I suggest we bring this meeting forward and have it tomorrow morning. The sooner we get this over with the better. We need to keep Isaac and Kelby busy enough that we can send men in and out of their courts undetected. If they have plans with the King and Queen, we will find out."

The storm makes an uncommitting sound.

"I will send word out tonight and have everyone ready for the morning. I suggest you make your arrival tonight to save struggle in the morning. I will get Lilly to prepare your rooms. And don't forget to bring her," the snowflakes form a hand and points to me where I'm still sitting, I wave my hand in a salute and hear him laugh. "I do like her. Now, I better go and prepare for your arrival. See you very soon, Alc, and do try to smile when you arrive, even if it's to save the mirrors from shattering from your sombre mood."

Alc nods once, causing snowflakes to fall from his hair, and flicks his hand. sending his shadows scattering into the room.

"Yes, see you very soon, Malik."

As quick as the snow arrived, it leaves, and the room drops back to the normal temperature. Alc runs a hand over his face and spins to me, the anger from before back in his emerald eyes.

"What was that? Didn't I tell you to keep your mouth shut? Next time you disobey me, there will be consequences. You're lucky Malik likes your quick mouth."

I stand and grip the back of my chair tightly, "You don't own me, and you don't have control over what I do and don't do. Why would you even bother with me anyway? I'm little miss unimportant, nobody that should concern you, the mighty High Lord."

My chest heaves as I fight to control my anger. I feel flames dance under my skin, fighting to get out, but I dowse them as I grip the chair harder.

"I didn't mean it like that, and you know that."

I laugh at him, the sound hysterical,

"Do I? All you've done while I've been here is shut me down and ignore me. I've only become interesting to you now because I have an ability that you don't understand. So, please spare me from your lies and save your breath for something important."

"Keilee, listen to me."

I hold up my hand, stopping him,

"I said save it."

Alc looks at me, his eyes cutting through me, and I fear they see everything I'm trying to hide.

"We leave in an hour, go and change. Don't worry about packing anything, I'll have it sorted."

I turn on my heel before he can finish and march from the room, my back stiff. As I make my way to my room, I pass Kai who tries to stop me but sees the look on my face and thinks better of it. He looks from me to the study and a frown passes over his face as he starts to make his way to the room I left. The halls are quiet, but as I get close to my room, I can hear running water and someone rustling through my closet. I push open the doors and see Tilly busy at work selecting a dress for me to wear.

"I'm guessing you heard the change of plans?"

Tilly just nods and holds up the most beautiful dress I have ever laid eyes on. Its deep blue fabric shimmering in the light like there are stars stitched into it. The neckline plunges deep, and the skirt is full and sways as she moves it.

"Is that for me?" I gawk at it and Tilly laughs.

"Well, I most certainly am not fitting into it. Go and bathe and I'll get it ready for you."

I do as she says and soak my body in the rose-scented water, enjoying the way the heat soothes my aching body. I feel my anger drain away until it is only a dull thud in my chest. As I climb out of the water, I grab my dagger from the pile of fighting leathers on the tiled floor and sheath it to my thigh. Once I emerge from the bathing chamber, I find Tilly humming to herself as she arranges my hair and face products on the vanity. I slide into the dress, marvelling at the feel of soft silk brushing my legs. The neckline comes to a deep end and the skirts are bigger now that it's on me. I run my hands through the folds, and I'm surprised that I can't feel the stitching that makes the star like pattern. I try and reach for my dagger but find the task futile as I can't get past the skirts without nearly falling over so I move to strap the dagger at my hip, hoping it won't pass the wrong message to Malik and his court. After I regain my balance, I slip on the heels Tilly supplied me and sink into the vanity chair while she does my hair into a messy updo. I stare at my reflection as she lines my eyes with kohl and paints my lips a pale pink. I go to stand but she puts a soft hand on my shoulder, her eyes glisten as she reaches down beside herself to bring forwards a small and elegant tiara adorned with blue gems that match the dress and diamonds that sit next to them in a beautiful design. I gape at it and shake my head as she places it atop my head.

"I can't take this, it's gorgeous," I touch the cold metal, surprised at the lightness of it.

Tilly slaps my hand away,

"Of course, you can, and you will, per Alc's orders."

I glare at her from the mirror,

"I'm surprised he would give something so regal to someone of no importance."

It's Tilly's turn to glare at me.

"Go easy on him, he's trying. I've known that boy from the moment of birth, and never have I seen him smile and laugh like he does when he's with you. You might not see it that way, but you've known him only for a little time, and I would hate to see you pass judgement before you know him truly. He's a kind and honest ruler and only keeps a few close. Very few are lucky enough to see him without that mask he wears."

I nod, feeling guilty despite myself, he has been kind to me while I've stayed and perhaps I've taken that for granted. My hand goes up and grabs my necklace and I feel calmer now that I have it in my hand. I suppose I could cut him some slack; I am the human he is stuck with because I killed his friend. After she's done fussing with my hair and face, I stand and look over the desk in front of me. My gaze catches on a ring sitting on the makeup box, and I grab it and tuck it into my pocket, not really sure why I have it with me. It's nothing of large value and I have only worn it once while being here when I had dinner with Alc. I make my slow way back down into the foyer, counting each step as I go to calm my rising nerves. I stop at the top of the stairs and look down to find everyone waiting there talking amongst each other. Naomi wears a deep emerald dress clinging to her wonderful curves, matching emeralds draped from her ears and lighting up her delicate bone structure. Next to her stands Ianira, who wears a simple red gown that flows gently at her knees, her feet clad in pretty sandals. The dress would look plain on anyone else, but her short hair and fierce eyes make the dress nothing short of regal. Kai and Neron are dressed in suits and the latter pulls at his tie like it's suffocating him. The suits, on closer inspection, have silver thread stitched into the edges and the buttons are sliver as well, marking them males of the Night court. Kai's hair is pulled back and tied with a black string, making him look smart and important. My eyes scan the room and all the occupants within it. Everyone looks so at home here and I can't help but wonder if they are used to parading around like Kings and Queens. The soft light from the hanging chandeliers makes the people before me glow and I feel dull in comparison to their Fae beauty. Even Neron, with his straight back and stern face, looks stunning. I nervously run a hand down my side and take a minute to appreciate that I haven't been noticed yet. I scan the room and my gaze is drawn to a figure clad in all black with silver stitching and a crown of deepest sapphire. My breath hitches as I take in Alc. He is a picture of power and strength, his dark hair gleams, showcasing the raven colours, and the crown makes him look like a god. Eyes of emerald green search the crowd and a smile spreads across his handsome face as he surveys his friends. I decide I've been gawking long enough and tip toe down the steps, praying nobody will notice until I'm on firm ground and there is no chance of me tripping and making a fool of myself. Alc's head snaps up from where he's talking to Neron and Kai, and I have to remember to breathe as emerald eyes clash with blue. My heart flutters so much that I have to come to a standstill to make sure I'm not having a heart attack. I wring my hands together as, one by one, five pairs of eyes pierce me. Slapping a smile on my face, I continue the rest of the way down and thank the gods for the small miracle that I don't fall on my face. Naomi skips over to me, her long blonde hair swinging, and embraces me. I hesitate, surprised by the action, but return the hug with a real smile spreading across my face.

"You look positively stunning, blue suits you and the tiara looks like it was made for you."

I pull out of her embrace and look her up and down,

"Please, how can you say something like that when you look like a goddess?"

A faint blush paints her cheeks as she links her arm through mine.

"I like you; I reckon we could be good friends, you and I."

I find myself liking the sound of that as I nod my agreement. Kai walks over and slaps my bare shoulder while Neron regards me with a softer expression than usual.

"Good to see you're still alive and haven't drowned in all the knowledge Alyssa has been sharing with you."

"It would take a lot more than a book to kill me, Kai, so don't get your hopes up."

Naomi laughs and pats my arm,

"Good friends indeed."

Ianira rolls her eyes, but a small smile spreads across her face at the light banter.

"I see you found yourself some food, girl. You don't look so much like a starved dog any more," she gestures to me, and I can't help but wrap my spare arm around my middle, still feeling self-conscious about it.

Neron nods at me and I nod back, enjoying the formal greeting much more than the hostile looks he often throws at me. I glance over to Alc, where he's still looking at me. I feel heat creep up into my cheeks and fight to keep eye contact with him.

"You do look lovely; I see you put my mother's tiara to use."

My hand flies up to the beautiful garment on my head and my fingers itch to remove the surely valued item.

"Surely I shouldn't be wearing it at all if it was your mother's?"

Alc shakes his head, but I see Naomi's, Ianira's, and Kai's eyes widen at the news of the tiara.

"It was made to be worn, and like Naomi said, it suits you."

I nod my thanks, not sure what to do with the compliment.

Alc clears his throat and addresses the room,

"I think it's time we drop in and visit winter wonder land."

Chapter 8

Frigid wind bites into us when we arrive in the Winter court. The first thing I notice as we stand in Malik's court is that everything is white. The ground we stand on is covered in snow, and as we walk, our footprints leave nothing behind but small holes in the ground where fresh snow is already filling in the gaps. Buildings are scattered everywhere in a brilliant white city, their roofs glisten blue under the weak light of the setting sun mostly covered in thick grey clouds. The walls of the buildings are white, and I can't tell if it's because of the snow or if it's just the colour of the stone used to build them. Despite being in constant winter, I see people milling around the streets, carrying things under their arms, or stopping and chatting with friends and strangers alike. My mind whirls as our group walks toward a building towering over all the other infrastructure. Even from this distance, I can see windows of glass frosted over by the freezing weather. Massive towers rise behind it, and I can see tiny figures perched there, no doubt watching us move closer. The castle is surrounded by a wall made of the same stone as the building but is parted by iron gates that twirl and reach for the sky. I've never seen anything so beautiful and dangerous before. This is the home of a High Lord, a King of winter. Alc comes to a stop in the middle of a street, and we all freeze next to him. He turns to us, and he has slipped on the mask he wears around others. The mask of a High Lord.

"Keep your wits about you and stay close to each other," Alc says in even tone, he looks over to me then adds, "I want you to stay close to me at all times, Keilee. A human is not welcome in a place like this, especially around a group of High Lords."

I nod my head quickly and walk closer to him as we continue walking. Kai and Neron flank the back of the group and Naomi and Ianira walk proudly with their heads held high in the centre of the group, with me and Alc leading. His crown glinting in the afternoon light around us, children run out of houses into the streets to look at the passing party. A girl no older than five in human years, with hair so white it's almost blinding, slides up to me holding out a deep blue flower, her tiny hands shake as she looks up at me. I stop and bend down so I'm her height and smile gently at her.

"Hello, what's your name?"

I look from her to Alc, and he nods slightly.

"Maria," she whispers, her blue eyes widening slightly as she takes in my face, her gaze landing on my ears that aren't pointed like hers.

Unease settles in my stomach, but I keep the smile on my face as I nod,

"That's a beautiful name, Maria."

She bobs her head and extends her tiny arms, holding the flower out closer to me. I grab it and smile brightly.

"Thank you, but don't you want to give this to someone more important to you?"

Maria just shakes her head and touches my arm lightly, like she's scared I'll bite.

"Every Princess needs a flower to match her dress."

I bite down on my tongue to stop myself from correcting her. I guess with the tiara and the dress I do look like someone regal. My hand slips into my dress folds and I pull out a ring with a pink gem that I took from my vanity before arriving. I don't know what made me grab the piece of jewellery, but I grab the little girl's hand and place the ring into her small palm. She stares at it and then puts it on her finger, her eyes glazed over as she takes in the gem.

"You take care of that for me, okay?"

She nods eagerly and wraps her arms around my neck. I bring mine around and hug her back, the simple gesture making my heart ache. Who knew I would be dressed like a Princess, hugging children I barely know? She pulls back and smiles.

"Thank you, your Majesty."

With a wave and a smile, she dashes over to a group of friends and shows them the ring. I don't have the heart to tell her I'm nothing more than a maid wrapped in silk. I stand and find Alc staring at me. My heart shutters and I become aware of the attention I have drawn, not only from our group, but from the people that were once milling around the street who now stand staring at me. I focus back on Alc's green eyes and smile weakly; he returns it, and we continue to walk.

He leans close to me a whispers in my ear,

"That was very nice of you. Not many others would take the time to get to know them, especially someone that's not from their court."

I blink up at him.

"Why?" I whisper back, aware of the people still staring at me.

"Because they are the children of the dead."

Shock makes me stumble slightly and I shake my head.

"That's horrible, what happened to their parents?"

Alc looks over his shoulder at the group of children growing smaller as we get closer to the iron gates of the castle.

"Most died as soldiers, but others were taken by illness or were executed for crimes they committed."

My heart aches for the children and I look down at my feet, "That's no way to grow up."

Alc just nods and comes to a stop at the gates standing tall in front of us. Two guards armed with long swords step forward, their uniforms a light blue with darker blue stitching. They are tall and burly with stern looks on their faces. One of the males with dark skin and darker hair speaks, his voice husky.

"State your business."

Everyone looks to Alc, and he smiles,

"Come now, that's no way to greet a guest."

The man nods his head once, seemingly happy with his rather vague response. I doubt anyone would be able to deny that Alc is the High Lord of the Night court just by the sinister smile on his face alone. The other man, with hair as white as the little girl's, steps forwards and smiles at us.

"This way, the High Lord has been expecting your arrival."

Ianira glares at the men as she passes through, and I'm amazed they don't wither away on the spot. We follow the man down a long, snow-covered path lined with bushes that have frosted over. I notice they sport the same flowers as the one I'm still clutching. We enter the castle through large doors of iron that match the gate and, once inside, I take in tall marble pillars that stretch to the ceiling and the tiled floor that opens up a large room, with many smaller areas branching off to each side. The colour theme in the room is much like outside, blues of different shades and white. Voices buzz around us as servants bustle past carrying trays of food and drink, but none of them worry themselves with us, they instead hurry through a room to the left of us, disappearing through a large set of white wooden doors.

My body is racked with shivers as the adrenaline of walking through the city fades. The male leading us through the castle stops and gestures a hand to the door I saw the servants pass through.

"He is waiting through there; I will leave you here, assuming you won't get lost on the short walk."

With a low bow to Alc and a nod to the rest of us, he walks back the way he came, I assume heading to the gate again.

It's then that Kai whispers, "I hope that food we saw is for us, I'm starving."

Alc laughs, the sound weaving around the huge pillars.

"Always thinking with your stomach," snorts Naomi, who is looking around the room with interest. "The last time I was here, we had to stop a fight from breaking out over Kai and Lilly having a heated discussion involving different types of sausages."

I raise my eyebrows at him, and he shrugs.

"All I said was that we make the best sausages ever tasted and she got all angry about it, saying the Winter court did."

Ianira slaps his arm and Neron turns his head away to hide a laugh.

"Don't be stupid, boy, that's not what happened, and you know it."

Kai grins sheepishly and Alc cuts further conversation off when a servant comes scurrying over. He is so short, he would only just reach my chest, his skin glows green, and his nose is more snout-like than anything I've seen before, not far from a pig's. Crazy black hair sticks up under his hat and he has eyes to match. He reminds me of a gremlin you hear about in children stories.

His nose twitches as he addresses Alc,

"Milord, Master Malik would like to speak with you now."

With that, he scurries away and opens the door the guard gestured at.

As we walk I lean over and whisper in Alc's ear,

"What is he?"

Turning his head slightly to me he answers,

"He is a goblin. Nasty little creatures, they like collecting hair and terrorising people, so keep your eyes open."

I blench and nod at the new information, my hand flies to my hair and I feel sick thinking about what they could possibly need hair for. Alc laughs at my obvious discomfort.

"You need to hide your emotions when we meet the other High Lords, they like to pick on weaknesses and will be looking for you to trip up, be careful."

He falls silent as we pass through the doors the goblin is holding open. The room is smaller than the one we just left but is grander in style. In the centre of the room, a round table stands with chairs all around it. In the middle is a fountain of ice flowing like water but solid, I'm mesmerised by it and have to tilt my head to see where it runs off to. Under the table, the floor is glass, and it looks like a storm of ice and snow is swirling underfoot. All around, banners of blue hang from the walls, their layout simple but beautiful, with snowflakes stitched into them. The goblin races ahead and pulls out a seat for Alc to sit in and we flank him; me on his right, Kai on his left. Naomi sits next to me, while Ianira sits next to Kai. Neron stands behind Alc like a bodyguard and the effect makes Alc look powerful and kingly. I fiddle with the flower in my hand and try to calm my sudden nerves.

"*Show no emotion.*"

I jump as I feel Alc enter my mind, I push him out and slam

up my mental shields, glaring at him, a small smile playing on his lips. Alc's words force me into action, and I move my face into practised calm and feign a look of boredom, placing the flower on the table and clasping my hands together. Doors open in front of us and two people walk through. The High Lord of Winter is gorgeous. His face is set in unreadable lines and his hair is so white it challenges the snow itself. Eyes of palest blue scan the crowd and a smile lights his beautiful face. The woman next to him is equally as striking, with long hair in the same shade as his and a delicate face with large eyes that would look doe-like on anyone but her. Instead of making her look vulnerable, they make her look like a warrior preparing for battle with the way they scan the room with efficiency. I feel rather than see Neron shift next to Alc as he assess any threats that may be nearby.

"What lovely timing you have, Alc," Malik's voice booms through the room and it sounds just like it did when he was speaking through the snowstorm earlier today.

Malik takes a seat across from us and the woman sits to his right, staring straight at me, and I have to mentally slap myself to stop from turning away from her scrutiny.

"It's good to see you, it's been too long since we last visited."

Malik nods and throws an agitated look in Kai's direction; who just smiles in return.

"Considering what happened last time, I think it was for the best we've had time apart," his tone holds something I can't place.

"Perhaps," is all Alc says before Malik turns his attention to me

"Now, if it isn't the beautiful flower with the quick tongue," he inclines his head to me, and I repeat the gesture.

"And if it isn't the bickering idiot."

From besides me, Naomi stiffens but Malik laughs and wiggles his fingers at me.

"I definitely like you."

I smile and the woman next to him frowns. Her brows pinching together with the action.

"Forgive my rudeness, Flower, but this is Lilly, my slightly overbearing sister and bodyguard."

I nod and turn my smile to her; she glares at me for a little longer but eventually nods her head at me. I take the peace offering and turn to Alc, whose face is unreadable, his eyes stern as he takes in the High Lord across from him.

"I wish to discuss a matter concerning the meeting tomorrow and would like to hear your opinion on what we plan to do if we can't get the other High Lords to agree to end this feud between the King and Queen."

His voice carries across the room despite his quiet tone and it sends shivers dancing along my arms. Malik's face falls into a look that means all business. Lilly beside him gestures to the servants to leave the room and I notice that the goblin takes his time to leave.

Alc continues, his voice carrying a deadly note, "As we all know, Isaac and Kelby are trying to form an alliance with the human monarch and I fear that it will do more harm than good in this battle. My spies have gathered information on the King and Queen..." he waves a hand at Neron, who straightens. "I have been informed that the couple is digging into the gods for reasons unknown. All we know is that they have been uprooting the less guarded sides of the Day court, overturning villages looking for something, and so far they haven't found it, only managing to make a lot of our people very unhappy. Last month, four children were killed by their majesties mercenaries."

I try to keep my face calm as shock and grief hit me. Alc told me that children are cherished in this realm, so to find out four were murdered is devastating. I glance at the faces around me to gauge if this news is new to them, but no one seems surprised, just sad and angry. Ianira's eyes glow and I'm glad I'm not sitting next to her right now.

Alc carries on, his voice becoming louder as he addresses the room again, "Kelby and Isaac joining forces with the King is betraying the lives that have been lost at their hands. We must find out what they are up to and why they are siding with them. What are they gaining from this? How are they going to use whatever it is against us, and why now after the tension has risen between us? This meeting is a chance to exploit any weak links between them and that's why we have agreed to have this meeting here as Kelby doesn't fair well with the cold, neither does Isaac."

I was right in guessing that they wanted to gang up on the young High Lord, I just didn't know the reason why. Malik speaks to us, and when he does, I can see a storm raging behind his eyes.

"I'm almost certain that Adian will see reason and join sides with us. He is smart and doesn't much like either of the High Lords after they nearly destroyed his house when getting in a fight. He is also wise and an old fart, so he won't want to see another war break out under his nose."

I grin at him, and he winks at me.

"I suggest we corner the bastards and break them until they bend to our will."

I groan and shake my head at him, and the room's attention shifts to me,

"What's with males and their need to kill and maim?"

I see Lilly cough into her hand and hear Naomi snort next to me.

"I suggest we go about it in a more subtle way."

Alc looks at me eyebrows raised as he asks,

"And what do you suppose we do?"

I glance at everyone in the room, finally looking back at Alc, hoping I don't regret this later, and say,

"We use base male instinct against them, because men like to do three things; fight, drink, and fuck. I'm not saying someone needs to sleep with them but seduce them enough to get them talking about their brilliant plans and, with a little alcohol to sway them, it could just work in our favour."

The room goes still as they consider my plan and a deadly grin spreads across Malik's face.

"You are a beautiful and sinful flower indeed; did I mention I like you? Because I might have to rephrase and say I love you instead."

I role my eyes at him and Lilly elbows him in the ribs, to which he just bats her away. Alc looks deep in thought but turns to me as he finally breaks from his trance.

"Isaac and Kelby know all the ladies in this room except for one, and that's you. Are you sure you're willing to go through with that?"

I want to say no, but the faces of dead children like Maria flash in front of me. I might be crazy, but I know that children can't keep dying because of whatever the King and Queen are looking for. I seal my fate as I nod once. Malik claps his hands together like a merchant finding a wealthy buyer, and Kai glares at me.

"What are you thinking? This is going to go horribly. You're a human, for crying out loud, they will destroy you before you can even lay a finger on them," his voice is laced with a growl and I'm shocked that he, out of all people, is defending me.

"I'm aware of the risks that are involved, but we need to do this to find out what they are up to," as I say this, Kai throws his hands up and shakes his head.

"Fine, but it's not on me when you get hurt. I warned you since nobody else seems to care."

He throws a pointed look over to Alc, whose firm tone answers,

"I don't have power over what she does, it's her decision. And frankly it's a good plan, they will think she's weak and find her of no threat."

Naomi nods along with his plan, a frown playing on her face.

"That may be true, but Isaac will see that she's friendly with us and will no doubt hesitate. What we need to do is separate ourselves from her, so it seems she means nothing to us and is only here so we can try to make amends with her people."

It's Ianira's turn to nod and unease settles in my gut at the forming plan. I fear that I have dived headfirst into something I don't understand at all. My heart is a rabid animal in my chest as Malik's voice catches everyone's attention.

"Now that we have that sorted, it's time to eat and then sleep, ready for the day to come."

It's the first thing I can completely agree with. Surprise catches me as the table becomes laden with dishes of food that is customary to the Winter court. Bowls of beef stew, plates of fluffy bread, and trays full of different meat makes my mouth water and I hear Alc chuckle as I lick my lips. I glare at him as I fill my plate. Alc frowns past me and I follow his gaze as it lands on Kai shovelling food into his mouth. Malik has just finished loading his plate and I see that everyone except Kai is waiting for him to take the first bite. Kai catches Alc's eye and stops his fork halfway to his mouth. A low growl comes from my left and I edge away as he passes his warning on to where Kai's seated. I see Ianira shake her head in disdain, her dark hair like a curtain flowing around her head.

Malik speaks and we all turn our heads towards him, "Let the feast begin."

My shoulders shake while I try to hide a laugh as Kai salutes and digs back into his food. Light chatter flitters around the room and servants come in carrying bottles of wine, filling up glasses when they get too empty. The little goblin with the long snout scurries around the room, asking repeatedly if the High Lord is comfortable, to which his answer is always the same.

"Quite comfortable, thank you. Go and enjoy the festivities."

As I watch the exchange for the fifth time, I notice how the goblin keeps leaning over the Lord's glass. My heart accelerates, and I shift in my seat to lean slightly over to Alc to see better. The goblin's green hands twitch and he glances around the room every so often to see if anyone is watching him. I stare down at my food that I've barely touched. A thought occurs to me, and I look up to catch the goblin's eye. As soon as I do, I feel the familiar sensation like I'm falling and then rightening. I open my eyes and it's like staring into a murky pond full of green algae. A stale smell hits me and I think I might vomit. I don't see the bridge that has been here the last two times I've done this, but I realise that I'm in the goblins head as clumps of different coloured hair floats past me. I shudder and try to avoid coming in contact with them. I scan the space, my eyes bouncing through the muck and landing on a clump of hair bigger than the rest. Its colour is dark and greasy. I'm not sure as to why it caught my eye, but I walk over to it and reach out my hand, which shakes slightly. Once my skin comes in contact with it, I'm falling and the world fades around me, opening me up to images as they flash past. Two large figures stand in the dark, their eyes gleaming in the poor light. Green hands stretch out and take a small vile wrapped in red silk. Then the image changes to letters plied on top of each other, the same green hands writing feverishly. Ink splatters the page and I notice words, whose meanings are foreign to me. Heir, ritual, and God, three words that snag my attention. What could a goblin possibly need with those words? Unless its gathering information for a third party. The image fades away and I stand back in the murky space. I scramble and will myself to fall back into my body. If I'm thinking straight, the High Lord of Winter is being poisoned. I feel myself slap back into my conscience and I look frantically around the room. Nothing has changed and I can still see the goblin leaning over Malik. Before rational thought settles in, I reach for my dagger sheathed to my hip and pull it free, keeping it hidden in the folds of my dress. Alc is immersed in conversation with Kai, and I don't have time to explain as I stand and walk over to where Malik is sitting playing with his wine glass, about to take a drink. It dawns on me that I could be very wrong about this and could be condemning an innocent to treason. The hilt of the dagger bites into my palm and the gems are surely leaving an imprint in my hand from how tight I hold it. I train my eyes on the goblin and see the sliver of a vile flash in his hand. Eyes around the room snap to me as I walk closer to Malik and Lilly. Dragging the dagger out into view, I cock my arm back, aiming for the wood of the table where green hands press eagerly. As I throw the knife, Malik's eyes widen and he thinks I'm throwing the dagger at him. It happens so quickly as the blade pierces through flesh and then wood, a scream erupts from the table and green skin pales as black, sticky blood oozes out of the wound in his hand. A small vile with clear liquid rolls across the table and stops when it hits the stem of Malik's glass. I can almost hear the snapping of necks as the people around the table look to me, still standing and breathing heavily, and the vile that rocks gently. Pain rips through my arms as strong hands grip me from both sides. I blink and look to my left to see guards dressed in blue and white strangle my arms. Their eyes hold murderous intent and I realise that it looks like I tried to kill a High Lord.

My heart stills and I stumble to explain,

"I wasn't going to harm you, Malik, I was stopping you from being poisoned. Your goblin is trying to lace your wine with some type of concoction."

I nod to the vile and his eyes leave mine to look at the bottle. A voice sounds from beside me and I look up at the burly guard to my right.

"My Lord, she could very well be lying. The goblin could be trying to warn you of the vile *she* was trying to poison you with."

I glare up at the guard, whose grip is cutting off circulation to my arm.

"And why would I do that, you idiot? Even if I were going to poison him, why would I draw attention to myself? It's not very assassin-like."

I see Alc stand, his eyes searching me. Maliks voice drags my attention back to him.

"How did you know that the goblin was trying to poison me in the first place?"

A small part of me wonders that too, but I answer regardless.

"I saw him leaning over your glass several times, but whenever he got too close, you would wave him away until the last time he came to talk to you. Who needs to ask one man how comfortable they are five times anyway? You would think that after the first time it would be enough, but he kept coming back to you. Plus, when you asked all the servants to leave the room earlier, I saw him dragging his feet about it."

A squeaky voice comes from the goblin as his eyes dart between us.

"My Lord, I would never I…"

His words are cut off when Malik rises his hand.

"Why would he try to harm me in the first place? To what ends would that achieve?"

My hands shake and I look to Alc for support, who just continues to stare at Malik. All the others are still seated and are watching the exchange with vicious interest.

"I… I saw it, I saw the goblin be given the vile, and I saw him writing letters to someone with the words heir, ritual, and God written over and over."

A dark laugh cuts through the silent room. Lilly's face twisting with the action.

"You saw all this within the hour you've been here? I find that very unlikely," Malik nods his head and a small smile creeps onto the goblin's face when he thinks no one is watching.

"I saw it through his head, in one of his memories."

The smile falls off his green face and the room stills, no one daring to breathe. I rush to explain, not caring about the yelling I will receive from Alc later.

"I don't know how, but I can enter a person's head and see their memories or make them bend to my will. I don't do it often at all and only did it tonight because of the way he was acting. I promise on my life."

My chest aches as I hold my breath, waiting for Malik to answer me, and when he does, I nearly collapse.

"Very well, let her go. I think we need to look to the creature with a knife in his hand."

Lilly splutters and grabs Maliks tunic,

"What are you thinking? You believe a human's word over one of our own?"

Malik shuts her down with a glare.

"I believe someone who isn't dumb enough to lie to my face and someone who threw a dagger through the hand of an assassin and spy. I want everyone out, except for Me, Alc, and her. Oh, and of course this little rat," he points to the goblin.

Lilly stands, outraged at his decision, but he just continues on, ignoring her.

"My sister will show you to your rooms and make sure you are comfortable."

With a final glare at her brother, Lilly stalks from the room with Neron, Naomi, Ianira, and Kai in tow, all of whom throw concerned looks our way but continue when Alc nods once. I fear more for what will happen when Alc gets me alone than the wrath that Malik can rain down on me.

"Now, flower, why don't you explain to me this power you possess, and I mean no offence when I say I'm curious as to how a human can hold something so valued."

I nod and open my mouth to speak, but Alc cuts me off.

"We don't know how she has come to hold this power and we don't know why she does. All I know is that when she entered the Night Court, she was able to control it. I thought it might be that she can borrow my power for small amounts of time, but it seems to not be the case as one of the times she used it, she was nowhere near me."

Malik's eyebrows raise, and I see the goblin squirm and wince as he pulls at his stapled hand.

"Are you suggesting that she could be a Shifter?"

Alc nods,

"That was my first thought, but now I'm not sure."

I flick my gaze between them as they seem to forget I'm standing between them. So many questions run wild in my head, and I grab onto one and ask.

"What do you mean a Shifter? I've heard stories of them when I was younger and I'm quite sure I can't shift into different forms."

Malik laughs, the sound holding none of his usual charm.

"There are two types of Shifters, the body type that belong to the Nether Lands, horrible creatures they are, and the other type are mind Shifters. They can use their power to grab a piece of someone else's power and use it for a short time as long as they are near the original host. As far as we know, they are extinct."

My natural instinct is to balk at them but I'm no longer in Fallen Crest, I'm in Thyithran and anything is possible here.

"So, you're telling me I'm a thief?"

Alc sighs and rubs his hands over his face.

"We don't know what you are, but we can almost rule out that you are a Shifter. You can use that ability for extended periods of time, and you don't have to be near me to do it."

I nod, letting it sink in.

"We could always test that theory, you know. Just see if you can borrow some of mine and see what happens."

My stomach drops as Malik suggests this. Stealing power from one High Lord is dangerous enough, let alone two. I almost jump out of my skin as Alc whispers from next to me.

"We could but we don't know what the repercussions could be, and we could be putting both you and her in danger."

Malik laughs and, his voice light, says,

"It's about time we had a bit of excitement around the place."

I want to argue with him as I think hosting a meeting with the most powerful beings in the world and having just avoided being poisoned would be enough excitement for a lifetime. But I bite my tongue as my attention shifts to the forgotten goblin, whose face is splotchy with pain. His hand is still pinned to the table, and he leans into the wound trying to take pressure off it. I address him and try to keep my voice steady and even.

"Why don't we focus on what you know and why you wanted to poison your High Lord?"

Malik blinks as if he's forgotten about the goblin and his plan to kill him. Alc moves and drags a chair from the table to sit in front of the goblin as he squirms.

When Alc speaks, his voice holds a deadly calm,

"I find it funny that someone like you would want to harm someone who could kill you in a blink of an eye. So, please tell me why?"

Black eyes widen and dart around the room, looking for an escape but when none arise, his green throat bobs.

"I was ordered to, otherwise it would be me lying cold on the ground."

Malik rolls his eyes at the vague answer before his face drops into unreadable lines.

"I want to know who sent you and what their motives are, don't make me force it out of you," Malik's voice carries cold authority and as he speaks, tendrils of mist floats around his clenched hands.

The goblin recoils but opens his snout-like mouth.

"I don't know who it was, I swear. All I know is that they are working with the King. I was told to kill the High Lord hosting the meeting so the ritual wouldn't be jeopardised."

Anxiety courses through me, making my limbs heavy. The host of this meeting is Alc. He is the one who ordered it, not Malik.

Alc makes the same assumption as me before he speaks,

"Well, I hate to tell you, but you've been hunting the wrong High Lord. Malik has graciously welcomed us into his home to hold the meeting, but I am the one who ordered the meeting in the first place and, if I'm correct, you should be trying to kill me not him."

The goblin's eyes widen further if possible and I can almost taste the fear radiating from him as he takes in the High Lord of Night. Alc lets the damper on his magic go and shadows encase him like a lover's touch. Malik laughs and claps his hands together.

"Isn't this just a lovely turn of events. I can rest easy knowing I'm no longer in harm's way," sarcasm drips from his every word.

I race to ask the goblin a question before both males lose their strained patience.

"What ritual is this that you speak of and how does Alc have anything to do with it?"

The goblin's eyes go to his pinned hand, then back to me, and he seems to decide that it's not worth another hand if he ignores me, so he answers.

"The ritual to wake the God of Death, the mighty Hugan. Your High Lord is hiding something of value and the King and Queen want it."

Nobody moves as we rush to process this new information. I look at Alc and can't tell if he is surprised by this or bored. My blood runs cold as realisation settles over me, does Alc know that he is hiding the missing piece of the King's puzzle or is it all new to him as well? Malik's voice is every bit the King of Winter when he speaks to the goblin.

"I want you to report back to your master and tell them that, if they want to kill anyone on my lands, they will have to try harder than sending a measly goblin to do their work," Malik flicks his hand, and a brand of ice appears on the goblin's forehead, a mark to tell the King that his footman is now property of the Winter court and it's High Lord.

Malik stands and turns to leave, waving at me to join him. Alc smiles and walks over to the goblin, pulling the knife out and making to walk away with us. But a scream pierces the air, making me spin back to the goblin.

"KIILL ME, DON'T LET ME GO BACK, KILL ME! IF YOU DON'T, I WILL BE KILLED IN THE WORST WAYS. PLEASE JUST KILL ME!"

Alc turns to face the goblin, his face holding a bored expression.

"And what makes you think that we will be any different? I can assure you Malik doesn't take lightly to vermin running around his palace. So, I suggest get going and do as he says before he loses his mercy for you."

Sobbing tears echo through the room and I almost feel sorry for him. Black blood drips to the floor as he moves to beg us.

Crouching on his knees and hands, he pleads,

"Please, you can't let them do this to me. I will do anything for you, I promise, just don't send me back."

Alc steps forward and places a booted foot on the goblin's injured hand, drawing a scream from him. I look away and fight the urge to hurl my guts up. Malik links his arm around mine and leads me to the door as Alc twists his foot on the hand. We leave through the doors but not before I hear the devil whisper into the goblin's ear.

"'Go."

The command sends shivers up my spine and the monster I feared would greet me when I first came to this godforsaken place has just arrived.

Malik left hours ago after escorting me to my rooms. His face had been apologetic, and he said he was sorry that I had to witness such activities. I had nodded and left his side to try and calm my racing heart. No matter how hard I try, sleep won't come to me, so I sit on the soft blue sofa near the marble hearth. I know that Alc was only doing what he had to do, but it still scares me. The force and the coldness in which he did it makes my insides twist. I have recently forgot that I'm not in the human realm any more. I'm sure humans are just as brutal, but it's the thought that I can no longer run home to my desolate hut and hide away from them any more that is rattling me. I stare around the room I'm to be staying in while here and draw a strange sense of calm from it. The room is large and comfortable; the curtains are a deep blue while the walls are the same stark white as the rest of the palace. A floor of marble that matches the hearth stretches beneath me and I have to put on thick socks to stop the cold from biting my feet. Everything, from the sofas to the bed, is in harmony with the blue and white that the Winter court values. It's beautiful yet it's missing something. I can't place what is missing, but it doesn't give me the same warm feeling as my rooms in the Night Court. I settle deeper into the chair and curl my legs under me as I watch the dancing flame in front of me. Would Alice be watching the flame in our hearth back home? Would Laura be sitting at the table, wondering when is the next time she can buy another dress? Questions about the family I left behind run through my head, but the one I try to push away keeps haunting me. Do they miss me or am I just a burden that has been lifted off their shoulders? I know I shouldn't care, but a part of me wants to know. I wonder who is doing the hunting now and who is keeping the family running if I'm not there to do it. My father would surely be drinking just as heavily as when I left and Alice will most likely be by his side, leaving only long enough to get him another drink. But Isabella and Laura, would they be wanting more? Wanting a way out and to get away from that horrible place? I feel a small twinge of pity for them, even though they have done nothing to deserve my sympathy. I long to run my hands over the ink-splattered pages of my mother's journal and to feel her close to me. The necklace is all I have of her, and while I love it, it has nothing compared to the journal, her fine handwriting sprawled gently across the page, and I loved how I felt as if I was there with her when she wrote about her day or something that interested her. Resentment flows in me at my father. Did she love him truly or was she stuck with him, not knowing a way out? I would like to think she did love him and he her, but I begin to wonder if that was the case. A monster like him doesn't just change, they are always there, lurking. They just hide it for the benefit of themselves. My mind whirls and I wish more than anything that sleep will come and collect me so I can feel nothing for a few hours. I glance over at a clock on the wall and groan as it reads two in the morning. I wonder if Alc is sleeping or sitting waiting like me. As if on cue, a light knock sounds on the doors. I stand and stretch my legs, padding over to the door. I open it a slit and see black, dishevelled hair. Opening the door further, I cross my arms and step back. Alc stands in front of me with his hands hidden in his suit pants. His green eyes scan over me and I realise I must look ridiculous in my silk shorts and simple tunic with my hair a mess from tossing and turning all night. His green eyes meet mine and he smiles at me weakly, and when he speaks his voice is tired and worn.

"Sorry, I didn't mean to wake you. I just wanted to see if you were okay."

I arch a brow at him, letting sarcasm enter my voice as I answer, "What? In the middle of the night?"

He laughs, the sound not in the least bit humorous.

"Sorry."

I frown, not liking the quiet and drowned way he is speaking.

"It's fine, you didn't wake me. I couldn't sleep anyway."

I step back from the door and walk over to the sofa I had vacated earlier and gesture for him to do the same. He sighs as he sits, and I tap my arm aimlessly on the chair, not sure what to say to the male across from me. He clears his throat and breaks the silence.

"I'm sorry you had to see that earlier. I shouldn't have done that in front of you, but it needed to be done. We can't have a spy running around without large precautions."

I nod and place my fidgeting hands on my knees.

"You don't need to apologies to me, I understand what you had to do."

Alc leans forward and shakes his head,

"No, I do. It wasn't right. You have been through enough without me adding that to the mix."

My heart clenches painfully at the sorrow in his voice. His mask is nowhere in sight and he's hurting. I wish I could soothe him, but I don't know how. I have to fist my hands on my knees to stop myself from leaning over and touching him.

"It doesn't matter, I've seen worse and been through worse.

He was a traitor. I understand that precautions had to be taken to ensure the safety of this court."

Alc's eyes darken, and I see anger flash in them.

"He will pay for what he did to you, mark my words."

For a second, I don't know who he's talking about but the images of the night I was taken by Alc flash in my head. I had a large bruise on my face from where my father hit me earlier in the day and he must have connected the dots when my father did nothing to stop him from taking me.

"I wouldn't waste my breath on him, he's probably died of starvation anyway."

Again, Alc leans forward but this time he reaches out a large hand and wipes away stray hairs that have escaped my braid. The tenderness in the action making me shiver.

"When I took you that night, I left them with enough money to move somewhere suitable with enough money to keep them fed, I didn't just leave them to rot."

I rock back but Alc catches my face in his hands, the impact of his words hitting me hard. He gave them so much when they deserved nothing. Guilt I didn't know I was harbouring lifts from my shoulders, and I lean into his hold.

"Thank you," my voice comes out in barely a whisper.

My pulse is too quick in my chest, and I am struggling to breathe.

"You deserve so much more than that, Princess," Alc kisses me lightly on the forehead and stands to leave but I grip his hand, tugging him towards me as I stand as well.

I wrap my arms around him and hug him, relishing in his warmth and smell. He embraces me back, his long arms wrapping me further into his warmth. I smile into his chest and as he lets go, I wish to tug him back to me but let him go and he smiles down at me.

His voice is husky as he says, "The things you do to me, Princess."

He shakes his head, clearing something unseen out of his head before he walks to the door.

"Be sure to get some sleep before the meeting. We all have roles to play tomorrow."

I nod and watch as he gently closes the door as he leaves. My head is swimming with so many unanswered questions but for now I walk to my bed, slip under the covers, and finally let sleep envelope me with the feeling of Alc's kiss still on me.

Chapter 9

A bird with the whitest feathers wakes me with its cheery song. I groan and shove a pillow over my head, but I peek out from under it to look at the clock on the wall. It is barely dawn, and as much as I like the sound of the birds singing, I would rather a few more minutes of sleep. I turn back to the bird sitting on the windowsill tilting its small head at me. I smile and sit up to watch it. It watches me curiously and it's so unlike the birds I used to see in Fallen Crest. Now that my eyes have adjusted to the light, I can see that its feathers are shaded with the lightest yellow. Its tiny black eyes scan the room I'm sitting in, and it hops closer to me.

I whisper into my empty room, "You just want someone to talk to, don't you?"

My smile widens as the bird ruffles its feathers as if to say, "Don't we all?"

My arms wrap around my legs, and I find myself talking to the little creature as it continues to just sit there.

"Do you ever wonder what it's like to be something different? Don't you get bored with flying around the same places over and over again?"

As if it can understand me, it looks over to a snow-covered tree below and I get up and walk closer to the window. In the tree is a nest made of small twigs and winter grasses. In the nest is three tiny birds calling to their mum, who is sitting on my window.

"You have a purpose here, don't you? Looking after your

babies in this cold place where even the sun hides from the snow."

I frown down at the bird and sudden anger surges through me. Even a bird has their life figured out better than me. I turn from the window and the bird flies back to her babies, who are waiting to be fed. Walking over to my wardrobe, I grab out a red dress that shows more skin then what I'm used to. Today is the meeting of the High Lords and I need to look the part if I'm going to be able to squeeze secrets out of Kelby and Isaac. My confidence in the plan I formed is slowly getting lower as the minutes pass. Kai was probably right in that the High Lords will most likely eat me alive before I can even look at them. As I dress and do my hair, I hear movement outside my door and, just as I put the final pin in my hair, Kai comes bursting in through the door, followed by the rest of Alc's inner circle. Ianira is the last to enter and she shuts the door with a bang, her face twisted into angry lines.

"The next time you come barging into my room at this early hour, I will personally skin you alive, boy."

I laugh at her words but stop when she shoots me a glare. She's clearly not a morning person, and by the smug look on Kai's face, he knows this. Naomi grabs Ianira's hand and pats her gently on the shoulder, ignoring the look she's getting pinned with.

"Calm down. Kai's like a toddler who needs constant reminders of what's right and wrong. Let's hurry and get this over with, we don't have long before the other Lords arrive."

Neron nods and sits down on the arm of one of the blue sofas, his voice echoing around the room as he speaks. I don't know if I will ever get used to the deepness of his voice, I hear it so rarely that when he does bless us with his voice, I can't help but be transfixed by it.

"Alc wants us to all play a role today, and unfortunately for Keilee, that means a plaything of the Night court. He has said that we are to mostly ignore her, but when we do speak to her, act as if she is vermin."

I recoil slightly, not liking the sound of how my day is turning out. Kai walks over to me and pats me on the arm in an affectionate way.

I smile as he says, "Don't worry, we will try to keep talking to a minimum. Hopefully Kelby will fall for our plan and make it easier for you, but remember, if they get too overbearing, everyone in this room will put them into the grave. You are part of this family now and you must remember that."

Even cold and distant Neron nods along with his statement and I feel my heart lighten. I never knew I wanted to hear those words so much.

A devil's grin spreads across Kai's face as he continues, "I say we get this party started."

And with that, Neron and he walk out of the room, patting me on the shoulder as they leave. Naomi and Ianira lag behind and the latter whispers to me.

"You call the shots here, don't let them push you over. Use that ability of yours to get what you want, when you want."

I smile down at Ianira, tucking her words away for later use. Naomi picks up my hand and presses a small clip into it. The red gem on it matches the dress I'm wearing, and I pin it into my hair.

"The clip will make you immune to any glamours they might try to use on you. As long as you wear it, it will work."

I touch the clip in my hair. I've heard of glamours that the Fae use, but I have never actually believed in them. I thought that they were just stories used to scare children away from the border. Many of the older children would spin tales that if a Faerie was to glamour you, you would be rendered useless to use your own body and would become their slave. Your mind would still be working but you had no control over your body. It would be like being paralysed. I shiver at the thought and thank Naomi, and the three of us then make our way to the meeting room we were in yesterday. I haven't seen Alc and lean over to ask Naomi.

"Where is Alc this morning anyway? Wouldn't he be walking in with you?"

Naomi shakes her head, but it's Ianira who answers me.

"Alc is known as a cold ruler, showing no sympathy to anyone, not even his closest associates. He has to maintain that façade to protect his people and his home. Nobody outside of Cassiopeia knows of the city's existence and he plans to keep it that way."

Ianira lowers her voice to a mere whisper as we walk past a servant cleaning a table near us, "The city is protected by many enchantments and spells and Alc does everything within his power to protect the city from outsiders."

"Why does he protect the city? What would someone gain from knowing of its existence?"

I follow Ianira's lead and keep my voice low and quite.

"Centuries ago, when the battle of the gods was taking place, Alc's ancestors hid away their people in a place where they could be protected from the bloodshed that the war caused. They built a city where children could play, and people could laugh. It is a sacred haven for the people of his court. It's the city of starlight and allows people in his court to dream. Alc has fought hard to keep it a secret and many of the people that have known of the city's existence have either forgotten or have been killed. Alc's mask is to show people a front that he doesn't care about his people's happiness, only their loyalty, and he has maintained this for a long while. Only his inner circle and Malik know of his façade, but not even Malik knows the true extent he has gone to in protecting his people and he most certainly does not know about the city."

I take all of it in and try to process it. Alc has been keeping the city secret for years to protect his people from hungry scavengers. The act would drain anyone and is a huge burden to carry around. I wish to ease it and help him in any way I can. Finding information from Kelby and Isaac will not be easy but I find myself more confident than when I first left the room. One question plagues me still, and I turn my head slightly to ask Naomi.

"How come Malik knew where to send his message if he doesn't know the city exists?"

Naomi smiles and answers, pride lacing her words.

"Alc worked a simple spell that allowed messages to pass to him and others within the city, but the address would be signed to a smaller city in his court where most think he spends his days. The spell can track him and allows for messages to find him wherever he may be."

I smile at her and go to reply but the doors of the meeting room loom closer and Ianira silences me with a delicate hand as she says, "Remember your role? It starts now. Don't speak unless spoken to and keep eye contact to a minimum. Good luck in there, we will try to help you as best as we can."

With that, she throws open the doors and struts past me with Naomi in tow, their heads held high, radiating power. The room is silent as they enter, and everyone knows that they belong to the Night Court and its High Lord. I follow behind, staring at my feet and keeping my shoulders slightly bowed. Voices flitter past me and I catch the deep timbre of Kai and Neron laughing at something. I look up under my lashes and see Alc sitting in his chair with arrogant grace, the perfect picture of nonchalant royalty. Alc sees me enter and nods to a wooden chair sitting near the closest wall to the table. Great, just great. I walk over and sit on it, the wood biting into me, but I keep my face impassable. Apart from Alc's inner circle, Lilly, and Malik, only one other male is sitting at the table. His hair is blond, and his eyes are ocean blue. He wears a thick coat of dusty yellow over a white tunic and pants, His court's insignia of a rising sun over a mountain peak is embroidered across his chest and I recognise him as the High Lord of Day. Adian runs his eyes over me and smirks when he finishes. I bite my tongue to stop myself from lashing out and wiping that smile off his striking face. His eyes are calculating, and I feel as if I'm laid bare before him. It's not the same feeling as when Alc does it, it's more like he sees only what I lay out for him, and he strips it into tiny ribbons. Malik clears his throat and drags Adian's attention away from me.

"It looks like Dorian is waiting to make an entrance once again, that man never fails to try and steal the spotlight."

Adian laughs, and when he speaks, I don't expect the accent to be there.

"I must agree with you, he is rather the dramatic type."

Alc leans forward and taps his fingers on his chair as if impatient and bored.

"If they don't get a move on, I'm going to start this without them. I don't like to be kept waiting."

I don't recognise Alc's cold voice and turn my gaze to where Kai and Neron are lounging in their seats. Kai catches my gaze and sends a sly wink my way. As if summoned, the doors of the room burst open and a man with swaggering movements walks into the room, his dark skin glimmering in the light. I can see hazel eyes scanning the room through blond waves of hair. Somehow, his lilac tunic and pants add to his relaxed persona and makes him seem completely at peace with the people before him. His gaze lands on me briefly before he gives a shallow bow towards the rest of the High Lords.

"You must forgive me for my late arrival, I was somewhat held up by Isaac and Kelby congregating out at the front gates."

Malik eyebrows rise at this, and he turns to usher a guard forward, his voice firm as he orders,

"Go and fetch the other Lords and direct them here immediately, we don't have time to waste on their antics."

The guard in blue and white nods and hurriedly leaves the room, going to find the stray Lords.

"It is good to see you, Dorian. How are things holding up at your court?"

Dorain glances at Alc before answering, like he wishes he didn't have to discuss this in front of the Lord of Night.

"We are faring well and have begun to get ready for the spring solstice."

Alyssa's description of the Lord of Summer didn't mention him being a man of little words. I look around at the table and see Adian glaring openly at Alc, who smirks to himself. Malik is calm and I don't understand how he can tolerate such tension in his home. It seems to me that both Lords of Summer and Day get along fairly well with Malik, while Alc is somewhat avoided by them. I wonder if the newcomers hate Kelby and Isaac as much as Malik and Alc do. Considering that the King and Queen killed four of the Day court children, I would think so, but they might not know of the forming alliance between them. I'm ripped from my thoughts when the guard that was sent to fetch the missing

Lords comes bustling into the room, holding the doors open for the two men following to enter. Isaac and Kelby strut into the room like they own the place. They don't bow to the seated High Lords like Dorian did, they just ignore them until they sit down. Eyes of raging fire land on Kai and I see a series of emotion flash across them. Kai smiles cunningly and wiggles a hand at his father, who ignores him and turns to Malik with an annoyed expression on his face.

"I suggest you get some new gatemen, Malik; the current ones ask too many questions."

Malik glares at him,

"Don't lecture me on what I should and shouldn't do in my own court, Isaac."

Adian smiles and opens his arms wide to the room.

"This is already turning out to be an interesting meeting and we haven't even started."

The High Lord I recognise as Kelby glares at Adian, showing his dislike openly, and my earlier assumption that the other High Lords don't like the younger Lord is correct. I try to sink into my chair and look the part of a scared, weak human and find that all eyes at the table turn to me as the chair scrapes slightly on the marble floor. My heart pounds as I keep my gaze facing forwards, cursing my lucky with inanimate objects. Adian speaks into the silence, and I can see the smile spread across his face.

"I was wondering what this little delight may be? I wonder if we may closer inspect it and see if it bites?"

Alc smiles and waves a hand my way.

"By all means, but I must warn you she has sharp teeth."

I flinch and lean back in my seat as all the Lords except Alc and Malik creep closer. Kelby's smile is deadly, and I fear that they may underestimate his evil.

"I'm fascinated. How did Alc come across such a specimen and be able to hide it from us until now?"

I want to slap him as he regards me as nothing more than a brood mare on show. Kelby smiles again as he sees his words have hit their target, except he thinks he's hurt me instead of angering me. My hands clench on the sides of the chair and I see red. My blood boils and I begin to taste blood in my mouth from where I'm biting my tongue.

"Tell me, does it speak?"

I open my mouth before anyone can answer for me.

"Yes, it does. But I'm afraid you might not like what I've got to say," I smile innocently at him and see that Adian smirks back at me.

"Sharp teeth indeed, Alc. How delightful," Adian's tone is full of curiosity, but I hear Dorian cough from behind him.

I turn my gaze to him, and he frowns at me.

"I don't trust it."

I bark out a laugh and nod my head to him. He seems to be the only one with brains in this group of curious bloodhounds.

"Very smart of you, my Lord."

Isaac and Kelby stand together, and I see their eyes trained on my every move, assessing if I'm a threat to them. Once they deem me harmless, they smile as one and I repress a shudder.

Isaac turns to Alc,

"After you're done with it, can I have my turn?"

I hear laughter and see Alc flourish his hand without turning away from his conversation with Malik. Even though I know it's a role he must play, I can't help when my chest constricts slightly at his words. It feels as if something is winding its way around my heart and squeezing till I fear it may crack.

"You might have more luck than I've had. So, again, by all

means."

Isaac smiles at this and both him and Kelby stand so close to me I have to lean back in my chair. My heart races and panic is trying to eat away at me, I push it down and swallow thickly. Dorian shakes his head and retreats back to the table, but he keeps casting wary looks my way. Adian seems to have filled his curiosity and follows Dorian back to the table. I can see his smirk on his face as he throws a look at Alc, then me, and I can't help but wonder if he is too perceptive for his own good. Isaac ushers me to stand and I do as he asks, not wanting to anger him when I'm supposed to do the opposite. Kelby sends a sly smile at Isaac and moves to his seat at the table next to Dorian, who frowns at the unpleasurable seating arrangements. Isaac places a hand on my back and pushes me forwards towards the table. I keep my gaze averted from Alc and the others while I walk, focusing on not stumbling. Isaac sits and taps his leg.

"Sit."

I grab my skirts and do as he says, resting on his legs while draping an arm around the back of his chair. I chose not to wear my dagger as it would be too much of a risk if he were to find it but regret my decision as Isaac places a hand on my upper thigh, marking me as his for the day. Playing my part, I paste a devils smile on my face and shoot Kai a look. He hides his smirk and looks to the rest of Alc's circle, giving them the barest of nods. Kelby watches me with a hungry expression on his face. Isaac notices and I feel him laugh from behind me.

"Don't worry, my friend, you'll get your chance."

My body is aware of every place his hand touches, and the longer it rests on my thigh, the more I wish to have my dagger to slice it off. Alc clears his throat and brings his attention to the room, never resting his gaze on me long enough for me to catch his gaze. There is something in his eyes that reminds me of jealousy.

"We all know that I called this meeting to address the hostilities that have been occurring between us and the King and Queen. I think we can all agree that overturning villages and killing our people has begun to wear on our nerves."

Alc sends a significant look to Adian, who nods his agreement, before continuing, "I for one don't want another tiresome war breaking out between us and the humans, it's a waste of resources and good fighters. I want to try and negotiate with the King and see if we can call some sort of truce between our people."

I notice Kelby frown deeply and look to Isaac behind me, who's hand has tightened significantly on my leg. Adian is also frowning and addresses Alc with anger lacing his every word.

"The King may be a dick but he's not stupid, He won't sign a treaty and keep true to his word not to attack. The loss of my children has been proof enough of this."

Alc nods and a sinister smile spreads across his face.

"I never said he would sign it freely, I said we will try and negotiate with him, and when he fails to do so, we will force his hand in our favour. The King is looking for something and I have every intention of finding out what it is."

Malik looks deep in thought and opens his mouth to speak.

"Do you have the slightest clue as to what he's looking for?"

I narrow my eyes on Alc and he regards Malik with impatience.

"If I didn't have a clue, would I be telling you all about this? My spies have informed me about their movements and I myself have been tracking them."

I think back to when Alc disappeared for three weeks and

wonder if that was what he was doing.

"The King and Queen are trying to form a plan on how to find this object and we must stop them before they find it otherwise war might be the last on our list of worries."

Dorian is the next to voice his concerns and Alc almost rolls his eyes.

"How are we supposed to find an object when we don't even know what it is?"

I glace around the room and bite back a smile at the confused looks on everyone's face when Alc speaks.

"You will leave the looking to me. I need all of you to form strong alliances between each other."

One by one, all the faces around the room drop into scowls.

"So, you want us to sit back and make cocktails while you go and find this object the King and Queen are looking for? Why are we to trust you?"

I move my body out of the way so Isaac can see Alc clearly. Alc nods his head and turns his full attention to Isaac.

"You don't have a choice but to trust me, and the reason you and every other High Lord in this room need to build alliances is because we need to show a united front against the King and Queen if we are all standing on the same ground in this fight. I will look for the object and bring it to your attention once I find it."

Isaac snarls but starts to rub a thumb on my leg, making me twitch with the need to get away from him. Adian looks to Kelby then Dorian in an attempt to see what they make of the situation. My gaze flicks to Naomi and Ianira, who both seem more interested in anything other than the meeting. Adian whispers into the room, drawing my gaze to him as he stares down Alc.

"I will do anything to protect my people, and if that's

showing a united front, then I will happily agree. But if I find that I've been played by you, Alc, I will make you regret it."

Alc nods once and speaks, his tone laced with arrogant authority,

"Thank you for your support on this. What of the rest of you?"

Malik smiles and grips his hand, albeit cautiously.

"I informed you earlier that you have my support, but my warning still stands, as does Adian's."

Dorian is the next to speak and I feel a strange calm settle over me.

"Not that we have any other choice in the matter, I will support you as well, but I am the same in my agreement."

Alc laughs a bitter sound and squares his shoulders.

"Ye of little faith. I will keep my word and your allegiance means a great deal."

Alc sounds not in the least bit grateful, and by the way Adian raises his eyebrows, he knows just that.

"Now that's four out of six who have agreed, what about you, Isaac and Kelby?"

I realise that Alc is trying to corner the Lords because to refuse now would mean they don't want to protect the people and save them from war. It would also raise suspicion about where their loyalties lie. Isaac shifts uncomfortably beneath me, and I fight not to throttle him when he grabs my hips and jerks me to him.

"I will pledge my alliance for now, but any hint of mistrust and I will withdraw."

Adian laughs and claps his hands once,

"And how is that any different from what you usually do, Isaac? It's always hide first and fight later with you."

My thigh heats from where Isaac rests his hand, his flame dancing under his skin, fighting to break free and no doubt burn the Lord of Day. I smile despite my discomfort and speak to Adian, my tone light and playful.

"Careful, I don't fancy being caught in the crossfire of two blundering High Lords."

Adian's smile widens, and he regards me with a nod.

"What is fun without a little danger?"

I laugh and rest back into Isaac, who calms slightly, and I feel I've played my part well. Kelby is the only one not to have answered and Alc continues to stare at him expectantly. With a sigh, he leans forward in his seat.

"Very well, I agree albeit reluctantly. I don't trust you or your people, Alc."

Alc just smiles,

"The feeling is mutual, trust me. Now, I want all courts to send a line of soldiers to the border between the Day Court and the Human Realm. It's the weakest link and is not as heavily guarded as the rest of the border. Am I right, Adian?"

He nods and I can't tell if he's offended by Alc's wording.

"All right, with that sorted, I suggest we rest up and take advantage of Malik's hospitality while it lasts. Tomorrow, we will go over the rest of the plan and set it into motion."

Various people nod and stand. My gaze floats around the room and I notice I can no longer see Lilly or Neron in the room. When had they left? I was so caught up in the moment that I hadn't noticed them leave. Hopefully I wasn't the only one not to have noticed as it means that they would have successfully gone to scope out the bond between the Lord of Autumn and Spring. Kai walks over to me, his face pressed into a disgusted expression as he regards me.

"Alc wants you to be silent and not cause any issue for the rest of the day. He doesn't want to see you until tomorrow morning. Try and keep your filthy hands off anything valuable."

He throws Isaac a significant look and Isaac loops an arm around my waist, claiming me as his for now.

"Tell Alc he won't have to worry; I will keep a very close eye on her. And as for you, I don't want to see or hear of you if I can help it, so leave me."

I want to laugh and spit in his face, but I resign to smiling coyly up at him.

"Very well, Father dearest," Kai smiles and mocks a bow.

With that, he walks over to Naomi and Ianira, who leave the room all throwing disgusted looks my way, but I see the concerned glint in their eyes as they do. Isaac's arm tightens on me, and Kelby comes up to walk next to us as we too leave the room, leaving Alc and Malik to reminisce with the other High Lords. My heart quickens as we make our way down unfamiliar corridors. I try and mark my way in case things go south, but find myself getting confused, so I resign to counting my steps; one, two, three. It calms me slightly, but the panic quickly grabs at me as I'm ushered into a dimly lit room much like the room I'm staying in except it doesn't have a window near the bed and I can't see the snow hanging off the trees. I'm not a claustrophobic person but I feel the walls closing in on me as the Lords turn to me with evil intent gleaming in their eyes and pulling at their lips. I clasp my hands to stop them from betraying my fear and I stand a little straighter. I don't want them to see me scared or weak, Alc's words ring through my head, *'Don't show any emotion. They feed on people's weaknesses and would love to see you fail.'* I steady my breathing and stitch a smile on my face in an attempt to look relaxed and compliant.

"I think we ought to have a little fun with her, what do you reckon, Kelby?"

Isaac's voice is laced with venom and lust. I have to shut down a shiver that tries to rip through me. Kelby smiles and nods his head, and I don't see how someone so twisted can rule over the lands that are known for the beautiful flora and fauna.

"*You've got this, you are strong and don't back down without a fight. Just get the information and leave. It's simple,*" I whisper these words in my head and try to build up my confidence.

It should be simple, right? My eyes are drawn to the large four poster bed in the centre of the room, and I note how it is unmade. The room remains bathed in dull lighting, causing it to give the room an eerie feel. The walls are white but don't seem to absorb the light, rejecting it and leaving the space darker and unwelcoming. My mind whirls with different ways to weasel information, and after much debate, I decide that a not-so-subtle approach would be the best way as it would drag any suspicion away from me trying get information from them. After all, I am just a plaything to them. I open my mouth and make sure to keep my tone confused as if I didn't understand a thing they were talking about.

!Do you know what the object is that Alc and the King are looking for? I mean, what could be of such importance that they would kill over it?"

Kelby eyes me cautiously and panic settles deeper into my chest. Without much thought, I imagine myself walking through their minds easing their distrust. Kelby's eyes glaze over, and he stares at me blankly. Isaac sighs and his words tumble from his mouth without much restraint.

"It's not an object but a living thing they are looking for. Those fools might as well walk around blindfolded for all the good it will do looking for an object. Alc thinks he knows but he's just going to end up on a wild goose chase."

I scrunch my nose in fake confusion and tilt my head slowly. I store the information away and turn to ask my next question to Kelby himself.

"Why do they need to look for a living thing? Aren't the King and Queen powerful enough without the help of someone else?"

Kelby nods and smiles slightly at my attention and apparent blondeness.

"This certain person will help them attain power to overthrow any Lords that stand in their way."

Isaac gives Kelby a look, but I interrupt with another question, trying to stay inconspicuous. A thin layer of sweat beads at my forehead with the effort of keeping the males' suspicion from arising.

"What power will this person bring them? Who is that powerful to be able to overthrow a High Lord?"

I'm unprepared for the firm grip on my jaw as Isaac brings me in close to whisper in my ear. Kelby smiles at me and my unease grows.

"So naïve, aren't we? The King and Queen are looking for an heir, a forgotten heir. The child of the mighty Hugan, God of Death. Once the heir is found, a simple ritual can be performed to awaken him and he can be bound to do the bidding of the person who woke him. The King plans to overthrow the Lords in Thyithran and rule over both lands, but little do they know that I don't intend for them to get that far. Kelby and I will kill the King and Queen as soon as Hugan is awoken and then proceed to kill every darn High Lord in this land to claim Thyithran for ourselves."

I shudder and pull back, not having to fake my disgust. Kelby laughs at my distress. The gleam in Isaac's eyes tells me that he doesn't intend to share the ruling of this land and that Kelby will become just another body to add to the growing pile. If the younger Lord isn't stupid, I can almost reckon he's planning the same thing as Isaac. It just comes down to who's smarter and quicker. I need to get away, but curiosity drowns all logic and I open my mouth before I can really think.

"What happens if the heir doesn't agree to help them?"

"It's only the blood of the heir that is needed, so if they prove to be too difficult to handle, then a blade comes to their throat. No loss to us," Isaac's voice is laced with malice, and he shakes his head like snapping out of a trance, his grip on my jaw tightens and I can feel the bruises forming.

"Now we can't let you leave this room with all this information, can we?"

I see Kelby smirk in response and my eyes widen as I let my fear finally show. Isaac shushes me like one would a spooked horse.

"Don't stress your pretty face over it, a simple memory erasing will do. We don't want Alc's little pet turning up dead, that would go horribly for our plan."

I swallow and try to step back but his grip remains firm. Isaac leans toward me and for a second I think he's going to kiss me, but instead he just blows on my face, the warm air wrapping around me. I notice the gentle scent of jasmine and pine and almost close my eyes. I blink rapidly in my confusion and look at Isaac and Kelby, who have taken a step back to observe me.

When he speaks, Isaac lets a seductive note into his voice, "What do you remember of this past hour?"

Again, I blink as realisation settles over me. He thinks my

memory has been erased, that's what the smell was. It was some sort of spell to erase my memory, only it didn't work because I remember everything. But I keep this from my face, tilt my head to the side, and press my lips together as if trying to remember.

"I'm not sure, all I recall is walking into the room?" I let my voice raise a question.

Kelby seems satisfied and sits down on an overstuffed chair near the hearth. Isaac nods and flicks his head in the direction of the door.

"Go."

I startle at the harsh command, but move as common sense settles back in. I swing the large doors open and step into a brightly lit hall. Torches adorn the walls and relief washes over me at the familiar sight. Casting a glace over my shoulder, I see Kelby rest his face in his hands and Isaac slam a hand into the writing desk next to the bed. Soft but angry words float over to me as the doors click shut.

"Fuck this shit show, I'm going to kill the King and Queen sooner than planned if they keep sending us in circles, chasing our tails."

I barely hear Kelby's mumble of agreement as I hurry back the way we came. All the information I collected swirls around in my head as it fights to break free. How were they supposed to find the heir if there isn't supposed to be one? What tipped them off that things had changed, and did Alc know about this? My footsteps echo on the marble floor and I slowly make my way back to my room. I can hear laughter from one of the doors lining the hall but slip past without stopping. I need to find Alc and pass on what I've learned about the King and Queen, and the Lords' involvement in their plans. Once I finally find the familiar white of my bedroom doors, I'm breaking into a sweat and ache for the comfort of my tunic and pants. I push open the doors and cool air greets me. Marching over to the window, I yank the curtains closed while scanning the room for my dagger. I spot it lying on the bedside table and grab it quickly, sheathing it and its holster to my thigh. Never again would I part with it. The amount of times I would have used it today surpasses the normal level of violence that's accepted for a normal person. I want to scrub my body clean of the feeling of Isaac touching me, his hands as greedy as his thirst for power. He is willing to let his people die so he can rule over Thyithran as its sole leader. I wonder how the Autumn court has fared so well over the years that he has been in power. Then again, I might be right in guessing that his mate has more to do with the politics than he does. My mind goes blank as I search for her name, I'm sure Alyssa and I went over it in the history lectures. Coraline. That's it. I wonder if she knows about his scheming and if she's in on it. Surely he would let his mate know? Alyssa said that to have a mate means the strongest form of love, but she also said she doesn't know how Coraline puts up with Isaac, so then again she might be completely ignorant to the fact that her husband and mate is conspiring with the enemy. I freeze mid thought as I run over my words again. When had the King and Queen of my people become my enemy? When had I accepted the fact that I was no longer part of their realm any more? It surprises me how easily I forgot where I came from and what these people took me from. I don't feel any anger towards the people I now spend my time with, I instead feel at home. I guess over the last few months they have become somewhat like family and have accepted me as one of them. No longer did Neron glare at me constantly, and Ianira smiled at me with an expression other than hunger on her face. Kai also seemed to drop his cold edge towards me and has been one of the first friends I found while I've been here. A smile spreads across my face and I can't help the feeling of belonging that creeps through me. I've found my family; it may not be the one I was born with, but it's the one I've made and love like they are of blood. While my father's face still haunts me, I no longer feel guilty about leaving them to fight for themselves. I can even say that I miss the banter between Alc and me. He may still annoy the shit out of me, but feelings I can't quite explain have pushed their way through my defences. It scares me and such feelings should be kept hidden as they are also dangerous, and even though I acknowledge them, it doesn't mean I care to explore them. My thoughts are interrupted with a knock on wood, but I look to the door and don't see any movement from the slight slit under the door. It comes again and I turn my head to the left, hearing the noise coming from my dresser. I edge closer to the noise that's become consistent and press my ear to the wall. I hear breathing and step back running, a hand along the wall. As my hand gets closer to the dresser, the wall bounces and pops open, revealing Alc standing with his fist raised ready to thud on the door again. At the sight of me, he drops his hand and smiles.

"I thought I was going to have to knock the damn door down before you answered," his words are light, and I can't help but wonder what's got his mood in high spirits.

"Maybe a little forewarning about a hidden door would keep you from waiting so long. I was about to stab anything that moved from behind that wall."

Alc laughs, "Wouldn't you need a knife for that, Princess?"

I roll my eyes and move my skirts to reveal the dagger attached to my thigh.

"Ohhh, I see you wanted a surprise attack. Smart but a little slow, you would be dead before you could reach for that dagger."

I slap him lightly on the arm and step aside to let him enter the room. He walks over to my bed and flops down on it, stretching his long legs. He is no longer wearing his suit but instead his shoulders and torso is covered by a thin white tunic and black pants that look to be made of the softest material.

"I hadn't expected you to be back so early, did Isaac tire of you?"

I don't miss the way his eyes darken threateningly, like he would like nothing better than to strip the High Lord of Autumn of his skin. I ease down on the bed beside him and smile.

"How did you know I returned? I didn't see you on the way back to my room."

Alc taps the side of his head and smiles down at me, even when sitting he's a whole foot taller.

"Excellent hearing, remember?"

Of course, I've forgotten that his kind have sharper senses. It used to make me angry but now I feel glad to be on a team with such an advantage.

"Good point, and Isaac did tire of me. I guess I ask too many question for his liking."

Alc nods his head in agreement.

"For once he's got something right, I've never known anyone who can ask as many questions as you. Now, did you find what we needed?"

I nod and launch into my time in the room with Kelby and Isaac.

"I asked them questions on their involvement with the King and Queen and they answered me assuming I was too dumb to be a threat to them. They said the King is looking for a person not an object and that they plan to wake the God of Death, Hugan, with his heir."

Alc's eyes widen but he lets me continue.

"They said that it is a rather simple ritual and that once they wake Hugan, the King plans to bind Hugan to himself, kill the High Lords of Thyithran, and rule over this land. But Isaac and Kelby are planning their own coop and are going to betray the King and Queen to take over Thyithran and rule it for themselves, killing all of you in the process," I take a deep breath and allow Alc to speak.

"Kelby and Isaac won't work together in the end, one of them will end up killing the other. There is no way they are sharing the rule over Thyithran if they intend to rid the land of its other rulers."

I nod and keep my voice low, like someone might overhear.

"That's what I said, and my bets are on Kelby. He may be young, but Alyssa said he is cruel, and I've seen that for myself. Isaac is hungry for power and that might blind him to his friend's planning. I was wondering if Coraline might be in on it as well, I mean she is Isaac's mate."

Alc frowns and shakes his head. His light humour from earlier long gone.

"That's not possible, Coraline isn't working with him."

I turn to regard him with a frown of my own.

"How do you know that? She is the High Lady of the Autumn court."

I hear Alc suck in a deep breath and let it go in one long motion.

"Coraline isn't working with Isaac because she's working with us. She's our spy for the Autumn court, and Thyithran doesn't have High Ladies."

Shock hits me hard and I have to calm my breathing.

"I thought Coraline and Isaac were mates?"

"They are, but she has long lost her love for him as the years have passed. He is a cruel and unfaithful male. I do not blame her, but she had chosen to stay in the Autumn court to protect her people and help us."

I blink, absorbing the new information with great interest. It makes sense. How else would Alc gather his information from the court? It's not like Neron himself could go marching around the place. Silence stretches between us and I'm the one to break it as my frequent curiosity burns again.

"Why aren't there any High Ladies? I mean, they are mates with the High Lords, so what does that make them?"

Alc is silent for a while but answers, his tone thoughtful,

"I don't know, I guess it never occurred to anyone to make their mate a High Lady. Once they marry, they just become a lady of their court, but I don't see why that can't change."

I nod and ask another question, hoping I'm not stretching his patience too much.

"What happens when the Lord dies? Does the power go to his partner? And if that's the case, wouldn't it mean they become High Lady?"

"Only the males of the ruling line can obtain the power to rule. Once the High Lord dies, his power is passed to the nearest living male relative. That's why only the male receives the power when there are siblings, not the oldest. The power also doesn't necessarily choose the oldest male, it chooses the strongest of the line, giving the court the best chance of growing and becoming stronger."

Nodding, I thread my hands into the soft sheets of my bed. So, there was no such thing as High Ladies and only the males of the line received the power of ruling. I wonder which of Kai's brothers will receive the power for their court and if it will be Kai himself. Kelby is young, so when his father died, the power passed to him. I don't know how he could be the strongest of the line, but maybe there was no other choice. Silence stretches between us and I'm conscious of every breath he takes. My heart beats loudly in my chest and I wonder if he can hear it. My mind runs over the meeting from a few hours ago, and something that Dorian said snags my attention. He mentioned a spring solstice. We used to have a winter solstice in the human realm, where we celebrated the turning of the seasons, but the tradition died long ago when the villages lost spirit and found the event took too much of their time and effort. I smooth my hand over the sheet that I crumpled and turn to look at Alc, who seems lost in thought.

"Dorain said something about a Spring Solstice, does everyone celebrate it?"

Alc blinks a few times to bring himself back to the present and nods slowly, running over my question.

"Yes, every court has some way of celebrating it. Naturally, the Spring Court has the biggest celebration, but all the other courts have small parties that start on the first day of spring. We dance and drink all night, thanking the Gods for the prosperity that Spring brings. In the Night court, we don't call it the Spring Solstice but the Everlast Moon. Every year on that night, the moon brings its orbit closest to the earth and covers everything in a pink glow for a few minutes. It's one of the most beautiful times of the year."

Images flash through my head, each more spectacular than the next. I can picture standing on the balcony at the house and watching as the moon passes, making the stars twinkle in the pink glow, the buildings being painted with the soft brush of a fine artist's hand. I sigh and find myself looking forward to it.

"I would love to see that. In the village where I grew up, we used to see the moon pass close, but it would just be the same ordinary grey-blue."

A frown pulls at Alc's face, and his eyes are sad. I resist the urge to lean over and grab his fisted hands.

"I would love nothing more than to show you the celebration at the Night Court but unfortunately you and I will be busy looking for the Heir before the King and Queen can find them."

My face pulls into a frown and my excitement drops away.

"Where do we even start looking for someone like that? It's not like they would be parading around yelling that they are the heir."

Alc shakes his head, anger seeping into his expression.

"We start at the source of all this. The Blood Wood Forest."

Chapter 10

Over the next few days, Alc and the other High Lords discuss the movement of troops that are being sent to aid the weaker border of the Day court. I haven't seen much of him and thankfully haven't been asked to attend any more of the meetings. It leaves me with much spare time to pad around the castle and play card games with Kai and Naomi while Neron and Ianira discuss anything that is of interest. Apparently the meetings are strictly High Lord only. I'm sitting on a cushion on the floor with a handful of cards in my hands, trying not to be beaten by Kai for the seventh time this morning. We play a game he made up and I feel as if he's constantly changing the rules for his benefit. Naomi is attempting to draw a landscape on a piece of parchment, but it resembles more of a house fire than a mountain peak. It's too cold to go out and explore the city, so card games and bickering are the main pastimes. Kai laughs and slaps down his hand as he wins yet another round. I glare at him and let fire enter my voice.

"That's not fair, you said last round that you can't put two aces down at the same time."

Kai smirks slyly at me and I slap his arm, he pretends to flinch.

"I think you've got yourself confused, sweetness."

I roll my eyes at both the pet name and his cockiness. Ianira looks up from where she's curled up on the couch with a book in her hands.

"Don't worry, Keilee, he's a dirty cheat and can't handle a

girl beating him in anything."

Kai gasps like she physically wounded him.

"That's not true, you beat me when we play monopoly."

Ianira lets out a harsh laugh,

"That's because you can't read."

Kai snorts, "I can read, I just don't like to. I would rather be outside playing with my sword."

Ianira is about to reply, but the doors across the room open and Alc and Neron come striding through. Naomi stands when she notices their stern expressions and Kai's face drops his usual charm.

"What's wrong?"

Alc glances around the room and his attention stops on me, causing my heart to plummet.

"We need to go now. The King has made a move on the southern border of the Summer court, fifty in total have been killed and more have been injured in a small village near the border. I'm sending our fifth legion out and I need you Kai…" he shoots a look Kai's way before continuing. "To lead them out. Ianira, I'm leaving you to look after the affairs at Cassiopeia while Keilee and I look for this missing heir and hopefully stop a full war breaking out."

Ianira nods and Alc turns his attention to Naomi and Neron, whose faces are set in unreadable lines.

"I need you two to get the Zeph forces together and send them out as soon as possible."

All heads in the room nod as Alc fires commands at them and soon we are packing our things and changing into fighting leathers. An hour later, we stand in front of Malik as he and Alc shake hands. I haven't seen Lilly since the meeting, and I presume she is still out gathering information from the Spring court. Malik smiles at all of us, including Kai, and his voice is happy when he speaks.

"It was wonderful to meet up again and I hope next time will be under a better situation."

Malik drops Alc's hand and walks over to me, grabbing both my hands in his, "You stay strong, Flower, and make sure you kick him in the balls when he steps out of line."

I laugh and look over Malik's shoulders at Alc.

"Don't worry, I will. It was an honour to meet you and I look forward to another meeting."

Malik smiles and gently lets my hands drop, his face looks pained now and he speaks in a low whisper to me.

"Any time you need somewhere to stay, the Winter court will always have a room for you. Not many people are as kind and as beautiful as you are, Flower, keep that and never let anyone take it from you."

I smile at him. I've grown to like the High Lord of Winter and his smart comments, I will truly miss him when we part ways.

"Thank you, Malik."

He nods and steps away to let me walk over to Alc, who turns to us grim-faced.

"Let's get this over with."

I nod and link my arm though his as the white world of the Winter court fades into a blur of colour.

Alc and I stand side by side staring up at the tall and thick trunks of the Blood Wood trees. They reach towards the sky as if they are trying to compete with each other for the warmth of the sun. Their leaves are just as red as I remember, and the air is no longer icy like the Winter court. A warm breeze floats past us, playing with my hair and the lapels of Alc's coat. My heart beats wildly in my chest, I can almost taste the trodden mud of my childhood. I'm so close to the village that I've grown up in and yet I have no desire to go back and revisit the past. I don't miss the smell of the market or the sound of chatter from the people inhabiting it like I thought I would. The leaves of the trees rustle as the gentle breeze floats through them. It sounds like the woods are offering a warning for us to turn back and leave it in peace, or maybe it's offering an escape from here like it did for me. I can't believe I used to hunt in these woods, I guess desperate times called for desperate measures. The trunk of the nearest tree twists to a point that the tree itself looks like it wants to grab us as we pass by it. Alc squeezes my hand and looks down at me.

"Are you all right?" his words catch me off guard and I nod.

"I have to admit, it's weird being so close to my previous home and yet still be so far from it."

Alc turns back to the trees and swallows.

"I understand. Do you want to see it before we go in?"

I shake my head quickly. That place was my keeper and forced me to become someone I was not.

"No, it's fine. I don't want to go back to that horrid place."

Alc nods, understanding my need to get away from that dark hut on the outskirts of the village.

"When we go into the forest, I need you alert and to never stray far from my side, understand?"

I sigh and rest my hands on hips, turning to face him fully.

"I used to hunt in these woods, remember? I'm not scared of the forest."

Alc's eyes narrow and he frowns.

"I know that, but the forest crosses over the Fae and human border, so we won't just be on the human side of the border. And while I have faith in your ability to hunt and defend yourself, it's dangerous and there are creatures that would tear you to shreds."

I gulp and shiver at the thought, I've barely explored the expansive lands of Thyithran and don't look forward to meeting its more hostile inhabitants. As I move to stand in the shade of the large tree, leaves crunch under my booted feet and I can't help but be reminded of the Autumn court forest where I first officially meet Kai and Alc. It seems such a long time ago instead of the few months that has actually passed. Alc glances over to me and nods his head in the direction of the forest opening.

"We may as well get a move on so we can find a suitable place to set up camp for the night."

I push off the tree and walk over to him, my voice seeming to echo through the trees.

"Where are we going?"

Alc looks like he wants to avoid my question but thinks better of it and sighs, making his shoulders hunch slightly.

"We are going to the resting place of Hugan to see if we can find anything that might help us."

I nod and look into the darkening forest, feeling like I'm being watched. It doesn't surprise me that we would be headed there, after all it is where the King would be.

"How long will that take?"

Alc smiles weakly at me.

"So many questions. It will take roughly a week as he's said to rest on the Fae side of the border."

I groan, my legs beginning to shake at the thought of all that walking.

"Of course he is. Why didn't you just take us there in the first place?"

Alc pins me with an exasperated look.

"The part of the Blood Wood Forest that is on the Fae side of the border is warded against any type of strong magic, meaning we can't get to it directly; we need to take the long way unfortunately. The only creatures that have any sort of strong magic are the ones that live there."

"Luckily I have good company then," a smile tugs at my lips and Alc smiles back at me.

"Come on, let's get moving."

I fall into step with him, as we pick our way to the edge of the forest. I can't shake the feeling of being watched but I don't make much of it as Alc doesn't notice anything amiss with his advanced hearing and sight. Soon we are surrounded by the large trees, and I feel somewhat at home in here since I spent the majority of my time hunting in these woods. I make sure to keep my eyes on the ground in front of me as roots and small rocks like to trip me up. The air around us grows heavy and humid as we advance further into the forest, like a storm is lurking on the horizon. I cast my eyes to the sky, but I can't see much past the thick coverage as the trees lean to block the sun. It's not the worst place for a god to be sleeping. As dangerous as the Blood Wood is, it's still beautiful. I love the way the leaves sparkle even when in the middle of summer and how the trunks have so many cuts and grooves, it looks like they have been in the middle of a raging battle. Jakarn, the God of Life, had good taste in a resting place for his brother. It bothers me, though, as to why the God of Life would trap him here. What did Hugan do to deserve that? Did he kill innocents, or was it more a family feud than anything else? As a child, I used to love hearing stories of the different gods and what they meant to us, which wasn't much, but it still allowed me to dream and hope. Then I grew up and the stories became more of a way to escape my father and his flying fists. My favourite was about how Pacarny, the ruler of War and Peace, fell in love with a human man. She was said to have given up her immortal lifespan for him, but I know that's not true because she's asleep with the other Gods. But it was a nice dream when I was younger, when I believed in happy endings.

A few hours pass and I resort to counting my footsteps. My calves burn, and I just want to sit down. Lost in my thoughts, I don't notice that Alc has stopped and is bent over the ground looking at something. I walk over to him and bend down as well. Trampled in the mud is a single set of footsteps, larger than mine but smaller than Alc's. I go to grab my dagger from its sheath, but Alc holds up a hand.

"It's a few days old, and whoever owns them is long gone. I'm just curious as to why they are here this deep into the forest."

I nod but I can't remove the uncertainty from my voice.

"Do you reckon they belong to the King and Queen's people who are looking for the heir as well?"

He rubs a large hand over his face as though he's already tired and sick of this place.

"It is definitely a big possibility."

Alc straightens and begins a brisk pace in the direction we were heading. I jump up and scramble after him, trying to match his large strides. I have to put a hand on his forearm, and he momentarily freezes, looking down at my hand on his arm.

"Slow down a bit, I don't have long legs like you and plus you're probably scaring away any potential dinner with your loud stomping."

"Sorry, I forgot how short you are."

A mocking smile is on his face, and I can picture myself punching him right now, but he continues speaking, "And you didn't really think I would let us go without food did you?"

His tone is gentle, and I can't help the strange feeling that rises with his soft words, replacing the feelings of earlier.

"I don't see you carrying any sort of bag with food, so I assumed we would be hunting."

Alc smiles at me and waves a hand, causing an apple to form in mid-air. I gape at it.

"We don't need a bag; I've got everything we need here," he waves his hand through the air like I'm supposed to see something.

I raise my eyebrow and he laughs, "It's called the void; I can grab anything I like from there as long I own it."

Again, I'm reminded of how little I know of the place I now live in, and I feel so very human.

"Won't the enchantments on the Forest stop you from using that magic?"

"No, its enchantments only stop stronger magic like my mind walking. The void is simple magic, so it should be fine."

I move my hands to mock his words. The void is simple magic, simple magic that could help me in a lot of ways. Alc laughs at my hand gestures and continues to walk at his brisk pace. I manage to keep up this time and soon silence again stretches between us, nothing but birds and the breeze to keep us company.

The sun moves steadily to the west and my legs scream at me while my stomach won't stop talking. The sun has begun to set and is casting a weak golden glow over everything. The light makes the crimson trees look majestical and for a second I forget that the reason the trees are stained is because of all the bloodshed that occurred in here. Silence reaches me and I realise that the birds I've heard over the last few hours have ceased their calls, leaving nothing but an eerie silence in their wake. My attention is so focused on the lack of sound, I don't notice that the trees have begun to thin out and that we are walking towards a small clearing with a small creek flowing through it. The grass is soft under my feet and the water is so clear, I can see my reflection in it. Alc stops and nods to himself, seemingly satisfied with the place.

"This looks like a good place to rest for the night. We shouldn't have much trouble with anything trying to attack us while we try to sleep."

Despite his words, which are laced with humour, my heart stills a little. I'm not afraid to rough it, I've lived in a hut on the floor for years. I'm afraid of what will no doubt be stalking the woods at night. While hunting in the forest, I never went too far in, I went further than most hunters, but I always knew when I was getting too close to uncharted territory. We are definitely in uncharted territory just by the unnatural silence that engulfs us. Alc stares at me as I turn in a circle, noting everything in the clearing.

"What?"

Alc shakes his head, "Nothing, it's just for a person that has spent most of their life in these woods, you seem a little tense."

I roll my eyes at him,

"That's because I've only been on the human side of the border in the forest, and I've never been this far in either."

"We are still on the human side, but we are close to the border. You'll be able to sense when we cross through."

"That's comforting," sarcasm coats my words, and he laughs.

His expression drops quickly into a serious calm, and I look around, half expecting something to pop out and attack us.

"You still need to be careful. This part of the forest is tricky at night. Not as dangerous as the Fae side, but still tricky."

I frown at him,

"What do you mean by tricky?"

"I mean the forest likes to play tricks on you. A thick fog will settle overnight, and many travellers get lost in it. It acts as a deterrent because we are getting close to the border, so I warn you not to interact with the fog if you can help it."

I stare at him, dumbfounded; he couldn't have told me this before we started?

"Thanks for the warning when it's just about to become nightfall."

A smile tugs at his mouth and he busies himself with getting bedrolls from the void. I stand and turn to him.

"I'm going to see if I can find some wood for a fire."

Alc nods and his words are muffled when he speaks because of the way he leans over to roll out his bed.

"You shouldn't have much trouble with that since we are surrounded by wood."

I bend over and pick up a small stone, pegging it at his bent head. He doesn't see it and it hits him. He groans and rubs a hand over his head.

"I was just pointing out the obvious, no need for violence, Princess."

I roll my eyes and march away towards the small creek. Its water flows gently downstream, and I can see small fish darting around the river rocks at the bottom. Gold fins shimmer in the dying light and for a moment I'm transfixed. I shake my head lightly and follow the stream down until I can no longer see or hear Alc. I stick to the water so I don't get lost and randomly pick up sticks along the way, piling them in my arms. My ears strain to catch any sound, but nothing reaches me. It's still so silent, not even a cricket screeches. I spot a large stick propped up against a tree and walk over to it, adding it to my slowly growing pile. The air is crisp and I can tell that it's going to be a chilly night. As I straighten, I hear a sound coming from my right across the creek. *Click, click. Click, click. Click, click.* It sounds to me like someone is tapping their long nails against each other and I squint my eyes, looking for the source of the noise. As if summoned, a thick white fog closes in from the other side of the creek and I freeze, Alc's words scream a warning at me in my head, *'The forest likes to play tricks. Avoid the fog, don't interact with it'*.

My heartrate quickens, and my flight instinct tries to kick in, but I shove it down as much as I can. Panic will only get me killed quicker. I take a deep breath and walk back the way I came, trying to look like I'm not about to drop dead of fright. I hear the clicking again as if it's following me, I quicken my pace and fight not to break into a run. Much slower than I like, the clearing comes into sight and I can see Alc carrying a pile of kindling too. I release my held breath and skirt over to him, adrenaline making my hands shake, Alc notices and I can see his shadows forming around his hands.

"What's wrong?"

I nod in the direction I came from.

"The fog, it was starting to form, and I heard some weird noises, that's all."

The dancing shadows creep up his arms, circling him like armour. The clearing darkens but instead of scaring me, it settles me down and I realise it's Alc's power that's floating around us. The distant rumble of thunder makes me shiver and I'm completely in awe of the male in front of me. His green eyes sparkle as he frowns and scans the trees across the creek. His black hair flutters around his head at the light breeze that's bringing in the storm. He looks powerful. He looks like a King. And in this moment, my fear seeps away. I am safe. With him, I'm safe, but I'm also not useless myself. I've protected myself for most of my life and I wasn't going to start relying on someone to do that job for me, although it is comforting to have him by my side. The fog that started to form is now lurking at the water's edge, watching from afar, not wanting to get too close to us. Alc glances around the clearing and frowns, I follow his gaze and notice that the fog has surrounded us but stays on the outside of the clearing. I look up at him and keep my voice a whisper.

"This is a bit weird, or is that just me?"

Alc shakes his head,

"Definitely a bit weird. I've never known the Picher to do this before."

I scrunch my nose at him,

"The Picher?"

Alc nods,

"Yes, the Picher. It's what controls the fog. It's the protector of the forest and it's known for its ability to take its job very seriously. And usually we would be fully immersed in fog right now."

"I thought the fog just acts on its own accord."

Alc smiles grimly down at me,

"That's what humans think, yes, but that is not correct. The Picher was created by the God of Life, Jakarn, to guard his friend's sleeping place."

"I'm liking the God of Life less and less as the days wear on," I grumble.

Alc laughs warily but sits down, letting his shadows disperse into the dusk air to arrange the fire, seemingly happy or at least satisfied that the fog, I mean the Picher, is staying put at the edge of the clearing. I sit down next to him and fiddle with the thin leather strap on one of the bedrolls while I watch Alc set the fire up. Soon, the soft heat of the flames chase away the growing chill of the night. The flame is blue, like the fire we had when I first arrived here, I like the way the flames dance on the logs, letting off a light blue glow. Alc and I sit in silence for a long while before my stomach eventually screams its protests. I laugh as it grumbles, and I look to Alc.

"Any chance you can get us something to eat from your void?"

"As the lady wishes," Alc reaches out his hand and two plates of what looks like quail and roasted potato lands into his outstretched hands.

He hands one to me and I dig in, savouring the mouth-watering taste. Silence again settles between us as we eat, and I find myself wishing that this moment would stretch on. I look over at the fog and find it's still in the same position as it was an hour ago. Even though the large trees cover most of the night sky, I can still see the strong glow of the full moon and the shimmering stars. It makes me feel at home and I again miss the town house in Cassiopeia. I regret not exploring the city and meeting the people. My thoughts drift to the event that Alc calls the Everlast Moonshine. Would we be able to see it from within the forest? I hate to think that Alc has to miss an event that means so much to his family.

My voice is barely audible over the crackle of the fire as I whisper,

"Will we be able to see the pink moon on Everlast night within the forest?"

Alc looks up from his empty plate and holds my gaze, Something I can't catch flashes through his eyes.

"I not sure, but I hope so as we will be in here when it passes. It's in two days and we will be well into the Fae side of the forest by then."

I nod and chuck the bones of the bird into the glowing embers. I sigh and fall back on my bedroll.

"How are we supposed to find the tallest blood tree if all of them are huge?"

Alc regards me with a funny expression, like he doesn't understand what I said.

"How do you know where Hugan is resting; I don't remember mentioning it to you?"

I rest my head on my hands and look up at him, his figure contorted by the heatwaves from the fire.

"An old merchant from my village mentioned it when I was selling him my products."

I avoided telling him I was selling him the pelt of his dead friend, not wanting to sombre the mood any more.

"Curious, only a few know of this tale and most that do think it's a myth."

I frown at him, thinking back to the day in the town square. The man was marked as a man that worked for the monarch, and I wonder if he's one of the men looking for the heir right now.

"The man was marked as a royal guard, albeit retired, but I wonder if he's helping to look for the heir."

I hear Alc sigh and also lay down on his bedroll.

"I wouldn't rule it out, but that's enough politics for tonight, we need our rest. Good night, Princess."

I smile to myself,

"Good night, Alc."

Chapter 11

My father's face pokes around the corner and his eyes are filled with rage. It's not an uncommon sight, so I look up from where I'm sitting on the floor of our manor playing with the nanny. Her name is on the tip of my tongue, but every time I try to grasp it, it floats out of reach. Today, she's teaching me how to write a letter. She keeps saying how it will help me later on in life. Father's face has lost the soft lines that appear when he looks after Mother. When he looks at me, all I can see is his anger. I stand up and brush my hands against the soft pink of my skirts, like the nanny taught me to do when addressing him. She also stands and gives him a small bow.

"Can I be of assistance, my Lord?" her voice is timid, and I stand straighter.

When she has that voice, it usually means Father is going to hurt something or someone. Most likely me. I refuse to cower to him and keep my chin up.

"No, leave us," his voice is harsh and there is no kindness as he addresses Lidia.

That's it, her name is Lidia! She nods and glances at me, offering me a weak smile. I try to return it, but it comes out more like a grimace. She always said I was older than my years and I'm inclined to believe her. I turn eight in a few weeks and already I can hide my emotions like an adult. The nanny leaves through the door my father came through and quickly disappears from sight.

"Come, Keilee, your mother wishes to see you."

I sigh and follow him out of the room. Mother is getting weaker by the day, and I often look forward to the few hours I spend by her bed. It's a reprieve from my father's horrid temper. As we walk through the grand halls of my home, I keep my head bowed and avoid bumping into my father. My feet sink into the soft carpet, and I can hear the kitchen and cleaning staff talking from downstairs. The house is always devoid of laughter and joy. If I was a stranger visiting, I wouldn't have guessed a child lived here at all. The house is immaculate, with its white walls and polished floorboards. Nothing suggests this is a family's home. Even my bedroom is white and has little personal touches. If Mother were well, I would have drawings and books everywhere. But since Father rules the house, I'm deprived of the life of a child. I'm instead resigned to live the life of an adult at eight. As we get close to her bedchamber, Father grips my arm and pulls me to a stop. His hand on my arm hurts and I repress a flinch. I often wonder if all fathers are like this and if I'm just being weak and needy. Arabella, my friend from tutoring, seems to have a nice father who dotes on her, but then again, looks can be deceiving. Under the public eye, my father plays the role of a wonderful husband and father who would go to the ends of the earth for his family, but in reality he's a bully who would rather have nothing to do with me if he could help it. I try to shrug out of his painful grip, but he just tightens his hold, strangling my arm.

"Stop squirming and listen to me, Keilee. You are not to stress your mother, and if I find you have, then we will need to follow up with your punishment."

I nod, eager to get out of his hold.

"I don't want a nod; I want you to say so."

"Yes, Father."

He rises an eyebrow at me.

"Yes father what?"

I swallow my panic and answer him, quickly sensing his growing anger.

"Yes, Father, I promise I won't stress Mother out."

"Good. Now go, and remember my warning."

I nod, hurrying down the white halls. I knock on my mother's door and her soft reply comes from inside.

"Come in," she coughs, and I flinch, hating hearing her suffer.

I reach up and turn the brass handle, opening the door to reveal her dimly lit bedchamber. I've always loved her decoration choices. Even in the dim light, the room is welcoming and homely. Portraits are on the wall opposite her large four poster bed. I can see my father and my mother smiling down at me on their wedding day. It's the only time I've seen his true smile and I hate it; it hides his monster. I'm also hanging from the wall in various pictures. My favourite is of me on the tyre swing in the garden with Mother pushing me. I was about five at the time and, most importantly, I was happy.

Mother smiles at me from her bed, "Hello, my flower."

I walk over to her and grab her hand. her grip is weak, and she looks pale even against the white of her sheets. Her hair is thinning, and her eyes have lost almost all their light. I try to swallow my tears and act strong for her. I don't know if she's aware of Father's cruelty, but I don't tell her, not wanting to upset her.

"Hello, Mother. Father said you wanted to see me?"

She nods and pats her bed. I lie down and snuggle up to her.

"I wanted to spend some time with my beautiful girl."

I smile against her and melt into her rose and jasmine smell. She coughs again, the sound painful, and I pull back to look up at her.

"Would you like some water?"

She smiles weakly and shakes her head.

"I'm fine, my beautiful flower. You help me just by being here."

I sigh and my voice comes out almost as weak as hers,

"I wish I could help you more, take the sickness away and make you better."

I feel more than see Mother frown against my hair.

"You don't ever need to feel like you have to do more, you help by being here and being strong, I would ask for nothing more. And as for the sickness, sometimes fate is kind and sometimes it is cruel, it just depends how you look at it."

I frown at her, and she continues.

"I consider myself lucky as I have a beautiful daughter with a kind heart. I've had love and I've had a good life. It's a blessing every day to wake and see you, my flower. Remember that for me."

I nod,

"I will, I promise."

My mother's arms snake around me, and she pulls me to her.

"Just rest here with me, flower."

I do and I have one hand on her arm and the other grips the necklace she gave me. Soon sleep drags me down, and I dream of a life where she's happy and healthy and we play out in the garden like we used to. I wake an hour later, according to the clock on the wall, and I gently roll out of my mother's embrace. I turn to her and find her face resting in a peaceful expression. I touch my hand to her cheek to wake her and say goodbye, but she doesn't stir. I shake her slightly, but deep down I know she's gone. Just like that, she's gone, she's left me. Tears run down my face, and I will her to wake.

"Don't leave me here! Don't leave me with him!"

I drop my voice into a whisper as the door bursts open and the maid comes running in. I whisper to her and only her.

"Don't leave me in this horrid place. I need you."

I don't remember opening my mouth to scream, but I do, and my voice feels hoarse. The maid wraps her arms around my waist, and I fight to break free, finding the attempt feeble. All of a sudden, I feel nothing and straighten. The maid lets me go and says something to me, but I don't hear it. I walk out of the room and head to my rooms. My father pushes past me, not seeing me in his haste to get to my mother's lifeless body. Once in my room, the tears start and a sob tears through my shaking my body. I slump on my bed and cry till my body runs out of tears to give me. She's left me. She's left me with him. Now there's nothing to save me from the monster that most children find in their closets, but unlike theirs, mine is very real.

I'm torn from my sleep when someone shakes me. Sweat coats my skin and I blink rapidly, trying to remember where I am, I look around and see the soft glow of dying embers. The Blood Wood. Someone shakes my body again and I look up at a figure with the greenest eyes.

"Keilee, it's all right, I'm here," his voice is hoarse and wary, like he's been yelling my name for a while.

I stare at him and wet my dry lips. My dream rushes back to me, and I sit up quickly, almost knocking Alc over with the sudden movement.

"I'm… I'm sorry, I didn't mean to wake you."

I shiver as the sweat turns cold against the cool night air.

"It's okay, as long as you're all right. You were screaming and thrashing around. I couldn't wake you."

I grab his arm to reassure him I'm fine.

"I promise I'm fine. I just had a bad dream."

Alc nods and sits next to me on my bedroll, his arm wrapping around my shoulder, holding me in place.

"May I ask what it was about?"

I'm silent for a minute but open my mouth to tell him.

"I dreamt of my mother's death."

The words hit me when I speak them out loud and I feel like crying. Alc pulls me closer to him and I rest my head on his shoulder.

"It's okay, you're here now and I'm here to protect you, Princess."

His warmth makes my eyelids heavy, and I lean against him, only now realising he's not wearing a shirt. His muscled torso flexes as he moves, and I can see ink swirling around his abdomen, creeping up to his shoulders.

"Do you think you can get back to sleep? We have a long day ahead of us."

I nod and he lets me go so I can lay back down. To my shock, Alc lies down next to me and snakes an arm around me, pulling me flush to him. I'm so shocked, I let him and find myself leaning into him. My body is aware of every place our bodies touch.

"Is this okay, Princess?"

I nod, not trusting myself to speak. His chest rumbles behind me as he laughs and he begins stroking small, calming circles on my arm as I fall asleep in his embrace.

His voice whispers to me just as I'm about to fall under, "You're killing me, Princess, and I don't know how to stop it." His words are so soft I'm sure I've imagined them.

CHAPTER 12

The twittering of a yellow and red bird pulls me from my slumber, and I go to sit up but feel a heavy weight around me. I look down and see Alc's arms wrapped around me in a tight embrace. I freeze, not wanting to wake him and startle him. My heart is galloping in my chest, and I try to gently wriggle out of his hold. He groans and whispers to me, his voice husky and sleep-thickened.

"Stop your wriggling, Princess, or you'll feel more than you bargained for."

I blink and blush as I look up at him.

"Sorry, I didn't know you were awake."

My face heats and I become aware of every place he touches me. Sometime through the night, I snaked my leg through his and we've become a tangle of limbs. He releases a tight breath as I brush my leg past him, trying to get out of the tangle.

"I'm serious, Princess, stop moving, you're killing me."

I freeze and he unwraps his arms from around me and gently pushes me into a sitting position. I stand and stretch my legs and back while avoiding looking at him and his bare chest. My muscles ache and protest when I move as the bedroll was nothing more than a thin mattress on uneven ground. My body has become used to the comforts of sleeping in a real bed. Alc comes around to me and hands me a mug of steaming tea. I raise my eyebrows at him and smile.

"Aren't you just a good housemaid."

Alc snorts at me,

"Mind your tongue, I might just slip something into your cup next time."

I laugh and look around at the clearing. The Picher has gone and with it the fog has receded, only leaving a thin veil of mist hanging onto the morning air. As I sip from the mug, Alc rolls up our bedrolls and places them into the void. The trick never grows old, and I wonder what else he has in there. I'm glad to hear the sounds of the woods as last night the silence was unnerving. The stream flows gently and birds chirp from their nests in the trees, it almost sounds peaceful, and I could find myself forgetting that I'm standing in a blood-splattered graveyard. Once Alc and I have finished packing up camp, I make sure my dagger is sheathed and we start to cross the stream, heading into the forest where the Picher was waiting last night. My breath comes out in white clouds, and I walk as close to Alc as I can, drawing from his warmth. Even though Spring has come, the chill in the morning air tries to hold on for as long as possible. We walk through the forest in silence, only speaking when something interesting pops up, which is not often as the trees all look the same and the ground we walk on is soft and bare. My mind floats away again but is ripped back when I collide with Alc's back. He is so still I think he's frozen in place. He has somehow become armed with a sword, making my heart race. I reach for my dagger and pull it free.

Alc turns his head to the side to whisper to me,

"In the trees about two hundred metres away are three men. They are crouched behind the trees watching us. They are human."

I nod and look to where he's suggesting and see the faint movement of someone crawling closer.

"The King's people?"

Alc doesn't answer my question as an arrow flies past our heads. I notice as it flies past that it's made of iron, and for the first time I really worry about Alc's safety. We duck down and stay close to the ground.

"You remember your training?"

I nod and clutch my dagger. Alc holds out his hand and a sword drops into his outstretched palm.

"Take this, it will work better than your short bladed dagger."

"Thank you," I wrap my hand around the cold hilt of the sword and get my arm used to the change in weight.

Alc keeps his voice low as the people slowly approach us.

"We need to get rid of the bowman first, those iron arrows won't do me any good. I trust your ability to fight on your own, but it won't stop me from warning you to be careful."

I nod,

"Can't you just kill them with a flick of your hand?"

Alc frowns and looks at me, "Usually I would be able to, but we are nearly over the border now and my powers have been trapped by the forest's protection."

I gulp but stand up, moving so I'm standing in the shadows of the trees. Alc does the same and I lose sight of him, but that becomes the least of my problems as one of the men jumps at me holding his blade in the air. He is thin and quick but I'm short and quicker, so I dodge his blow easily. I bring my blade down on his and hear the satisfying clang of metal hitting metal. He pushes me back and I let him think he has me. But I swiftly jump to the left, throwing him of balance. I see an opening and lunge forwards, driving my sword through his stomach. He looks at me, surprised, before his eyes go dull and he is no longer breathing. I place my foot on his middle and shove him off my blade. Another man of stockier build comes running at me with his blade swinging. He has more power behind his swing than his friend and I find my arm shaking as I block the blow. I push against him, my muscles straining as I swing his blade to the right. I somehow manage to nick his arm, but he swings low and pain sears through my thigh. I ignore it and lunge forward as he rightens himself from the low swing. His head tumbles from his shoulders and his body slumps to the ground. The dirt under my feet is painted crimson from their blood mixing with mine. I look around for Alc and see him standing over the soldier he has killed. The man's bow is slung over his shoulder, and I think it would have been better for him to use it instead of fighting Alc with a blade. He looks over at me and I smile weakly. My leg hurts like a bitch, but I'm more concerned with scanning the area for any more soldiers that may be lurking. Alc's voice sounds from my right, and I look over at him.

"I've already checked, there's no more for now at least."

I nod and bend to pick up the dead man's blade. His skin is still warm under my touch, and I repress a flinch. On their coats is the royal insignia, confirming my question earlier. I flip through the scrawny man's jacket and look for anything that could be of use to us. After finding nothing, I walk over to Alc trying not to limp. Alc notices and his gaze snaps to my leg.

"It's fine, it's just a scratch."

Alc shakes his head,

"A scratch could mean infection, and by how much blood you're losing, it's more than just a scratch."

I shrug and tell him,

"It's not like we have any first aid to wrap it anyway."

This time Alc smiles, "Ahh but, Princess, you forget I come prepared for the worst."

He clicks his fingers together and a small leather bag appears, "Sit."

I do as he says and stretch out my injured leg. The pain is throbbing and travels the full length of my leg, I breathe in deep and glare at him.

"Don't do anything funny or you'll be missing a hand."

Alc smiles at me mischievously,

"So little faith. Now, this is most likely going to hurt so do you want something to bite on?"

I shake my head,

"No, just get this over with."

Alc nods and grabs a needle and some sort of white thread. He threads the string through the eye of the needle and grabs a gauze pad out of the bag, along with some alcohol.

"I need you to remove your leathers, I can't see the wound clearly."

My hands go to the numerous buckles, and I begin to undo them. My hands tremble slightly as the adrenaline wears off. Taking off my leathers proves more difficult than I expected as I can barely move my leg without a new wave of pain ricocheting through my thigh. Eventually, I do get them off and lay them on the ground next to me. Alc leans over and a hiss escapes him.

"You are lucky you didn't damage a major tendon; this is deep."

I glance down at the wound and almost gag, the flesh is parted in two deep ridges and it's pink and puffy. Blood oozes out of it when my muscles tense and move.

Alc pats my hand, "I'm going to have to hold the sides together while I stich it up. It's going to hurt like hell, but I need you to be strong."

I nod, not being able to speak through the pain. Alc cleans

around the wound with the pad and washes alcohol over it. He then pushes the sides together and holds them in place with one hand while the other grabs the needle. A whimper escapes me and my vision dots. I lean back on my elbows and fight the urge to kick him.

"I'm going to start the stitching now, so hold tight."

Before I can reply, he sticks the needle into my leg and I yell out. I feel like vomiting again but bite my tongue until I taste blood. I don't look down at my leg and try to focus on breathing evenly. The heavy metallic tang of blood hangs in the air and I can't tell if its mine or the dead men. I killed people, I killed two. They could have had families waiting for them and I killed them. Despite myself, I look over at the cooling bodies. The men I killed lay close together. The skinny one's face is frozen in a mixture of pain and surprise while the stockier one's head is discarded at the feet of his body. I expect to feel sick but instead I feel scared. How far am I willing to go to help Alc? How many people do I have to kill? I know the answer and it terrifies me, I will do anything; I will kill anyone, and I will sacrifice everything. This is my home now and I've grown to love it like I've grown to love the people. Alc finishes one stitch and moves onto the next. I hold my breath and release it when he pierces my skin. I need a distraction from the pain, so I open my mouth and my voice comes out breathy.

"How did you learn to stitch up a wound?"

Alc looks up at me and frowns, trying to remember, then he smiles.

"My brother and I got into a fight when we were younger, and mother said we were to stitch ourselves up as punishment."

I grimace,

"That's rough, I would have fainted."

I knew from experience; I've had to stitch myself up a few times, granted not to this extent, but the first time I did it, I passed out every time the needle first went through.

"It taught us a life skill, I guess, and trust me I did vomit a few times when I first had to do it, but now I don't even flinch."

I nod and he continues, "You would think that being a High Lord, you would have personal healers everywhere you go, but I've had Kai stitch me up more times than anyone."

I laugh through a new stab of pain.

"Only you would choose to have an idiot like Kai stitch you up over a trained professional."

Alc chuckles, "Yes, but healers can be scary. Always bossing you around."

I snort and flinch as the action sends a jolt of pain down my leg.

"Look at that, the big and mighty High Lord of the Night court is scared of an old woman with a needle."

Alc leans back and I look down at me leg. The once gaping wound is now closed with neat little spiders holding it together. I look up at him, surprised.

"You did a good job."

Alc laughs,

"Your lack of confidence in me is alarming, Princess, and as for the old lady with a needle, Beth would hate for you to call her old, and quite frankly she terrifies me."

I smile at him and stand gingerly. He reaches out a hand and holds me while I find my feet.

"Are you all right to carry on? We can rest here for the night if you wish?" concern laces his words and my heart jumps at it.

"No, I'm fine. I would rather get away from all this carnage before someone comes looking for these men."

Alc nods, understanding my urgency to get away, and packs up his supplies, pushing them back into the void while I gingerly put the leathers back on. He comes to my side and loops my arm around his middle to support my weight as we begin to walk again. We are slower than before, and my leg hurts with each step, but it's no longer bleeding so much, and the pain is bearable. I'm glad for Alc supporting me otherwise I think I might stumble and fall on my face more often than not. We walk through the shade-speckled forest for at least an hour before Alc stops and looks down at me.

"See that tree there?"

I look to where's pointing and nod,

"Yes, what about it?"

Alc walks me close to it and I see similar markings to that on the tree in the Autumn court woods.

"These markings show that it's on the border line. Once we move past it, we will be on the Fae side of the Blood Wood."

I nod and he tightens his grip on me.

"I don't know what the side effects will be for you when we cross, so just hold tight and stick close to me."

I roll my eyes at him,

"It's not like I can go far from you at the moment anyway."

I wave to my leg, and he smiles.

"Ready?"

I nod and we move forwards and pass the tree. I feel no difference, still waiting for something to happen. The only change I can notice is the sounds of the forest. It seems more alive and sinister. I blink and turn to Alc to find him breathing heavily.

"What's wrong?" I tap his arm and he looks at me.

"It's heavy in here."

I study him in confusion, and he opens his mouth to explain.

"The forest is trying to make me think I'm suffocating. It will pass in a few minutes."

He looks from me to the trees, and I can see he's in pain.

"Are you sure you're all right? I can't feel anything."

He nods, his voice tight when he speaks.

"Yes, I'm fine. This was one of the things that was said to happen to people who try to pass through."

One of the things? I hope he doesn't have to experience any of the others. Alc gently guides me through the trees, and I shiver at the eeriness of this place. The trees are the same colour and build, if not a little brighter in colour. It's only the sounds that catch me. I hear a screech from somewhere distant and there's a constant tap from somewhere to my left. Alc's face is set in a frown, but he's breathing easier, and he's not tensing, so we must be fine.

"What's that tapping sound and the screeching?"

Alc smiles at me,

"It's a mockingbird banshee."

I gape at him,

"A mockingbird banshee? What is that supposed to be?"

Alc laughs and waves a hand around us.

"A mockingbird banshee is a bird, as the name implies, but it copies sounds of the banshees that lurk around in here. For some reason, they only copy the sound of the banshee and nothing else. They are harmless and only like to scare travellers. It's the monster they mimic that you should be wary of."

"That doesn't make me feel any better at all."

My gaze keeps going to the bird hidden somewhere in the branches.

"How do I know when there's a real banshee or not if the

bird mimics them so well?"

Alc frowns at this,

"Trust me, you'll know; your ears will bleed if it's a real banshee's call."

I shudder and I feel not in the least bit relieved. The fake banshee keeps calling as we make our way through the forest, and I begin to tune it out. Dusk is settling quickly, and we soon stop in a small clearing, smaller and less protected than the one from yesterday. I sigh and sink to the ground, resting my back against a small sapling. Alc makes a fire pit and gets the beds set up again. By the time he's finished, the Picher's fog has made its claim and this time it doesn't hang around the outside of the clearing, it engulfs us, and I can barely make out Alc's figure near the fire. I'm too sore and tired to be alarmed and stay seated at the tree. He wanders over and gestures at me to stand. I groan and pull myself to my feet.

"Come and sit by the fire, you don't need to be dying of frostbite."

I follow him to the fire, limping on my leg, but at least I can put pressure on it. We sit down on the bedrolls, and I snuggle into his side, enjoying the warmth. I tell myself that it's nothing more than for body warmth, but my heart begs to differ. Alc's arm comes around me and we sit in silence before he breaks it and speaks, his voice low and cautious.

"I'm sorry."

Shock hits me and I glance up at him,

"Sorry for what?"

He looks at me, his eyes sad.

"I kidnapped you from your family and forced you to live amongst people that want to kill your kind."

I smile,

"I was mad, and I hated you at first, but I've grown to love it here. And it's better than being in a hut with a drunk for a father. Besides, you kept me fed and you taught me how to protect myself mentally and physically. I owe you an apology for killing your friend."

Alc looks at me and I can't read his expression.

"You shouldn't apologise to me; you were acting out of fear and it's still not right of me to have taken you."

I nod slowly and place my hand on his cheek, feeling the rough shadow of stubble that had grown over the last few days.

"I'm glad you did, Alc, I would never have learnt I have an ability and I hated it at the village. I also like the company of a certain overbearingly arrogant High Lord."

He smiles at this, and before I can blink, his lips crash onto mine, my body tenses but I relax into his, wrap my arms around his neck, and kiss him back. The forest melts away as nothing else matter but the feeling of him and his lips on mine. I ignore the bite of pain in my leg as he drags me onto his lap. The kiss ends too quickly and we both pant for breath. He runs a thumb gently over my bottom lip and I whimper at the action. Tears spring to my eyes and he kisses my forehead, melting my heart even further.

"You have no idea how long I've waited to do that, Princess."

I smile at him and steal another kiss. I don't know why I feel so reckless, but I don't let it bother me. I will worry about that later, right now all I care about is Alc. A blush paints my cheeks and I try to look away, but Alc takes my chin in his hand.

"You are beautiful, Princess, inside and out. Don't let anyone tell you any different."

I smile at him, "Thank you."

He smiles at me and something inside me changes. My heart rages at me and my head seems to be in line with it for once. This feeling has been growing for a while, but I've chosen to ignore it, not wanting to believe it, but I knew, I knew from the moment in his dining room when we bantered back and forth. I knew from the moment he apologised for his outburst, and I knew from the moment he wrote me the note about the dagger. I love him and it's dangerous, but I love him regardless. His black hair is tousled, and I almost jump back as his massive wings spread behind him. I reach out a hand and brush it lightly against them. I'm amazed by their beauty, and if I could paint, I would make sure they went on canvas. Alc shivers under my touch, his breathing heavy.

"Princess, don't do that."

I laugh,

"Why?"

He shudders again as I brush a finger over the small veins running through them.

"Because you are killing me, and wings are very sensitive."

Smiling, I poke him,

"You're saying you're ticklish?"

Alc runs his hands down my side and settles them around my waist.

"I'm not ticklish, they are sensitive."

"Same difference."

His hands move from my waist to tickle my sides and I thump him on the shoulder, trying not to move my leg too much.

"Stop that."

He smiles,

"Say I'm not ticklish."

I sigh and squirm on his lap, the action sending a weak pain through my leg.

"All right, all right. You're not ticklish, your just sensitive."

"Good, thank you."

I mumble under my breath, and he gently lays me down on the bedroll and kisses me softly.

"Get some sleep now, Princess, we move early tomorrow."

I nod and straighten out so my leg has enough room to be comfortable and I close my eyes. Sleep claims me but not before I feel Alc place something hard and rectangular next to me.

A screech pierces the air, waking me from my sleep. I bolt upright and ignore the throbbing in my leg and, strangely, my head. It sounds like an old man screaming in pain. Before I can grasp where it's coming from, it stops and drops the forest into complete silence. I feel around my bedroll, looking for Alc, but the fog is thick and it's pitch black, the fire has died and no embers glow.

"Alc? Are you there?"

Silence. I fumble with my dagger and pull it onto my leg.

"Alc!" I raise my voice and stand, trying to keep my balance with my crook leg.

Still no answer. I walk around the clearing and freeze when I see an arrow protruding from one of the trees. I walk over to it and the slick metal makes me freeze. Iron. Panic settles heavily at the bottom of my stomach and I move around the clearing, looking for any sign of him. I find none, only the arrow and a small trail of blood leading into the trees. I pray that it's not his, but my head knows better. There is no way he would leave here without a fight. I just wonder why I didn't wake. My question is answered as I bend down to pack up my bedroll as quickly as I can. A small sack tied with string sits next to my pillow. I pick it up and instantly feel drowsy. I throw it away. What sort of enchantment is that? Next to the sack is a book, I pick it up and almost fall to my knees. It's my mother's journal. The leather is well kept, and I flick through the pages, the smell of old ink blinding my senses. When did he give this back to me? I clutch it close to my chest and cast a final glance around the clearing. The fog is thick, but I know where we were headed, so I grab the bag that the bedroll is kept in and throw in the journal and anything else that might be useful to me, including the sword and scabbard of the man I killed. I limp over to the tree and pull free the arrow; I will find him no matter what it takes, and when I do, I will kill anyone who's harmed him. My mind buzzes and I feel something tugging at my chest like a piece of string is tied to my heart. The screeching returns and I look up into the trees. My ears aren't bleeding, so I assume it's the mockingbird. My fingers scratch to reach for my dagger and end the bird's pitiful life. As I walk through the forest, I keep all my senses on high alert. I can barely see, but I keep walking in what I hope is a straight line. My leg drags slightly, and I curse at it. A small stream appears in front of me and somehow the branches throw shade over the already dark water. I don't have the agility to jump it, so I walk through, soaking the insides of my boots. A *click, click* makes me pause and I look around my surroundings, trying to see past the thick fog. The clicking sounds again, but closer, and it's followed by a laugh that makes me shiver. It sounds like it should belong to a little boy, but it's slowed and slurred.

"*Hehehehe.*"

I startle and back into a tree, trying to hide in the shadow and fog. The creature laughs again, closer to me.

"Keilee, Keilee. You can't hide from me."

Click, click. I shudder and freeze, it knows my name. I work up my courage and step out from behind the tree. The sight in front of me makes me want to vomit and scream at the same time, but I settle for standing frozen. The creature's body is black and emaciated, It looks like a human man. Its head snaps to me and it smiles. Its lipless mouth opens, and I see rows of jagged teeth. It lets out the laugh again and clicks its long fingernails together. *Click, click.* Eyes that are a creamy white stare at me from large sockets and I flinch slightly.

"*Hehehehe.*"

I grip my dagger tighter and stand taller, trying to hide my fear.

"What are you? Are you the Picher?"

The creature laughs and tilts its head at me.

"Oh no, I'm much worse. The question is, what are you?"

I blink at him, and he smiles.

"I said what are you?"

Click, Click. I don't know what unsettles me more, his click or his laugh.

"I am what people call a Nymph."

I stare at him, he's a fairy? As if reading my mind, he continues.

"I'm not the type of Nymph your thinking of; I'm a Death Nymph. I assume you don't need to know what that means?"

I shake my head and edge my dagger to point at him.

"What do you want? Where is Alc?"

The Nymph taps a hand to his cheek and smiles, it's all teeth.

"Your mate is somewhat occupied. And you called me, I did not seek you out."

His words sink in, and I stumble. Mate.

"What do you mean, mate?"

His expression changes to complete joy and I recoil from him.

"Your mate, your soul partner. I must say, fate has good taste for you. The High Lord of the Night court, master of dreams and nightmares. Such a fascinating combination."

Alc's my mate? Is that what this tether is that's pulling on my chest? Is it a connection to him? I process the Nymph's words and I snag on the second part of his answer.

"What do you mean I called you here?"

Now it's the Nymph's turn to look confused, which just makes his face even more horrid.

"I heard you calling my name, I could smell you. It's the same when you called me at the stream with the Picher."

I'm shocked and I tell him,

"I didn't call you. I don't know how to do that."

He laughs,

"Such a surprise, you are. You've been calling us for a while, we've just never had you this close to us before."

"What do you mean by us?"

He smiles. *Click, click.*

"Me and the other creatures in this wood. The Picher, the Mockingbird, the Banshee," he pauses and clicks his hands together. "I don't suggest meeting with the latter, though. Nasty little devil, she is. We have heard you ever since you entered Thyithran. Weak at first, but then stronger as your power adapted. We cannot harm you, I do not know why, but I think it has something to do with what you are."

This time I laugh, the sound more erratic than joyous.

"I'm a human, and you're saying you can't harm humans? Because if you are, you're a liar."

His face drops into what would be a scowl, except his teeth are clattering together.

"I am many things, but a liar is not one of them. I have been gifted, or cursed, with the fact that I cannot lie."

I frown and drink in his words.

"And you are not human nor Fae but both."

Click, click. I stare at him and feel like my head is about to break open. Words rush back to me, and the merchant's voice from town rings through my head, *"They are both and neither, only the heir knows this."*

The Nymph's voice breaks my trance and I look at him clicking his nails together.

"You have questions, ask them."

"What am I if not human?"

His teeth gleam yellow, and I shudder.

"The forgotten heir."

I stumble back and crash into the tree, my thigh aches but I ignore it as a new pain rips through my chest.

"I am not an heir. I'm a poor girl from a village, with a dead mother and a drunk father. I am nobody."

The Nymph moves closer to me, and I hold my ground.

"You are the forgotten heir, and your father is not the drunk man you lived with, he is the God of Death."

I lift my dagger and step towards the Nymph.

"How do you explain that? He's been asleep for centuries and I can guarantee that I am not that old."

"You seek answers I do not have. Only Hugan can give these to you."

The dagger feels heavy in my hand as I take another step towards the Nymph. His breath fans over my face and I try not to gag at the potent smell of death that hangs off him. Milky eyes track my movements, and he smiles down at me.

"If you wish the answers to your questions, then may I suggest a family reunion?"

"What about Alc? Where is he?"

The Nymph smiles,

"He is where you are headed."

I frown at him,

"What has the King taken him for, and why to the resting place of Hugan?"

The smell of death hits me as he lets out a deep breath.

"The King doesn't like things that get in his way, so he removed it. But the High Lord of the Night Court is too valuable to kill, so he keeps him locked away at his side. They assumed you too weak to be of any harm to them, so they left you here to be finished off by the creatures in the forest. Like me. But it seems they underestimated you, which means they don't know you're the heir."

"How am I supposed to end a war before it has even started? I don't even know the full extent of this power."

"These are all things you have to figure out for yourself. I cannot help you in this. All I can say is, save your mate and wake Death."

His voice is low, like a warning, and I nod despite the whirlpool of thoughts in my head. Alc is most likely hurt and is a prisoner to the man that wants him dead. My mate is prisoner to someone who wants him dead.

The Nymph speaks to me again, but he's receding into shadows, "You have a journal, it has the ritual in it. The King thinks he has it, but he's mistaken, only you do. Read between the lines and fight proudly."

I want to speak back, but he's gone. The shadows have enveloped him, and he's gone. The forest is quiet again and my ears strain to hear any sign of the Nymph or the Mockingbird. Nothing reaches me, so I begin walking again. The forest is still dark and the fog strains around me. The thought of the Picher watching me as I walk around is unnerving, but I feel slightly at ease if they can't harm me. My mind is stuck on three things, waking Hugan, saving Alc, and killing the King and Queen. Something akin to primal rage rushes through me and I feel a tug on the tether in my chest. If Alc is harmed, I don't know if I will be able to stop myself from ripping this place apart.

CHAPTER 13

I've been walking for hours, and my leg has reached its maximum pain threshold. A stitch has torn and blood runs through my leathers, but it's not enough for me to worry about, so I keep pushing myself through the trees. The ground under my feet has become littered with leaves and it's hard to stay silent as I walk through them. I passed a stream a few miles back and I wish I had a canteen of water; my throat is parched, and I feel as if my head is floating on my body. I know I should rest, but the thought of Alc near the King makes me push on. I feel nothing but anger. I have no tears to cry, and weakness isn't going to get me anywhere. Alc is alive and that is what matters. I will find him, and I will free him. The Nymph's words ring, and it sours my mood even more. I'm the forgotten heir and I don't know anything about it. I don't know how to wake Hugan, apart from using my blood and a ritual that seems to be hidden very well. I've scanned through my mother's journal until I felt like my eyes were going to bleed. I've found nothing that could help, unless the ritual is about my mother explaining her day, which seems unlikely. I step through a thick wall of ferns and my ankle twists off a hidden rock, causing me to fall to the ground. I groan and I have to drag my injured leg into a kneeling position. It feels heavy and lethargic. Using a tree as a leverage, I push myself to my feet and brush my hands on my leathers. I need to find a stream and somewhere I can camp for the night. The sun is crawling lower by the minute, and I don't feel like hunting around in the dark and fog for a place to sleep. Making my way down a stray animal track, I keep my ears open for any sound of running water, and sure enough, I hear the faint tinkle of water against stone. Sunlight peppers the ground, lighting my path, and I'm reminded of summer when I was younger, playing in the garden with Mother before she fell sick. I wonder if Kai and the others are wondering where we are, I haven't heard from them and I have no way to tell them Alc has been kidnapped. Naomi and Neron were sent to get the Zeph forces ready, so I wouldn't have the slightest clue where to find them, and Kai is leading a small army to the Summer court, which rules him out completely. I only know where Ianira is, but I have no hope of getting to Cassiopeia, I don't even know where the city is located. I'm going to have to do this on my own, which isn't a comfort at all since I'm heading into this almost completely blind. The stream is getting louder, and I will my legs to move faster. I hold back a cry of relief as the clear water rushes in front of me. I bend as much as my leg allows and scoops some water into my mouth, it's cold and beautiful. I sigh once I've drunk my fill and sit down, stretching out my tired legs. I remove the sword from my hip and place it next to me. Removing the bedroll bag from my back, I pull out my mother's journal and flip through the worn pages, stopping when I find an entry I've read a thousand times. It's about when my mother's request was approved for the trade of fish and crab between the small town of Fallen Crest and the bigger city closer to the royal castle named Royal Crest, which seems a bit ironic to me. All the sad and tired souls live in Fallen Crest while the rich and lucky ones live where the King and Queen reside. I look down at the entry and read her delicate sprawl.

Spring 18th

Dear beloved Friend,

Today I received news that my proposal for trade between Fallen Crest and Royal Crest has been approved. It brings me great joy that we will be able to enjoy the delicacies that the richer city receive. I thought it unfair that the coastal city didn't trade between the less fortunate towns. Lord Habbel of Winston house wants to request a meeting to discuss prices of transporting the goods, but I don't fear as we have plenty to spare in our coffers. Richard might not be happy when he learns that he'll be paying for this, but he will come around when he sees the benefits it will bring to our town. For the good of all, let them rise.

Yours truly, Mary.

I trace a finger over the ink and flip to another entry of the day I was born; the page is splattered with the stains of tears and my heart clenches at the sight. My father may not have loved me, but she did, and I will hold that close to my heart. I close my eyes as a faint breeze floats through the trees, it settles me, and I begin to read.

Autumn 26th

Dear beloved Friend,

Our baby girl was born today, and she's beautiful, her eyes are blue, and she has a thick head of hair for her age. She's a happy baby and doesn't cry often at all, only when food is late. I named her Keilee, like the warrior. She's so small and the healers said they were surprised she came out healthy, but I never had a doubt. She's strong, like her father, and will one day make us so proud. Richard is quiet, and I fear he doesn't like the name

choice. He wanted to name her Rose or Ivry, but I wanted a fierce name for such a fierce babe. She is one and she is many. Our daughter, Keilee.
Yours truly,
Mary.

My eyes catch on her first sentence, and I have to read it again to make sure I'm seeing it right. The words *'our baby girl'* stills me, it's as if she's talking to a different person when she writes. She doesn't use my baby, or Richard's baby, she uses 'our baby'. I read the passage again and run my finger over the last sentence. *'Our daughter, Keilee'*. Is it possible she was writing this book for Hugan when he was woken by me? Did she hope she would be here to give it to him? My hands shake and I flip through the book, going to the back, trying to find anything else that might confirm my suspicion. I scan the back cover and do a double take as the leather near the top of the book is peeling back slightly. I move a finger over it and find it lifts away with a little pressure. In between the leather and the back of the book are two letters, hidden neatly away. I shimmy them out and sit up straighter while I unfold them. The air around me has suddenly gone cold, and I shiver and draw a deep breath. The first bit of parchment is battered and worn, and the paper is thicker, implying it's from old. The sprawl doesn't belong to my mother and is larger and more elegant, like a king wrote it. It reads:

My dearest love, Mary

How I have missed you and your presence. I find it boring without your wit and bright smile. I also find myself wishing for your return, but I know this is forbidden. My brother has warned me about the tension rising between your people and the Fae, he seems sure that a war is going to break out and I am inclined to believe him. Promise me you'll stay safe and away from the conflict. I will personally kill anyone that so much as touches you against your will. I've had Jakarn warn the others and we stand by awaiting a time when we will need to interfere and stop an unnecessary bloodshed. I love you, my angel, and I will see you again. But until then, stay safe and stay strong.

    Yours always, Hugan.

My eyes widen as I read Hugan's name at the bottom, the acknowledgement that this *God* is my father seems surreal and I struggle to grasp it. The message is written with such love, it hurts me that they couldn't live their life together. I fold the parchment and tuck it back into the book, making sure I don't crumple it as I do. My hands are unsteady as I grab the next note. It's made from the same paper, but when I open it, the paper is outlined with gold dust that is slightly faded with time. I also notice that the message is significantly smaller than the last, like it was written in a rush. The writing is in Hugan's elegant sprawl and despite the rush, I find it easy to read.

My dearest love, Mary
    It has been some time since we parted, and the battle has ended between the humans and the Fae. I hate that I have to rush this, but I have little time. Jakarn is hunting me, and I fear what he has planned. I wish I could explain this to you, but for now I hope this letter helps. I miss you as always, my angel, stay safe and stay strong.
    Yours always, Hugan.

I reread the letter and try to keep my hands from clenching. What did Hugan do to make Jakarn punish him like this? My mother is dead and never got to see her lover again because of him. Then again, I was born so they must have seen each other, but he's been asleep for centuries and I don't see how that could work. I blink and look up at the small sliver of sky that is poking through the leaves. The sky is a riot of colour as orange, yellow, and red signal the end of another day. I sigh and tuck the letter in with the other one. Slowly, I flip through the book page by page and read all the passages. As I read the last one in the book, my hands freeze and my heart gallops. At the bottom of the passage, the last sentence is four words. *'Let the heir rise.'* I try and get my rioting heart to settle and close my eyes before reading it again. An idea pops into my head and I flip through to the two other messages I read tonight. Sure enough, at the end of each entry, there are words that stand out. *'For the good of all, let them rise. She is one and she is many.'* I hold my breath, wishing I had a pencil or pen to write them down. I go to the beginning of the book and read carefully through the passage. At the end, four words stick out, *'Born of darkness and death.'* The entry is about Richard's mother, and she says that she is an evil woman born of darkness and death. I flip through the next page and find nothing of interest, so I move on. I begin to see a pattern, where every five or six entries has a sentence at the end that seems innocent at first glance but is a hidden message. As I move through, I find two more strings of words; *'A babe of strong and brave, A saviour of the grave.'*

    I shuffle around the small clearing, looking for anything that could be used as a pencil. I find a stick and a clump of toad stools. It will have to do. When I was living in the hut and we ran so low on resources that we couldn't afford writing tools, I would go out into the forest and collect mushrooms, then mash them up till they formed a paste. It worked well, if not a bit thick, but it was the best I could do. I walk back over to where the journal is and sit back down, I grab the stick and clump of mushrooms and put them on the canvas of the bedroll bag and begin to mash it up. Once I'm happy with the texture, I flip through the journal to a blank page and dip the stick into the paste. It's a little messy and smells like mould, but it will have to do. I calm my shaking hands and write:

Born of darkness and death.
A babe of strong and brave.
They are one and they are all.
A saviour of the grave.
For the good of all, let them rise.
Let the heir rise.

Once I'm done, I hold it out in front of me and smile. It's not the best, but it will do. As soon as I place the book on my lap, the page begins to glow and the paste falls away, leaving the message in a perfect replica of my writing. Around the edge of the page is the same gold dusting as Hugan's letter. I brush the page with my hand and close the journal. The sun has set, and I curl my legs up to my chest, trying not to strain the stitches too much. The fog has settled, bathing everything in white. The trees somehow look more sinister, and the ground seems so far from my feet. The mockingbird banshee screams from above me and I look up at a branch that hangs slightly lower than the rest. A bird with all black feathers and yellow eyes blinks at me, its beak opens, and it screams again. I contemplate throwing my dagger at it to shut it up. Its feathers almost make it impossible to see, but the yellow eyes follow me as I shuffle closer to a tree to lean on it. I find a small stone near the stream and bounce it around in my hand. The mockingbird goes to scream again, and I peg the rock at it. The bird squawks and jumps up, flying to a branch further up out of my reach. Its scream pierces through the silence, and I curse at it.

"Shut up, you stupid bird."

As if teasing me, it screams one more time before ruffling its feathers and flying away. Silence settles around me again and I'm conscious of every rustle of the leaves or trinkle of water. My stomach is almost as loud as the mockingbird, and I have to put my hand on it to still it. Even though I've found the passage that will wake Hugan, I can't help but feel as if I've gotten nowhere. I'm in the middle of the Blood Wood without food or a bed, I've lost my mate, and I have to somehow kill a King and Queen without dying myself. Easy peasy. As I sit on the ground, the fog around me turns to a shade of pink and I scramble to my feet. Through the thick tree cover, I can see the moon's large silhouette blocking out the stars, it's beautiful. The fog looks as if it's sparkling and the trees are no longer black masses in the dark, they too glow pink and seem to soak in the light. I move around in a circle and smile, it's the Everlast that Alc was talking about, and he was right in his description about the beauty of it. At this thought, my heart aches for him and I hopes he's all right. I hope at least he can see this and feel the tiniest bit at home. The tether on my heart pulls and I fist a hand to my chest. I whisper into the night, letting the fog absorb my words.

"I will find you."

A noise from behind me makes me crouch down and pull my dagger out of its sheath. Voices float to me and I still my movements, trying to hear them. They are too far for me to make out what they're saying, but I can tell they are males. There seems to be two of them and they are moving quickly. I move to a large blood wood tree and look up, there are two notches that could be used as foot holds to help me climb it. I sling my bag over my back and tie it around my waist. My stolen sword hangs at my hip, and I hope it doesn't make me fault in my climb. There is a branch that I can reach if I jump, and then I can pull myself up to the two notches. I check that my dagger is sheathed properly and bend my knees to jump. The voices of the men float to me, clearer this time, and I push off the ground, clamping firmly onto the branch. Heaving a breath, I pull myself up and arch my back so that my feet can grab onto the tree. I silently thank Kai for the many push ups he forced me to do. The sword doesn't help me as it almost catches on the branch I'm holding; I use the strength in my arms and flip myself over the branch and eventually stand to reach the next one. My feet strain on the holds and I quickly scramble up the tree. Once I'm happy with the height, I lean against the trunk and hide in the fog. A pink glow still surrounds us, and I use it as an advantage to blend in with the tree. The two voices of the men are clear now, as if they stand right under me. One of the voices is thick and carries an accent, like he comes from the eastern side of the country.

"The King ain't paying me enough gold for this, I nearly shat myself at that fuckin bird."

He laughs and I hear a slap as someone hits the other on the shoulder.

"Hold in there, Tommas. We are close, according to the word of the King. Plus, it was a stupid bird. As long as we don't run into any of those Faeries, we should make it out of here alive."

The first man with the accent sighs through his nose and they sound like they've stopped under the tree I'm perched in.

"I will be grateful if I never have to see those fuckers while I live. Although apparently the King has one as a pet."

His eastern accent is thicker when he cusses, and I bend lower to catch the other man's reply.

"It's true, I've seen him. He's a High Lord, I think."

Tommas laughs and I hear a *thunk* like he's hit the tree.

"And how did you see that?" Tommas sounds untrusting and the other man sighs.

"I was part of the royal guard, but the King sent me to go find you as we are in need of your skills."

I hold my breath and will him to continue, luckily Tommas seems to have the same amount of curiosity as me because he asks.

"And you saw this High Lord get captured?"

The other man answers, his tone proud,

"Yes, I helped in the capture. There was also a girl with him, but she was small and not worth the fight, so we just left her in the clearing. She's probably long dead now, knowing what resides within this forest."

Tommas coughs,

"That's harsh, Cody, she was just a girl."

Cody snorts,

"A girl that was camping with a High Lord in the middle of the Blood Wood. She was most likely a prostitute."

I bite back a laugh and stand on the branch, ignoring the pain in my thigh. I grab my dagger and flip it in my hand. The fog is thick, but I trust in my judgement that they are directly below me because I can hear their voices clearly. I climb down to the first branch and, through the thick white wall, I can see a head of red hair and another of chocolate brown. I assume the redhead is Tommas, as our eastern neighbours are known for their red hair and pale skin. Cody stands facing the tree and I make sure I stay out of sight. I steady myself on the branch and clench the dagger between my teeth. Letting my legs drop, I swing from the branch and hit Cody in the chest, knocking him to the ground. Before he can react, I hold the dagger to his throat. He chokes and lets out a strangled sound. Tommas' eyes go wide, and he steps forward as if to fight me with his hands. I smile and reach out, grabbing hold of his mind and bringing him to his knees in front of me. I've never held someone's mind in my hands before and a rush runs through me at his inability to fight me. I smile wider and pull Cody up to whisper in his ear.

"Don't you know its rude to talk about a lady behind her back? And as for the dead part, I hate to disappoint but I'm very much alive."

Tommas gapes at me, not being able to move and Cody chokes on his words as they spill out of his mouth.

"You're… you're the…"

"Yes, I'm the prostitute. Nice to meet you. Now, I want to know what you know about the King's plans."

Cody's throat bobs and I press the dagger harder against his neck, drawing blood.

He whimpers and speaks,

"I know nothing, he doesn't tell anyone his plans except for the Queen."

I nod and smile down at him. I move my free hand and pat him on the head like an obedient dog.

"Unfortunately, I don't believe you. You are from the royal guard, so as much as you claim innocence, you must know something because secrets are only secrets if the keeper is dead."

I tap my hand against my throat and smile at him, "Although, if you don't want to speak, I can always use persuasion."

This seems to startle him, and he hesitates, but speaks to me with his voice full of fury.

"The King is looking for the missing heir, and he believes he's found him. He plans to wake Hugan tomorrow at midnight."

I nod, not showing any emotion.

"See, how hard was that?"

Cody closes his eyes and mumbles a prayer.

I laugh, "That's not going to get you anywhere."

I stand up, remove the dagger from his throat, and release Tommas from my hold. They both stumble and climb to their feet, reaching for their short fighting knives. I pull my sword from its scabbard and smile at them. Tommas steps forward and raises his arm.

"What are you? Are you a witch?"

I laugh and throw the sword between each hand.

"I'm much worse. So, I suggest you kneel and listen to what I'm going to say."

Tommas frowns and lunges at me, his knife aiming for my chest. I dodge it easily and kick my leg out, he tumbles to the ground and I'm holding my sword to his chest before he can regain ground.

'Tsk, Tsk, how silly. I don't want to hurt you, but I will if you prove to be ignorant and stupid. Are you ready to listen to me?"

I can see the conflict in his eyes, but he kneels and nods. I smile and, before I can speak, Cody tries to run and I pull my dagger. Aiming and throwing, it flies through the air and pins his cloak to the tree. He jerks to a stop and almost falls to his ass.

"Wow, I would have expected the royal guard to be at least smart and practiced in situations like these. I must say, I'm disappointed."

Cody glares at me and I roll my eyes, holding out my sword to point at him. Tommas stands and his gaze flicks between me and his friend. He must find it's not worth the risk to attack again because he walks over to the creek that's ten feet away and sits down.

I almost laugh but Cody drags my attention to him, and he speaks,

"Once the King finds out that you've captured and hurt a royal guard, you will be hung."

I do laugh then and walk over to him; I lean down and whisper into his ear,

"I'd like to see him try."

I pull back and remove my dagger, placing it back into its sheath.

"And as for him caring about anything other than himself, that's just a joke and you're the clown for believing it."

Cody rubs his neck where the cloak pulled tight and looks over to Tommas. I follow his gaze to the man sitting on the ground. The fog has lifted, almost as if it wants to watch what happens next. The clearing is still pink but it's beginning to fade. Tommas is resigned to cleaning his already spotless fighting knife. I nod and chuckle to myself, turning back to Cody.

"The King thinks this man is the heir, doesn't he?"

Cody nods reluctantly.

"Yes, he does. I was ordered to find him and bring him to the tallest Blood Wood tree."

I laugh at the irony. The king has it all wrong, he's hunting the wrong man, and he doesn't even have the gender right. And this is the man that's supposed to be ruling our country.

"Do you know what the King is going to do to him?"

Cody nods again and his throat bobs slightly at the thought. I walk over to Tommas, and Cody must follow because I hear leaves crunch behind me. He comes up next to me and sits next to Tommas. They whisper something to each other, and I clear my throat, bringing their attention to me.

Tommas speaks, and his accent is heavy in his fear, "Are you going to kill us?"

I smile but shake my head,

"Not yet, I need you to take me to the King. I have a bone to pick with him."

Cody coughs and mumbles under his breath, but I hear it anyway.

"Yeah right, like we are going to do that. I would rather fall on my own sword."

Tommas looks up at me but quickly glances away when he sees me watching him. I walk up behind them and speak, making Cody jump.

"Well, that can be arranged if you would like."

Tommas curses and I smile.

"Right, now I suggest we head off because the sooner I find the King, the sooner I can be rid of you two."

I glance around the clearing. The pink of the moon has completely faded, and the fog has crept in again, leaving my sight short and restricted. I would need my wits about me if I'm to travel with one of the King's royal guard and a random man that I know nothing about. Movement sounds from next to me and I glance over to find Cody looking at me, his gaze a mixture of distrust and anger.

"Are we going or not?"

I smile at him and wiggle my fingers.

"We are in quite the mood aren't we?"

Cody grunts and starts walking into the bush, Tommas hurries to follow and I wonder if he knows the King is going to slit his throat for a ritual that won't work. He seems to trust Cody too much for his own good and it will most likely get him killed sooner rather than later. I follow the two men and make sure to keep my sword in my grip. Silence lapses and I begin whistling to myself. As if not liking being out done but in annoyance, the mockingbird banshee screams, sending both Cody and Tommas ducking for cover. I laugh and march past them.

"Come now, boys, we aren't scared of a bird are we?"

Tommas grunts and his voice betrays his unease,

"That fuckin bird, I'm going to kill it next time it screams like that."

I smile at him, and he seems startled by the action.

"Not if I get to it before you."

He smiles at that and seems to relax the tiniest bit. Yep, definitely too trusting.

"We will see about that, Miss…?"

"Keilee, the name's Keilee."

He nods and says my name to himself, his accent drawing out the K and shortening the E. Cody grunts and I turn to face him.

"Is there something wrong?"

"Yes, only that you are holding a royal guard and a subject of the King hostage."

I snort and wipe my free hand across my face.

"You are barely a guard. You can't even hold yourself in a fight and all you do is whine. And as for the King's subject, he is nothing more than a pawn in a massive game of chess. Except for him, he doesn't have a chance to checkmate because he will soon see his throat cut. So don't lecture me on your sad life and how I'm holding you hostage. The King doesn't care for you, and you'd be lucky if he remembers the colour of your hair."

I take a breath and Tommas' eyes go wide. His gaze darts to my hands and back to my face. Cody has also stopped and he's staring at my hand around my sword. I look down and almost jump back in shock. The sword handle is glowing cherry red, and steam rises into the air in thin spirals. Tiny sparks of pure white dance around my fingertips and I raise them to my face. They look like tiny stars. I turn to a tree and place my hand on the bark. The wood sizzles and pops, and when I remove my hand, in place of it is my handprint burned into the wood. It glows white and slowly fades to leave a black mark. I hear Tommas' voice from behind me, he sounds amazed and horrified at the same time.

"Holy fuck."

Cody grunts his agreement,

"What the fuck are you?"

I turn to them and blink in my shock. My hands have turned back to their normal temperature and the sword has cooled with a permanent hand hold from the melted metal.

"Nobody of importance," I use the words that once hurt me to try and turn suspicion off me.

It doesn't work as Tommas snorts a laugh,

"Yeah, and I'm the King. Are you a witch?"

It's my turn to snort. But before I can open my mouth, a voice so angelic floats to me and I freeze, the hairs on my neck standing up.

"She is none and she is all. Good evening, your Majesty."

I turn quickly and come face to face with a stunning woman with a black curtain of hair framing her large blue eyes and red lips. She is cloaked in a black dress that would make the Queen blush. She bows deeply and straightens. 'Your Majesty' is a new greeting, and I can't help but balk from it.

Cody and Tommas have gone still behind me, and I feel their eyes flick between me and the woman.

"Who are you?" my voice is breathless, like I've run a mile, and she smiles.

"I think there's a bird named after me, and it was quite offended when you threw a rock at it."

My mouth drops open and the air around me turns sinister. The mockingbird, sensing we are talking about it, screams and the men jump, still transfixed by the beauty in front of us.

"The Banshee," I bow slightly to show my respect and her smile widens, revealing perfect teeth.

"The one and only. I must say, I was quite excited to meet you, your Majesty."

I frown,

"Would you stop calling me that?"

Her own frown paints her face, and she looks offended,

"And why would I do that? You are the daughter of a king, so the title fits."

I laugh and Cody's voice pierces the tension, his voice hoarse.

"You're the King's daughter?"

He shoots to his knees and places his hands in front of him. Tommas looks between me and Cody before quickly following.

The Banshee laughs a magical sound, "No, you idiots. She's not the daughter of the King you're thinking about, she is from a much more regal line."

I glare at her, and she smiles.

"What? It is the truth."

"It doesn't matter if it's the truth, they do not need to know what they can't understand."

She laughs again and the air around me turns cold.

"They do not understand because you were supposed to be impossible. That is why Jakarn placed that curse on his brother, because it was impossible," she twirls a hand around me and I shudder. "You are a queen by blood and right, as was your mother."

Her smile grows in size, and she looks less beautiful and more hungry. Cody and Tommas have frozen completely, listening to the conversation with focused intent. I wish to throw my dagger at them and spill their blood to have some privacy.

"I'm afraid I don't understand what you mean," I keep my voice level so as not to betray my fear and growing unease.

Somethings not right and I can't put my finger on it.

"Your mother is Princess Mary, daughter to King Dunkin and Queen Eliza, rightful heir to the throne of Glendale. Although she is dead now, so I am mistaken and the throne belongs to you. Princess Keilee, daughter of Mary Whitewash and Hugan, King of the dead."

I gasp and stumble back. The Banshee looks proud of herself, and I can no longer hear the sounds of the bush or the water. I'm a Princess and a God's daughter. How could my mother keep this from me? Tommas swears from behind me, and Cody lets out a low whistle.

"Fuck me, Imma need some good, aged whiskey after this," Cody laughs but shuts down quickly as both me and the Banshee turn to them.

They are both standing but drop down again as I face them.

"I do apologise, your Majesty, please forgive my rudeness," Cody's voice is low, and I almost want to laugh at the genuine fear I hear behind his words, but I instead ask the Banshee.

"How do I know you're not lying?"

She shakes her head at me.

"You don't, but why lie about this? I'm your loyal subject, I wouldn't lie to my Queen."

Genuine respect sounds behind her words, and I almost take a step back.

"You're a Banshee, you aren't ruled by anyone."

This time she laughs,

"I don't listen to the human monarch. You're not solely from the human blood, you have the blood of a god running through your veins. And Hugan is the king of this realm, so he is the king of me and my kind."

I smile at her, my shock hitting me like a stampede of horses. I don't know what to do with myself and I hate the fact that Cody and Tommas are still staring.

"Right, well that doesn't get me any closer to finding Alc and stopping a damn war from breaking out. So, if you'll excuse me, I'll be on my way," I pause, not wanting to sound rude or to piss her off. "And thank you for the information."

The Banshee bows and straightens, a smile plastered on her face.

"It's my honour, your Highness. We will be seeing each other again soon, and next time lose the luggage," she nods towards Cody and Tommas and the latter's face drops into a scowl.

The Banshee laughs and turns walking off into the fog. I stand still, watching her recede, and hope to whatever god that may be listening that I don't ever have to encounter her again. My legs feel weak, and my breathing is sharp. For some reason, the fact that I'm an actual Princess is not settling in, and I feel like I'm dreaming.

Tommas' voice is like an angry wound ripping open as it pulls me from my trance,

"Forgive me, your Highness, but I'm a little startled. We just ran into a Banshee and survived, and now we are in the company of royalty from both a God and our King."

"Cut the bullshit, Tommas, you know my name so use it. And this doesn't change anything, I need to get to the King and you're going to take me there. By the way, grow some balls, you're a grown man for fuck sake."

Tommas swallows but nods and looks away from me. I don't mean to be so rude, but my world has been turned upside down and not only do I have to kill a King but apparently my grandfather as well. I don't ever recall hearing about the King and Queen having any children, but then again I don't hear much about the royal family, especially when I lived in Fallen Crest. My heart squeezes weirdly and I shrug it off, turning my focus to Cody, who stands silently watching me.

"We don't have long, so let's get going. Can you take me to the King?"

Cody nods and starts walking into the thick fog. I think about the Nymph's words to me. It is indeed time for a family reunion.

CHAPTER 14

The night soon turns into day and the weak glow of the sun is shadowed by the leaves that glisten with early morning dew. Birds chatter to each other and it's like walking through a city of wildlife. Tommas whistles to himself and his movements are slow with exhaustion. We've been walking for most of the night and have only stopped to drink from shallow streams along the way. Cody's face is stony, and I get the feeling he's not happy being involved with an assassination attempt on the King. He refrains from saying so, though, as I am apparently the King's granddaughter. Despite the gloomy tension that's settled over us, I feel energised and eager to get to the King and free Alc. The string in my chest is pulling tighter and I struggle to keep my breathing even. I hope to god that it's a good sign that we are getting closer and that he's not injured or dying. I shake my head at the thought and Cody glances at me but doesn't say anything. I glare at him until he turns away and walks faster to match Tommas' pace. Both men seem to have bonded, even though Cody planned to kill Tommas. It's funny what being stuck in a magic forest will do to you. I for one have learned my family heritage and have developed more abilities that I don't know how to use. I've tried everything, from getting angry at Cody to punching trees as we pass them, but it's only earned me a bruised knuckle and a cranky royal guard. Again, I wish for Alc and his calm manner, showing me how to master this newfound ability. Thoughts of him drag me to the Night Court and I wonder how everyone else is holding up. I haven't heard anything from the Summer court or Cassiopeia, but then again, how could I if I'm here and they are miles away. I miss my home and I miss the people that made it so. Cody mumbles to Tommas and he grunts a reply. They both look over their shoulders at me and I lift a shoulder and place my hand on the hilt of my sword.

"What? If you have something to say, please say it."

Tommas waves a hand to Cody as if to say you deal with it and Cody grunts but speaks to me as if I'm a spooked animal.

"We need to rest. The place you are looking for is a day's walk from here and we should reach it by tonight if we are lucky."

I regard him for a moment before replying. If we keep walking without stopping, we will get there sooner, but if I push them too hard, I will kill my only guide. So, I nod and Tommas sighs in relief.

"Here will have to do. I don't know how far the next clearing is and we don't have time to go exploring."

Cody nods and unstraps his sword from his hips, laying it down next to one of the many blood trees. Tommas keeps his swords strapped to him and I wonder how that's comfortable. I sit along with the men and make sure I can see both of them from where I am leaning against a tree. Its bark bites into my tender muscles and the dew slowly soaks through my leathers. What I wouldn't give for a hot bath and clean hair. Chatter soon settles around us as Tommas and Cody lapse into conversation. I sit and watch them, taking in every movement they make. After a while, I drag the bedroll bag over to me and grab out my mother's journal and the letters hidden inside. The note with the passage is safely tucked away and I glance over at the men to make sure they aren't watching. I grab the letter and fold it into one of my pockets. When the time comes, I don't need to be ruffling through a book to find the ritual, a ritual that I don't know how to work. It seems pointless that I should be the one to wake Hugan when I didn't even know he was my father until a few days ago. The King was looking for the heir in the country of our eastern neighbours, this means he either doesn't know I exist and that I'm his granddaughter, or he doesn't care and has disregarded his daughter from the family. How did a princess end up living in the poorest town known to the kingdom? And how did she meet a god, anyway? The question seems to have no possible answer and only Hugan can answer them since my mother is long dead and buried. I reach a hand up and grab the necklace that once was a comfort to me. Now it sits cold in my hand, like frostbite on a sailor's fingers. So many secrets and I fear they will ruin me instead of saving me. My chest aches and I ignore it, looking over to Tommas and Cody.

"How much do you know about this ritual?" my voice startles them both and Cody looks from me to Tommas.

"The King was tipped off that the heir had fled with his family to Shalhigh, our eastern neighbours. He had searched our kingdom high and low for the heir, but no man was found with the right lineage," Cody takes a deep breath and looks at Tommas with something like sympathy before continuing. "A group of sentries were sent to bring the supposed heir to the King in the Blood Wood. Unfortunately for Tommas, his family was slaughtered, and he was brought here against his will."

I snort a laugh and Tommas looks at me, disgusted. I quickly drop my face into a frown and rush to apologise.

"Forgive me, I was not laughing at your misfortune. I am truly sorry about your loss. I was merely finding it funny that anyone would have a choice with the King involved. As far as I know, it's either give and die or refuse and die. There seems to be no winning with him."

Tommas nods and Cody looks uncomfortable. I raise an eyebrow at him, and he shakes his head.

"I'm not used to speaking ill of the King. I swore my life to protect his and it is not an easy vow to break."

I nod, understanding his tension, but he long ago committed treason when he accepted my offer for him to lead me to the king. A true guardsmen of the royal family would sooner fall on their own sword than help an assassin. Cody seems to realise this and shrugs.

"Well, I'm going to die anyway, so might as well help the so-called heir in her path I suppose."

I truly laugh at this and a smile cracks across his face.

"The King has kept the ritual close to his person and not many people have seen it, but the few that have can't help but brag. All I know is that the heir must spill their blood against the tree and say the passage, but there is also a key of some sort that the heir has on them."

I frown,

"I don't have anything that could resemble a key."

Cody shakes his head,

"You do, you just don't know what it is. That part of the ritual is absolute, the heir has the key."

I nod slowly, thinking over every possession I own. Nothing comes to mind, and I shake it from my head for the moment. Tension stretches between us and I'm the one to break it.

"I will do my best to protect your life when we encounter the King. You are helping me in many ways and for that I am grateful."

Tommas frowns at me and looks to Cody before speaking,

"I want to return home. Why keep me here when I am not

the heir and are of no real use to you?"

I cringe, hating what I'm about to say.

"The King still thinks you're the heir, so we need you to act like it until I can get close enough to wake Hugan myself."

Tommas frowns at me as a plan starts to form in my head.

"How are we supposed to hide you long enough for you to get close to the tree? The King is not stupid."

I nod,

"You will take me in as your prisoner. One that you found on the road. I tried to steal from the royal chest, so that should get you enough leeway to smuggle me in. We need to be careful, though, as there will be three High Lords there, two of whom will want me dead."

Tommas makes a sound of distraught and I continue, ignoring him, "All three High Lords will know my smell and know what I look like, so I'll need to have a heavy disguise. The King will be blind to me as his focus will be with you, Tommas. Cody will be with you long enough that I will be discarded to lesser guards. Then I will fight my way out and make my way to Hugan's resting place."

My plan seems more ludicrous the more I explain it and is based on chance, which I should know is like building a house on the top of an avalanche. Tommas notices my fault along with Cody, and they stare at me like I'm crazy. I begin to wonder if they aren't wrong.

"There are many things wrong with that plan. One of them being that you trust in the King to give you enough time to reach the tree."

I frown and Cody continues, "The King wants his plan known by as few people as possible, so you will just be someone he will kill without thought."

This time I smile and nod my head in his direction.

"If that is the case, he may want to talk to his granddaughter before he kills her. And I have abilities he does not know of, so I have a small advantage."

Tommas laughs and says something in his native language, "*Filla sorra.*"

Both Cody and I look at him in confusion and he realises his mistake.

"I apologise, your Majesty, a slip of the tongue."

I continue to glare at him while Cody fiddles with his sword belt and tries poorly to hide a smile. I grow more agitated and let deadly calm enter my voice.

"Tell me what you just said."

Tommas looks away and blushes, Cody turns to me with a wide smirk.

"I do believe that *filla* means stupid in Shalhighish, but I'm afraid I do not know what *sorra* means."

I turn my attention on Tommas again and smile cruelly at him.

"Tell me, Tommas, what does *sorra* mean?"

He looks at me then Cody like he's looking for help, when he finds none he gives in and keeps his head bowed.

"*Sorra* means woman."

My eyes widen and I laugh. He seems startled and lets go of a weak smile.

"So, I'm a stupid woman? I must say that is quite tame from what I'm used to. Let me assure you, though, that I'm afraid you're the *filla* man here as you insult me when you have no defence."

At this, his smile drops and he scrambles to his knees, holding out his hands.

"Do forgive me, anything I have is yours."

I laugh harshly and turn away.

"Get up, Tommas, before I give you a real reason to beg. And call me by my name, for god's sake. You know it, so use it."

He rushes to sit, and his voice is shaky as he whispers, "Yes, of course, your high… I mean, Keilee."

I get up and walk over to the never-ending tree line and squint, trying to look past the receding fog. Daylight presses firmly around us, and I begin to feel restless. I hear rustling of leaves and turn to find Cody standing next to me. I look him up and down and he nods his head in the direction of Tommas.

"Come on, sit and rest. We will leave in a few hours and get you to the King."

I smile weakly at him and follow him over to the shade of a large blood tree, who's branches spread like warm arms waiting to embrace life. If only I could look on life with the same energy.

The heat of the day suggests it's time to move. I strap my sword belt round my hips and check my dagger strapped to my thigh. The bedroll bag is slung over my shoulders, and I try and keep my nervous energy at bay. Cody and Tommas glance at me from where they too strap on their weapons. Despite the rest, I feel worn and tired and it has started to rub off onto the others. Tonight, I could kill a king and my grandfather while waking my father. It all seems like a nightmare I have no way of escaping, not when the King has Alc. The tether in my chest has gone silent and that scares me the most. I feel like I'm walking on thin ice that could shatter with one wrong foot. Tommas' eastern accent drifts over to me and I look up from the sheathed sword.

"This has to be the stupidest plan I've ever taken part in, and that's saying something."

Cody slaps his back and try's to shoot a grin my way, it looks more like a grimace.

"Don't worry. Keilee has a plan, we just have to follow her lead and it should be fine."

I glare at Cody as he passes the weight of this to me, I'm not only responsible for my life but two others and I don't know if I can promise their safety. Instead of offering a comforting word, I march into the trees, not looking back to see if they follow. Tonight, will end in bloodshed and I can only hope it's not mine or Alc's. But the more I think about it, the less likely that seems. I walk with purpose and the forest seems to heel to my urgent pace as no roots trip me and I can see clearly. Cody and Tommas follow as I hear the occasional nervous chatter or anxious laugh. My mind whirls and I try to keep the steadily growing morbid thoughts to a minimum. Each scenario is worse than the next and they all end in the same way; Alc's blood spilt. My heart stutters and I breathe deeply.

Cody widens his pace to match mine and he glances at me, his dark hair swinging as he looks me up and down.

"You are tense."

The statement is a question I wish to ignore, but I have dragged these men along and I owe then some sort of explanation.

"I'm to kill a king that is also family, and I have just found out I'm a god's daughter. So yes, I am a little tense."

Cody nods and looks into the thick wall of never-ending trees.

"You are also a queen by blood and right. I don't know what the King has planned after he wakes the God of Death, but it can't be good, and I am tired of the bloodshed the Whitewash family has caused. And I mean no offence to you."

I smile at him and it's genuine.

"None taken, the King and Queen have slaughtered enough innocent blood to turn their hands red and I will not stand for it."

"That is not a lie, my Queen."

I balk at the title, and he looks just as startled at my reaction.

"I am not a queen, and I am most certainly not your Queen. Your Queen sits beside the King."

His smile widens and I study him. He is young but brave, he has a good heart that has seen too much blood for such youth.

"You are a queen; a queen is not defined by a crown but by her actions. The people choose who they follow, and I choose to follow you. That makes you a queen that has *earned* her crown, not taken it. Royalty is a privilege and a burden, only the strongest and loyalist can bear it without turning against themselves. You, Keilee, are that person. You may be new to this, but your courage and kindness is what makes you different. The crown was made for you and the people will follow you."

I slow my pace and run his words through my head. I am a queen whether I like it or not and it's up to me if I choose to rule or pass that burden on to another. I don't know how I earned Cody's loyalty, but I am grateful for it.

"Thank you, it means a lot to me to have you on my side."

"Of course. This world has been separated for far too long and I believe you are the change this land needs. The High Lord the King has captured is someone I believe can help the change as well, he seems different from the other Lords."

I nod and blink back the tears that try and force their way out.

"He is. He's doing this to stop a war between the Humans and the Fae."

Cody nods slowly while looking at the ground.

"He means something to you, doesn't he?"

Again, I nod and smile to myself,

"He's my partner. My mate."

"By the heavens above, that is really something."

I look at him in confusion and he laughs.

"How do you know about Mates?"

"My grandmother was a storyteller, and she was a firm believer in the mysteries of mates and the unbroken bond between the two lovers."

I laugh and my muscles relax slightly at the easy chatter between us.

"Your grandmother sounds like my mother. She loved anything that concerned the running's of the heart."

This time Cody frowns. Tommas has also caught up and walks on in silence, staring straight ahead.

"Mary Whitewash was the queen the people needed and wanted. Even as a child, she was full of hope and love for her people. The King and Queen fought to keep her as schooled as they could, but she always listened to the people and fought for them as she grew older. Then she just vanished. The King blamed it on the Fae, but you are proof she ran away to make a life for herself. Somehow, she found the God of Death and you were born."

I go to speak but Tommas cuts in before me.

"The God of Death was put to sleep thousands of years ago, how did he wake and fall in love with a mortal?"

Cody looks from me to Tommas and his frown deepens.

"I am also stuck on that, but I guess that can only be answered by the man himself."

Silence laps around us and we march on until the sky turns from gold to navy, branches from surrounding trees waving us on. The fog has vanished completely, and it leaves me more unsettled than calm. Cody and Tommas have become agitated and jump at the smallest of noises. I for one can't tune my ears away from the forest. I expect the King to pounce out from behind the trees and ruin our plan, but the forest stays the same and I can't decide if it's a good omen or a death signature. The only change in anything is the soft scent of smoke clinging to the evening air, it's the only indication we are getting closer to our destination. Nerves take flight in my stomach, like butterflies on a spring morning, and if I were to eat anything right now, I would vomit all over myself. Cody pulls up next to me and crouches down, pulling the sheepskin bag over his back. The strings are tied tightly, and it takes him a good minute to open the bag. Tommas creeps up next to him and bends down, also removing his bag, but instead of untying it he stuffs it behind a berry bush, grunting as he does so. He reminds me of Big Ben from Fallen Crest; his wife tried to have him on a diet to keep his weight down, but he would stuff food into an old bag and hide it in a bush near his shop. He thought no one knew of his secret, but the village children would sneak in and steal the food after he left. He would return and think a bird or squirrel stole his food. Tommas straightens and startles as he finds me watching him.

"*Faltaey.*"

I smile at him, confused, and he slaps a hand over his face.

"What does that mean?" I keep my tone light, so he knows I take no offence at his slip of language.

"My people use it when something scares them or when they are angry at someone or something," he looks at me sheepishly and continues. "And I was not angry with you, just startled."

"Completely understandable, you just reminded me of someone I once knew."

He smiles at this and turns back to his bag, making sure it is well hidden behind the berry bush. Cody finishes untying his bag and begins to pull out a bundle of clothing. He turns to me and places black slacks, an old hat, and a black tunic in front of me.

"This is what you'll wear when we meet the King. It's not much, but it's a better cover than the leathers you're wearing. A thief doesn't dress in top end fighting leathers. Tommas and I will flank you. I will lead, and he will follow you. The King expects me back soon and he will not tolerate being let down. It's nearly midnight, so we best get moving again."

I nod and pick up the clothing, heading behind a blood tree for some privacy. I strip from my leathers and pull on the disguise. The material is scratchy, and my skin begins to itch, but Cody is right, I need to look the part if I'm to get close to Hugan's resting place. I strap my dagger to my hip and make sure the tunic overlaps it. My hair is twisted into the hat and only a few flyaways dangle around my face. Gathering up my leathers, I make my way back to the men and pull out the folded piece of parchment with the ritual on it. I tuck it away in a pocket, hoping the walk to the camp doesn't damage it. My bedroll bag with my mother's journal hangs over my back, banging awkwardly on my shoulders. Cody and Tommas nod to me and we fall into line, with Cody leading and Tommas tailing, their faces are cold and immoveable. We move at a brisk pace, and with every step, my heart jumps further into my throat. What am I getting myself into? Fate either has a cruel sense of humour or gets bored with dead lovers and evil men. Close to half an hour passes and the glow of dancing flames run along the already red bark of the surrounding trees. Cody's movements become stiffer and his training with the royal guard slips into place, much like the mask Alc wears. Tommas stumbles slightly and I feel fear radiating off him, it makes me feel uneasy. Through the smoke and haze, voices drift to us and I can count at least eleven men, Cody stops and turns to me, only breaking his façade to cast a weak smile at me and Tommas. I try to return it but my heart hammers too loudly.

"Whatever happens in there, I am glad to have met you, Keilee, for this place needs a new rule and I believe you will help bring peace to this place."

I smile truly this time and slap him on the shoulder.

"Now, now, we don't want to get all soppy. We will make it out of this alive, trust me. I don't break promises."

Cody nods and we begin walking again. I can make out the silhouette of two guardsmen walking up and down a narrow path that I presume leads to the King. Cody coughs and the guards' attention snaps to us. They draw out their swords and we freeze. I keep my head bowed and my hand near my dagger as Cody speaks.

"I have the 'someone' for the King."

One of the guards looks from me to Tommas and nods once, "Follow me."

The second guardsman falls in behind Tommas and jabs him roughly in the back with the hilt of his sword. The silver imprinted with the royal crest of a crown surrounded by delicate vines twisting and turning around the elegant head garment. I used to think the vines were portraying the meaning life around the crown and its people, but now I know it's symbolising the way the crown suffocates and traps its subjects. Tommas grumbles and marches forwards. I keep an even pace, keeping my eyes to the ground. For we have just entered hell and are soon to meet the devil.

CHAPTER 15

Despite myself, my eyes flicker up to the approaching crowd. A dozen men in uniform stand watching as we approach, their faces are covered in a black leather and I automatically class them as the Royal Guard. One of them holds a sword out and the two guards with us come to a stop ten feet before the man. I can't see much past the guards, but I hear laughter and the loud crackle of a fire. The man with the sword nods to the guards that have us surrounded and he whispers something I can't catch. Tommas stumbles forward and the guard that was poking him grabs him by the arm and drags him through the line of soldiers. Tommas looks back and smiles at me. I keep my head down but I can't help a frown spreading wide across my face. Cody moves forward and drags me along with him. He stops directly in front of the guard with the sword.

"I caught this one trying to steal from the royal guard, Commander."

The apparent commander uses the tip of his blade to bring my face up to him. I gulp and can feel fire dancing under my skin. I pray silently that it stays there and doesn't give me away.

"Ratty-looking thing, isn't it? The King will want to know what it was looking for, so bring it through."

The Commander drops his sword and I want to spit at him, but he continues, 'Oh, and Lieutenant Bishop, next time you come across something like this, kill it."

Cody nods and I try not to gape at him. He's a Lieutenant?

The wall of guards open and we step through. I notice more men gathered around the fire, but they are dressed in finery, so they must be guests of the King. I keep my eyes open and pray that Kelby and Isaac are occupied somewhere else. Cody keeps his grip on my arm, and I match his brisk pace. He leads me around the fire and down a small forest track almost overgrown by ferns and black berry bushes. Strangely, the trees begin to thin and we step into a very large clearing. It's larger than any of the other clearings and the trees seemed somehow dwarfed. Again, men dressed in armour and finery walk around and talk to each other. It's like watching ants scurry around their nests. A man with a big beard and small legs laughs at something another man says, and I can't tell if it's genuine laughter or just court bullshit. A few of the people surrounding us stop and stare, but most carry on ignoring us. Cody leads me to the back of the fire, and we walk through a line of trees. It's like crossing a bridge. One moment we are in the clearing with merry men and soldiers drinking themselves to oblivion, and the next I'm boxed in by huge trees that reach further than the clouds themselves, with hooded figures turning to look at the new incomers, their faces hidden in the shadows of their hoods. A tall man around six foot has a golden circlet place upon his hood, marking his power and status. I look away from the priest. Despite the eerie crowd, the thing that grabs my attention is the trees or rather one tree in particular. The largest tree I've ever laid eyes on is standing near the edge and its bark bleeds. The blood runs down its trunk and pools near its roots before disappearing into the soil. Hugan's Chamber. The leaves are wilted like it's barely hanging on to life and small bushes surrounding it are completely dead, their stiff branches never again waving in the wind. A gruff voice drags me from my curiosity and Cody edges me closer to the circle of men, which has begun to gather around us. The priest among them. His eyes flash in the firelight as his gaze travels over my body, finally landing on my face. His attention is also grabbed by the rough voice.

"What do you have for us, Lieutenant?"

Cody straightens and bows slightly, not low enough when addressing a king, but to someone of importance nonetheless.

"A thief, Lord Cummins."

Cummins smiles and turns to face me fully, his blonde hair scraping his strong brow. I hope the hat throws enough shadows over my face to hide my shudder at the eager look in his eyes.

"How interesting. The King would surely be intrigued to meet this pretty specimen."

I glare at him and keep my chin held high, like an arrogant idiot. and the Lord snorts at me and flicks a hand behind him.

"The King is talking to his... how do I put it? Ahh, yes, guests."

I look behind him and two broad figures make me pause. Kelby and Isaac are bent over land papers discussing something akin to war plans. Cody notices my rugged stance and nods a farewell to Lord Cummins as he pulls me away from the circle to a more secluded area.

"What's wrong? Has someone recognised you?"

Panic laces his words, and it draws my attention to him.

"No, nobody has noticed I'm here."

I leave the 'yet' out of my sentence, but it hangs there like a heavy weight.

"I've noticed the King and his accomplices, two of which know me just by smell."

Recognition flashes through his eyes, making them bulge out of their sockets.

'The Fae High Lords.' I nod and he leans in close but angles his body away to make it look as if he's scolding me from the eyes of an outsider. 'Have you seen your High Lord?' I shake my head and my chest begins to ache; I haven't even felt him since the last time in the forest.

I nod and sigh, wishing I could feel even the slightest twinge from the tether, but I can't and now is not the time to dwell over things I can't help. Right now, I need to be focused on waking Hugan and stopping a war. I look at Cody and nod once.

"Let's do this."

Cody swallows thickly but nods in return before he drags me around the swarm of men to the front of the clearing. To where the King is seated alone now, apart from a bowed man with peppery hair and a large middle, half covered by a heavy cloak. Cody bows low towards the King, and he pushes me to do the same.

"Your Majesty."

I straighten before Cody and look at the King, keeping my face immobile. His features are sharp, and his hair is the colour of my mother's. Everything about him shouts royalty, from the knee-high boots on his feet to the fur-lined cloak around his neck. His nose is slightly crooked, as if broken a few times, but even in his older age he is handsome. I wish for the strings to tighten and strangle him. He looks me up and down and I am conscious of his piercing eyes.

"What do you have for me, boy?"

Cody swallows and nods his head once,

"A thief we found trying to steal from us. your Majesty."

The King tilts his head at me and laughs.

"A girl try and steal from a trained guard? How brave or rather stupid."

The fat man next to him lets loose a fake laugh and the king silences him with a glare.

"Take her to the holding yards, I will deal with her later. I have business to attend to now that we have the missing piece."

I glare and Cody nods, not wanting to disobey the King's orders. He goes to grab my arm, but the King stops him.

"No, not you. Eric, come take this rat to the yards, this young man and I have things to discuss."

Eric, the fat man that laughed earlier, comes closer and grabs my arm roughly, leading me away from Cody and the King. Eric makes a path through the crowd gathered near the King to a dark corner of the clearing. His breathing is laboured, and he doesn't take notice of my free hand sliding to my dagger until I have his arm bent back and the blade at his throat. He makes a strangled noise and tries to call out, but I press the blade harder against his neck, kicking out my leg so he falls to his knee with a gulp.

"Ssshhh, we don't want the King to hear about your incompetence to hold a rat still."

Blood gathers at the blade pressed against his neck, and it slowly drips down the front of his cloak.

"Now, when is the King planning to perform the ritual?" my voice is so quiet it's almost drowned out by the chattering people in the large crowd.

Eric struggles aimlessly in my hold and when he speaks he sounds muffled.

"I would rather die than tell you."

I smile and drag the dagger across his neck, "Fine."

His body drops from my hold, and I unbuckle the cloak from his neck and throw it over my shoulders to hide myself better. It smells of cigar smoke and red wine, which will hopefully help me blend in. The so-called holding yard is nothing more than sturdy trees with chains around their bases hidden partially by the midnight darkness, which is more of a comfort to me than any light from a fire. I look around the corner of the clearing and my breath catches, and my knees almost buckle under me. Within the darkness, green eyes flash at me so bright they drown out any stars. At the base of a large tree is Alc, staring at me with wide eyes. I rush over and drop before him, catching his face in my hands. His hair is messy, and he looks weak and tired.

"What happened?"

He leans into my touch and sighs.

"Now is not the time for that, Princess. The King is nearly ready to wake Hugan."

I nod,

"I know, but let me get you out of here first."

Alc reaches up and stops my hand from touching the jingling metal.

"No, don't. They've used iron and laced it with old magic. Only the key will open these and I don't know what it will do to you. Leave me here and go stop the King."

I frown and shake my head, but he grabs my face and places a kiss on my lips so light I have to question if I imagined it.

"Save them, Princess, just like you saved me."

I smile and fight the moisture building up behind my eyes. I squeeze his hand that's on my face and stand.

"I will fix this, I promise."

He smiles and looks up at me,

"I have no doubt in that, Princess."

And with that I leave him on the ground and creep around the clearing, pulling the hood up so I'm hidden. My dagger is in my hand, and I grip it tightly, trying to keep silent. The blood wood tree stands tall, and I make my way to it, weaving in between the crowd. I eye the King and Cody still talking near the head of the clearing. I'm so focused on them, I don't realise someone's standing in front of me until I crash into them. I grunt and go to tell them to scoot but I'm met with pale blue eyes that hide more secrets than the King himself. Kelby looks down at me and smiles. It's pure evil and I repress a shudder. I go to move out of his way, but he grabs my arm and holds me in place.

"Such a surprise to see you here. I smelled you as soon as you entered."

I shudder and cringe,

"That's very creepy."

He laughs and his grip on my arm tightens.

"I never got to have my turn with you, and I must say I was quite upset about that. How about we change that now?"

I try and shove him as anger rises.

"How about you fuck off?"

Kelby laughs again and drags me to the tree. I almost thank the gods when he lets me go, but he pushes me up against the tree and it's not until blood wets my back that I realise it's Hugan's tree. I freeze as a plan forms in my head and I find myself leaning forward as I take action. I place my hand on Kelby's face and look into his eyes. He smiles but soon freezes, and that's when I know I have him under my control. He lets go of me and I make him move to my side to block me from the King's view. He follows my order like a doting dog. I reach into my pocket and grab out the folded piece of parchment with the ritual on it. My dagger is back in my hand, and I take a deep breath. I have no idea how to do this and I hope it works in my favour. Kelby's eyes widen slightly as my control slips while I concentrate on the words before me. A voice comes from in front of me and I go still. The King stands before me with Isaac by his side, he smiles at me and I shudder, swinging my hands behind my back, hiding my knife and paper.

"What are you doing, little thief? And why is one of my associates standing next to you?"

He looks from me to Kelby, who is staring blankly at the King, his mouth slightly open. My breath catches as he frowns, like pieces to a puzzle are clicking into place. But then he laughs and it's more unnerving than the frown.

"I see. I haven't met someone like you for a long time. I must say, I am surprised."

I frown at him, and he continues. Isaac laughs and looks between me and the King, eager to see how this will play out.

"A Shifter is quite rare, but here you are, standing before me practically shouting your ability."

My heart gallops in my chest and I want to collapse out of relief that he doesn't know who I truly am. Gently, I drag the dagger over my hand and bite back a wince as pain sears across my palm. I look to the King and keep my focus on him as I lean back against the tree.

"You caught me. Such a shame I didn't get to play before you interrupted, I was quite looking forward to it."

The King laughs at this and shakes his head.

"We have a jokester among us. Let's see, I have a deal for you, little thief. If you lend me your services, I will let you walk freely with no punishment."

I hold my cut hand near the tree and show my other hand to him, smiling as I do so.

"I fear we are not on the same page, for I would never play with a fox pretending to be a wolf. I have much more urgent business that requires my attention. I do apologise in advance."

The King is no longer smiling, and he glares at me. His

guardsmen step closer to him and pull their swords. A crowd has gathered, and they watch the tension with caution. Nobody wants to see the King lose his temper.

"I have offered you a deal that could save your life and you throw it in my face. Guards, seize her."

I smile as they step forward and press my hand fully to the tree. The King notices my movement and looks at the trunk where my blood fuses with the tree. It begins to glow, flowing down the bark like veins, and the King's face falls into a shocked expression.

"You see, I would advise you to keep a better check on people entering and exiting your grounds, but I see that you have to learn that the hard way. And who best to teach you that than your own granddaughter?"

Gasps bounce through the crowd and the guards freeze their pursuit at my claim. The King looks me up and down, then smiles.

"You may think you have something over me, but I'm the one with the ritual, you merely have the blood I need."

This time I smile,

"That may be what you think, but your daughter was smarter then you, so I think you have your words crossed."

I open the parchment in my hand and the King lunges at me himself, but he's too slow. I breath in and read the words on the paper, keeping my palm to the tree.

"Born of darkness and death.
A babe of strong and brave.
They are one and they are all.
A saviour of the grave.
For the good of all, let them rise.
Let the heir rise."

The King yells something but I don't hear it, I'm too focused on the golden glow that begins to surround me. The blood on the tree flashes white and draws up out of the ground in small drops. The liquid swarms around me and rushes to regroup in front of me. The tree itself splits down the middle and the golden light explodes through the crowd, knocking people off their feet. The King watches and his guards have surrounded him in a protective circle. I can't see Cody anywhere and I hope he's taken the opportunity to find Tommas and get out of here. The light begins to fade and in its wake stands a man like no other. His silhouette has a white aura surrounding him. His hair is shoulder length and brown like mine. Eyes of beautiful blue pierce the crowd and it's not hard to guess why my mother fell for this man. He's stunning and proud. Like a true King. He looks around at the crowd and turns to face me. His eyes scan over me and he freezes, looking shell-shocked. The King looks eager but stays within his wall of guards. Kelby has been released completely from my hold and he stumbles back into the crowd, watching as the God of Death stalks me. I'm not prepared for when he speaks, so I back into the once whole tree that's now split in two.

"Mary, is that you?"

My heart clenches and tears form behind my lids.

I shake my head sadly, "No, I'm her daughter. I'm Keilee Whitewash."

Hugan looks at me with soft eyes and steps forward.

"I'm your daughter."

"My daughter? You look just like her, what a family reunion this will be," his voice is so soft, and I want to kill Jakarn for commending him to eternal sleep.

"My mother is dead, she died many years ago, it's just me now."

Hugan frowns and that's as much emotion he allows to show before turning to face the crowd that's stares in bewilderment. The King glares at Hugan and the God of Death laughs. I stare at him, and he claps his hands together.

"Ahhh, I should have known you would be up to something, my dear friend, for you could never keep your hands off something that could give you power. I must say, this is not the way I envisioned waking from my curse. Where is your lovely wife? Finally had enough of your greed?"

Hugan stares at the King and no humour can be found on his face.

"The Queen is busy."

Hugan nods once and addresses the crowd,

"Leave us now. I do not care where you came from, but leave and go back to whatever place you crawled out of."

The crowd watches him with unease and many freeze in their places.

Hugan sighs, "Very well."

He clicks his hands and the crowd disappears in fumes of smoke, leaving the King, Isaac, and Kelby standing before us. I look at Hugan and he sends me a weak smile.

"Don't worry, I just sent them back to the castle grounds."

Hugan turns his attention to Kelby and Isaac, whose faces are nothing short of greedy.

"What brings the High Lords of Spring and Autumn to the Blood Wood?"

"We have come to wake you, but it seems your daughter got to you first," Isaac gives a mock bow and Hugan laughs again, the sound hollow.

"You have come to start a war between the Kingdoms and Courts of this land. I must say, I am surprised peace has lasted this long with males like you ruling."

Kelby goes to step forward, but Hugan waves a powerful hand and they both freeze in their places, not moving. They seem to be fading, hands of once solid flesh and bone fading to almost glass, and if they could express emotion, I would guess pain would be written on their faces. The King watches and claps his hand at the spectacle.

"Thank you for doing that for me, friend, it saves me one task. Now for the second to begin."

The King walks forward and Hugan glares at him, watching as he approaches. I grab my dagger and hold it forwards, pointing towards him.

"What are you doing?"

Such a universal question, with so many answers, all different and unique. The King looks at me and stops.

"I'm fixing what was broken many years ago."

"And what would that be?"

I keep my tone level and look him in the eye.

"Killing the Fae. For the humans need to be free of them, they have caused enough suffering to them to last centuries."

Hugan walks forward and stops in front of the King, but I get in before he has a chance to open his mouth.

"There has been peace for many years between the Humans and the Fae. Why start a war now when it will only lead to humans being slaughtered?"

The King really does pause this time and he takes his time to answer.

"Because as long as they live, no true peace will come. And if that means losing some human lives, then it's worth it in the end," he takes a breath. "One of my many joys in life is watching the humans live their life with all the struggle and loss and I have grown to envy their riches. And I have a weapon this time, for what is a better weapon then death himself."

This time it's my turn to pause, and I look to Hugan. The King laughs and claps his hands together.

"Oh, you don't know do you, my dear Granddaughter? Has your father left out the details of the family tree?" he looks at me and I try not to shrink back. "Considering your father lived under a tree for a few centuries, I would have thought he would know all about them, but even gods can be mistaken."

I glare at him, and he smiles sweetly at me, Hugan places a hand on my shoulder, and I'm shocked at how cold it is.

"Why, Malki, you are the God of Earth and Sea, so one would think you would know about the life cycle of a tree."

I stare at both of them dumbfounded, partly because they are bickering over a tree's life and purpose, but also because my grandfather is a god. I feel light and have to swallow a few times to free my throat.

"So, not only do I have a god for a father but for a grandfather as well?"

Malki smiles and nods,

"Unless you have a hearing problem, then yes, that's what we are saying."

I shake my head and step forward towards him, angling my dagger so it points at his heart.

"What is your true purpose in this? Why did you truly want to wake Hugan? If you are a god. You can easily kill the Fae yourself, you don't need the help of Hugan, for the Fae are powerful but they have nothing on a god."

Malki frowns and seems at a loss for words before he steps forward and squares his shoulders.

"That is true, but I needed something as a disguise. A scheme for people to fall for so I could get closer to the main reason I'm here. Because if Hugan woke, then I could kill him with my own hands."

He turns his attention to Hugan, ignoring me.

"My beautiful daughter was happy until you took her away from me. You ruined her life and then left her to die."

Hugan almost shudders and that scares me the most, the God of Death shuddering.

"I would never harm Mary. I loved her, and you know that."

Malki laughs,

"Why couldn't you leave her alone and let her live her life?"

His hand slips to his sword and I follow his movement.

"The moment you fell under your brother's curse, we thought that would be the end of it and that she would be able to live her life and rule the kingdom like she was raised to do. But then you woke and eight years later she was dead from a mysterious illness."

Malki's breathing is heavy, and his eyes are red where anger fights to control him. I look at Hugan who has gone still.

"You know that's not true; Mary and I had the bond and we loved each other. You were the one keeping her in a cage, you were the one that slowly killed her."

I freeze and look between the two males, who seem to forget that I stand beside them. My head spins and I feel weak. They both blame each other for the death of my mother, and I don't know what to think. My hands tremble and the dagger shakes with it. A shuddering breath rips through me. It was Malki, he was the one to put Hugan to rest. The God of Earth and Sea put Hugan to sleep to protect his daughter. Jakarn was a mask he placed to protect himself. The God of Life only placed the ritual on his sleeping brother to protect him from the King being able to wake him and kill him. The stories were a lie with only one truth, created to form the plan Malki has worked on for centuries. I stumble back. My mother died because Hugan was gone, their bond weakened to the point of breaking.

Alyssa's words wrap around me, *"When the bond is broken and one dies, the other becomes a shell of their former selves, almost worse than death."*

The pit in my stomach where I shove all my worries and insecurities begins to strain and I place a calming hand on my chest. She is dead. She died of an illness, an illness of the heart. She is gone because her father unknowingly killed her. Malki pulls his sword from its scabbard and swings into Hugan, who blocks the blade with his own weapon. The two men begin to spar, each of them looking for an opening that doesn't present itself. Malki grunts and lunges forward, driving Hugan to level ground with him. His blade flashes silver in the pale moonlight streaming through the trees.

"You killed my daughter and for that I will kill you."

Hugan laughs, the sound holding no joy as he swings low to try and disarm Malki. It almost works, but the King is quick and agile. He side steps and draws his arm back to bring his sword through with full power. I step back into the shadows and bump into the split tree. I turn and run my hand across the cold bark, stopping when I find something floating in the middle of the split. The men behind me have forgotten I exist, so I lean forward. Floating in the middle is a golden flower the size of a small pendent, it spins slowly and I'm mesmerised by the familiarity of it. Searing pain grabs at my chest and I stumble back. I reach up to where it burns, and I come in contact with my mother's necklace. When I touch it, my hand burns and I wave it around trying to cool it. Reaching around, I undo it, careful not to touch the flower. The pendent strains towards the identical flower still rotating, so I let it go and it flies to the golden sister. Once they connect, a flash of light bright enough to blind me spreads across the clearing.

Chapter 16

I open my eyes, feeling it dim. Hugan and the King have frozen in place and even a stray bird has stopped mid-squawk. I stand on ground that shimmers like gold, and everything is silent. My heart beats loudly in my chest.

"Hello?" my voice comes out muffled, like I'm trapped in a glass cage, which seems not too far from the truth.

Even my footsteps are hollow as I walk around the golden box. I turn to face the once glowing flower, which now stands frozen with the necklace interlaced through it. Something makes me shiver, and I feel as though I'm being watched. My eyes narrow and I scan the surrounding area. Nothing moves, it is as if it's frozen in time, waiting for the clock to continue its cycle. Both Gods' faces are contorted with rage so primal that I don't doubt that the forest could be changed to the deep red of blood if a battle was to rage between them. My thoughts drift to Alc, hidden in the shadows where he's chained in iron shackles. Anger at the King rises in my chest and the tether in my chest pulls tight. Warmth surrounds me and a voice pulls me from the depth of my mind.

"Rage is sometimes the poison and the antidote if one knows how to use it right. I'm afraid, though, that these two barbarians are not equipped in that art."

I startle and look to my right where a woman stands; her hair billows behind her in a phantom wind. It's gold, like the rest of her appearance. Her face is kind, and she smiles down at me. An eerie glow surrounds her, and she has to be the most beautiful being I've laid my eyes on. I must stare for a while as she laughs, the sound floating around me and encasing me in warmth like that of a summer breeze.

"My dear, what troubles such a youthful mind?"

She turns her gaze fully to me and her features resemble someone familiar, but it's lost in a haze that my mind can't untangle.

"What has caused the hatred between these two men, truly? I mean, why start a war when peace reigns between the two realms. It would just cause so much more hurt to both sides."

The woman hums her agreement and turns back to watch the frozen men.

"They blame themselves for the death of a Princess and a goddess. When in fact it was no one's fault but her own."

I turn sharply to face her when she finishes. That's my mother she's talking about, and what does she know about her anyway?

"Don't talk about my mother like that. I don't care who you are, but you cannot speak about the dead when they are not here to defend themselves."

The woman smiles at me and her eyes shine under the mix of moonlight and gold.

"Ah, but that is where you're wrong. She is here to defend herself, but she will not because she knows it's the truth."

Spinning around, I try and find my mother's face but all I see is gold and the woman in front of me, who stares at me with sad eyes. Realisation dawns on me and I stumble backwards, hitting the solid wall of transparent gold glass. My hands tremble and I stare at her.

"Mother?"

The one word bounces around the dome and she nods, tears staining her perfectly arranged face. My heart clenches and I feel sick. I sink to my knees and draw from the cold of the ground under my pants. Movement flickers in my vision and the goddess that is my mother bends down to sit with me.

"I've watched you grow into the young woman you have become, and I am so proud of you. To face what you have would bend even the strongest of men. You show strength and compassion that I am envious of," she pauses and wipes an elegant hand across her face before continuing. "I was foolish and naïve; I never worried about the consequences of my actions. I didn't think of the pain it would cause the people I loved most. That is why this is my fault."

She stops and stares at Hugan where he's frozen, holding his blade in the air.

"What did you do to cause this? How could anyone be at fault but the people who continue to fight against better judgement? You died because your bond was snapped."

My heart pounds in my chest but I feel weak.

"It is best I start at the beginning of this mess. I assume you are familiar with the story of the six gods and the battle that turned this land red from the blood spilt?"

I nod my head as no words form in my tight throat. I swallow, trying to clear it.

"There was only meant to be the six gods that ruled the world we walk on, but when two fell in love, a miracle was made in the form of a baby girl," pausing, she looks to me and smiles. "Pacarny and Malki, gods from different sides of the battle, fell in love and had a baby. She was said to be a weak and measly child that they kept from the sight of the people they ruled over. But when a story becomes told throughout the centuries, people begin to twist the tale to benefit their needs."

I interrupt, finding my words even if they are stuck in my throat.

"I thought Pacarny fell in love with a human man, not another god, let alone the King of Glendale?"

My mother nods once, her expression coming close to anger.

"That, my flower, is why people should keep to stories they know. My mother and father broke the laws that were created for the gods to follow to keep the balance between the realms. Once I was born, I tipped the scales and created a crater to form in the centre where many of the magical people pull their power. I never learned from my parents' mistakes, so I fell in love with a god myself and had a child with him. Jakarn opened Hugan's portal to let him see me for one last time. He warned us against the consequence, but I ignored them and then nine months later you were born. Never do I regret this, but it caused the scales to tip further, sending a plague across the lands. It is what caused my illness. The world is trying to righten itself through dark magic. Yes, the bond weakened me to almost mortal health once Hugan was put to sleep for good, but it was the plague that killed me. You need to fix it, my flower, and right the balance between the worlds. For you, my flower, are the Goddess of Balance and Power. You alone hold the power needed to balance the world again."

I freeze and stare at her like she has gone mad. How could someone fix something like that? I would imagine it would take years to master a power like that and I only have a matter of hours.

"What do you expect me to do? I don't know how to control this."

My mother's face pulls into a smile, and she places a delicate hand on my shoulder.

"You have it within you, my flower. All you have to do is believe and follow that feeling. For I am the Goddess of Knowledge and Truth. I believe in you, and so should you."

Grim understanding settles over me and I nod, a knot forming in my stomach.

"I will fix this as best I can, I promise."

She smiles and stands, pulling me to my feet as well. Before I'm ready, she wraps her arms around me and I feel her begin to fade. I latch onto her, not wanting her to go for a second time. She steps back and smiles at me, watching as she slowly fades, taking the gold dome with her.

"I believe in you, my flower; you have always been strong. Let the Heir rise."

Then just like that, she is gone and I'm back on firm ground and the sound of battle continues behind me. Birds continue their cries, but I stand and stare at the flower pendent still in front of me. I look at Kelby and Isaac, who have faded almost to their chests, and a calm fills me. Moonlight circles me, and I breathe in deeply, closing my eyes for a brief moment before my heart finds peace. I can do this; not only for myself but for my mate. Taking a step down from the dais, I walk steadily towards the men, whose swords clash against each other. My gaze shoots to Alc, who strains at his restraints trying to get free. He stills when he sees me, and I nod my head once. His eyes widen with fear, and I smile to soothe his worry, but it does little. He continues to strain, and I hear his voice over the clash of steel.

"Keilee, don't!"

Somehow he knows what's happening and he tries to fight. I reach down to the tether pulling at my chest and send words down the bond. As soon as they reach Alc, he sags and stares at me, sorrow filling his eyes. His words reach me through the bond and my heart aches terribly.

"You don't have to so this, take me instead. Please, Keilee, don't do this."

"Don't worry about me. I have to make this right, for the balance is tipped and only I can fix it. Please forgive me. I love you."

Alc shouts at me and I close down and focus on the men in front of me. My heart jumps into my throat and I feel dizzy. With all the courage I can muster, I step in front of the blades; Hugan pulls his blade away at the last second, but Malki doesn't, he drives the blade through me and pain spreads until it suffocates me. Alc screams, the sound making me cry out. Hugan freezes and drops his sword. Malki's eyes widen in shock as he pulls the blade from my body. Everything is cold and I shiver, falling to my knees.

"No, no, no. What have you done?" Malki's voice is faint, and I sigh as darkness so complete pulls at me to follow, begging me to fall into a sleep that I will never return from, and for a moment all I want to do is listen, all I want is for the pain to stop and for the ache to leave me for once.

All I want is to be free. But I can't, I have something to do. Something important. And I promised Alc I would come back. My eyes flutter closed, and everything fades, but not before I feel the earth shake with the fury of the King of Night breaking his chains and cloaking the land in eternal night. For his mate was dying.

Chapter 17

I'm standing in a vast span of black. I feel nothing and hear nothing. I only see endless black shadows; I never knew there was so many shades of the colour, but I was mistaken. I blink and turn slowly, trying to grasp where I am. Something flickers before me, and I watch as stars blink into existence. It smells like jasmine and orange blossom. A smell that reminds me so firmly of the Night Court that tears swell in my eyes. The stars form a path under my feet and I walk on, following them. All is dark but something is pulling at me to follow, so I do, and when the path fades, the sight before me has my breath catching; for I am no longer surrounded by shadows and night. It is as if I crossed a threshold and entered a forbidden palace. Pillars of black stone rise above me and disappear into the darkness. Walls form on either side of me where ivy and jasmine climb. Windows that show nothing are open and a phantom breeze makes the heavy navy curtains wave. The floor is cold and of solid marble. My mind swirls, this isn't just a place, this is a throne room. Gold runs through the marble like snakes trapped in stone. At the other end, a throne stands tall. It is as dark as the shadows surrounding me, but gold lines the edges and spiralling gold shards spread from the back making it look as if the sun's rays are rising above it. My footsteps echo as I walk closer to the throne. Once I ascend the dais, the floor around me glows and the gold in the throne spreads out painting a picture of scales that have tipped too far to the left. I look above the scales to the ceiling. A glass mosaic is stretched before me. Six figures stand tall over a world so familiar to me. The two middle figures stand side by side, one surrounded by light and youth the other stands amongst the dead. Jakarn and Hugan. Next to Jakarn is Malki, surrounded by towering oaks, and Danti, holding the rays of the sun. On the other side of Hugan, Pacarny holds a sword of the blackest metal and Dakota holds the moon in her hands. Under the Gods is Thyithran and then Glendale. The former had been split into its courts, not with words but items, like stars for the Night Court and Flowers for the Spring Court. I look back down at the tipped scales. This is what I've been brought here to do, I need to fix this. Heart hammering and hands shaking, I lean back and sit on the throne that is surprisingly warm. As soon as I rest my back on the stone, light blinds me and I blink it away. Pain lances through me, grabbing hold of my lungs and squeezing tight. I try and step out of the throne, but it holds me firm. My hands turn on their own accord and a staff of silver and sapphire falls into my waiting palm. It's cold to the touch and I startle as something is placed onto my head. I reach up and touch it. A crown. My mind is muddled, and I don't understand any of this. I try and stand again, finding the throne has released me. I walk towards the scales that shine brightly. I'm stopped in my tracks as I feel something tug at me. It comes from inside me, from the depth of my soul. I close my eyes and reach for it. I touch it and my eyes shoot open and my breathing quickens. Images flash through my head, from new and old, some so primal I'm not sure even the Gods walked the earth at such a time. I gasp as the images stop. I found it. I found what I must do. Falling to my knees, I grab my dagger from its sheath and slice my palms before placing each hand on the tipped scales, making sure each plate is covered. I speak into the darkness and feel warmth spread from my hands to my chest.

"Born of darkness and death.
A babe of strong and brave.
They are one and they are all.
A saviour of the grave.
For the good of all, let them rise.
Let the heir rise.
Through dusk and dawn, ice and fire, tip the scale back.
Through war and peace, righten what has been wronged, for let the scales balance.
Let power restore."

The warmth settles around my heart, and I open my eyes. Before me, the gold lifts from the floor and swirls around me, moulding into figures of dancing Fae and singing women. The image changes to a babe laughing and children running around. It is showing life and the balance of it. The dust falls back to the ground and runs through the cracks in the marble, forming scales once again. The plates settle evenly, and a new figure has been added to the formation. At the bottom of the scales kneels a woman with a crown and a staff. At the bottom of the scales, I kneel. Standing, I walk back to the throne and sit once again. A band of gold forms around my wrist and I stare forwards, watching through the eyes of another as trees of red melt to the colours of green and deep brown. I watch as rivers run full, and crops grow tall. My eyes drift to the mosaic and it has also been altered, for two more figures stand there. My mother stands with a book in her hands, smiling up at the other gods from where she stands just under them. The other figure is me. I stand with scales in one hand and the staff in the other, and adorning my head is a crown. I look down at the Gods and Goddesses smiling also. Words written in a delicate sprawl shine down upon me:

"A crown that has been earned. A Queen who has made her Kingdom."

"Balance and Power."

It is done. The world has tilted back and balance has been restored. I whisper into the room, "Take me home."

CHAPTER 18

Inaudible noise floats in and out of my consciousness. I'm surrounded by something soft and comforting, like the embrace of a loved one. Pain laces through my arms but I ignore it as I'm lured into the blissful quiet of sleep. I feel my body slipping into the pulling darkness, but something prohibits me from fully submerging. A firm grip on my hand pulls me from my haze and I blink, staring at a white ceiling etched with intricate designs that resemble the night. The noise from before now filters to me clearly and the voices are whispered. It sounds as if someone is trying to have a quiet argument that is turning louder by the second. The hand that grips mine so tightly jerks as he speaks. Alc. A smile plasters itself to my face and I turn my head to him. His hair is messy, and his eyes are tired, but he's dressed in his lord attire that I've grown to love so much. He doesn't notice me, and I scan the room at all the other people in it. Kai sits on a sofa near the fire, watching it with killer intent. Neron twists rays of light around his hand and my smile grows at the familiar frown plastered on his face. Ianira and Naomi talk near a writing desk, they seem deep in thought and my heart clenches at the people I have grown to love so fully. Alc is still focused on a figure I cannot focus on, so I try and sit up. This drags his attention to me and the smile that I receive sets my heart ablaze. Kai looks over at me and his face splits into a grin.

"Look who's finally graced us with their presence."

Naomi and Ianira walk over to the bed and Ianira looks as if she could kill someone.

"If you do something that stupid again, girl, I'll make sure you're dead for good next time," despite her harsh words, a smile makes its way across her face.

Naomi laughs,

"I think it's time for a drink."

A cough comes from where Neron stands, and he shakes his head.

"I think you have had enough drinks to last a while."

I laugh and my head pounds at the action, but I ignore it. Alc is still staring at me, and I smile at him.

"What?"

"Nothing, it's just you had me scared there for a moment, Princess."

I smile brighter,

"Just for a moment?"

He raises his eyebrows and Kai's voice interrupts.

"More than for a moment, he was weeping when he carried you through the doors. If I wasn't so worried myself, I would have been laughing at his expression."

Alc picks up a book from the nightstand and pegs it at Kai who narrowly avoids it.

"He's exaggerating."

I laugh again and swing my legs over the side of the bed.

"I'm sure he is. Now, I need food and a bath."

Alc stands and extends his hand to me, which I gladly take. Once I can stand, I look around at the people who have become family. My heart is full, and I smile as tears gather in my eyes. This is my home.

CHAPTER 19

The bath is deliciously warm, sending steam into the room, and my body relaxes into the water. I never knew how much I would miss this when I went into the forest. Even if it was only for a few days, it felt like months. Alc informed me when the others left the room that I was out for two days and that he was beginning to worry that I wouldn't wake. I settled his worry with a kiss, and he told me to freshen up because he had a surprise to show me. As much as I love the water that caresses me, I stand up, the action sending a small wave of pain through my abdomen where a wound was supposed to be but now only a scar shows. Somehow I was healed when I returned from the throne room I visited. I asked Alc about Isaac and Kelby, he said they are nowhere to be seen but he does not worry as all the High Lords of Thyithran are on the lookout now that the borders around the Summer Court have been secured. I also learned that Malki was banished by Alc and now sleeps in the same place Hugan once inhabited, but unlike the God of Death, there is no way to wake the sleeping god. The queen of the human lands still rules, but she shows no sign of knowing what her husband was up to and is happy to negotiate with the High Lords about the continued ruling of her realm. Once I dry myself, I head to my bedchamber and find a beautiful gown of blue draped over the bed. I also notice two familiar figures smiling at me. Tilly runs over to me and wraps her arms around my middle. Alyssa stands watching, smiling at me.

"Oh, dear, you had us all worried. I am most pleased that you are all right. Now, let's get you dressed."

Tilly looks to Alyssa, and something passes between them.

"What?"

Both women smile and shake their heads.

"'You'll find out soon enough, dear, but for now let's worry about that hair of yours."

Half an hour passes with Tilly doing my hair and Alyssa fussing about my dress. My curiosity grows as the time wears on and soon Tilly has to pat my shoulder to keep me still.

"There we go, all done, and don't you look stunning."

Tilly slides the last pin into my hair, and I stare at my reflection. It's hard to believe that I was once a shadow in a world that should have feared me. I stand and thank the girls. Alyssa tells me that Alc is waiting in the garden. I nod and make my way down the familiar path. Double doors soon loom in front of me, and I push them open. My breath whooshes out of my lungs at the sight before me; stars twinkle so brightly above, and the moon illuminates the flowers growing in neat rows. Jasmine climbs the trestles of the house and the paved path glows under the light. Alc stands at the other end of the path under a spreading oak that has fairy lights twinkling between the branches. Fae light bobs up and down, bathing the area in more light. Once he sees me, his face lights up in a smile that stops my heart. The man I love stands before me clad in a black tunic and pants that are lined with silver. He again reminds me of the King of Night. I make my way over to him and he grabs my hands, squeezing them tight.

"You look absolutely stunning, Princess."

I smile,

"As do you. I must say the night suits you well."

He laughs and shakes his head.

"Well I hope so, otherwise my job as High Lord of the Night is wasted."

"I suppose it would be," my voice echoes around the garden and I smile; at peace.

Alc stares at me and before I can grasp what's happening, he gets down on his knees and holds my hands firmly in his. My heart stills and I feel tears prick at my eyelids.

"Keilee Whitewash. My mate, my soul bonded. Would you do the honour of becoming my wife, my Lady of the Night? I promise to cherish you for the rest of my days and to work with you for the centuries to come. I love you, Princess."

Tears I had no hope of holding back flood my face. The King of Night who kneels for no one is kneeling for me, his mate. Without hesitation, I speak the words in my heart.

"Alc, High Lord of Night, I would want nothing more than to become your wife. Your Lady of the Night. For you have given me a home and a family I love so dearly. I want to fight and laugh by your side for the rest of my days. I love you."

Alc stands and his lips crash onto mine. The world fades away and I wrap my hands in his hair, loving the feel of him pressed against me. He eventually breaks away when we both need air and the smile on his face is brighter than the stars above me.

"Oh, I forgot something."

He puts his hand into his pocket and pulls out a velvet box. Opening the lid, he shows a ring of sliver with sapphires and diamonds encasing it. I gasp at its beauty, and he slips it onto my ring finger. I hold it out to the light, relishing in the way it sparkles.

"It's gorgeous, thank you so much."

I lean forward and kiss him again and he smiles.

"It was my mother's and now it's yours."

I smile and hold it close to my chest. Alc grabs my other hand and leads me back inside, where Kai stands at the door apparently listening to the conversation. I laugh and Alc pushes him away.

"Busybody."

Kai laughs and replies,

"I was just making sure we didn't have to pull down the decorations if she rejected you."

Alc laughs and Naomi hits Kai on the shoulder and says something to him that I can't hear. Neron walks over and grasps Alc's hands.

"Congratulations, you will be a lucky man."

I smile at his kind words, and he smiles at me before he wraps his arms around me in an embrace. I laugh against him and hug him back.

"Not so big and scary now, are you?"

Neron laughs and pulls back.

"It was you that was the scary one."

I laugh and doubt his words, but before I can reply, Ianira clears her throat.

"As much as I love the celebrations, we must be on our way otherwise we will be late."

I stare at her confused and she continues, "Alc, didn't you tell her?" she sighs and shakes her head when he smirks.

"I was a little distracted, but yes, I do agree that we need to head off now."

I stare back and forth, confused.

Alc leans into me and whispers, "It is time you explored the real castle of the Night court."

And with that we disappear.

Chapter 20

Stars fill my vision before the sprawling towers and rooms of a castle filter into view. I'm struck by the beauty of it and Alc laughs from beside me.

"How come I never knew about this place?"

Alc laughs again,

"Because I never had time to show or tell you about it. But here it is my formal home."

I stare out at the view before me, lost in the beauty of it. A massive courtyard filled with climbing white roses twinkle under the moonlight and huge willow trees line a river running around the castle. The building itself is cut from the deepest black stone, like it was pulled from the sky itself. Windows glint with light from inside and I can see doors gleaming in front of me. A black peacock strolls across the grounds and I turn to Alc, who watches my expression with a smile.

"You have a black peacock? I didn't even know they existed."

His laugh wraps around me and I smile despite myself.

"They don't outside the Night Court. Now, we must hurry. People are waiting for us."

I nod, voicing my confusion,

"What is so important it couldn't wait till morning? And why are they waiting for us?'"

"You'll see soon enough, don't worry."

I trust him and we walk through the doors in silence. The

inside of the castle is striking, and everything matches the Night court. From the tapestries with the crescent moon to the marble flooring that stretches before us. Alc leads me down a hall to the left of a grand staircase. Double doors that reach from the floor to the ceiling loom in front of us and two guards stand stoic and silent. They bow when they see Alc approaching. One of them steps forwards.

"Your Majesties."

He pushes open the door and I freeze. A throne room twice the size of the one I fixed spreads before me. Two thrones are seated at the front draped in the colours of night. Pillars of white shoot for the ceiling that resembles the night sky. It even winks like stars are actually imprinted in it. Fae mill around but freeze when their eyes fall on us entering. Alc grips my arm and smiles at me, moving us through the watchful crowd.

"Relax, Princess, you are their Queen."

I glance at him and frown, but he looks away and we move quickly to the dais. Alc's inner party line the bottom and a figure stands at the top, smiling down at me. My chest constricts. Hugan. A smile spreads across my face and my body relaxes as we get closer to my father. Alc climbs the dais and I follow, making sure to keep my footing. Hugan steps forward and embraces me, he's warm and smells of orange blossoms and cedar.

"It is good to see you well, my child. Now, sit on the throne you earned, show the people their queen."

I frown and he grips my shoulder.

"It will all make sense soon."

I do as he says and Alc sits beside me on his own throne. I draw courage from his touch and from my family standing below me. Hugan steps forwards and addresses the crowd, who have all faced the throne, watching and waiting.

"Subjects, friends, and family of this court, it brings me great pleasure to introduce Alcinder, the High Lord and King of the Night Court, and his mate, our saviour and Queen, Keilee Whitewash of Glendale, The heir of both realms."

The crowd applaud us and someone whistles, drawing my attention to Cody and Tommas standing waving at me, Next to them stands Malik and the other High Lords. The former is waving like an idiot and bystanders look at the King of Winter with slightly startled expressions. My face breaks into a smile and I manage a small wave back before Hugan continues.

"We have gathered here tonight to crown our Queen and welcome her to the Court that rules the stars. Keilee Whitewash, would you please step forward."

Alc grips my hand and smiles, urging me on. I smile back and stand, walking over to where Hugan stands. He nods to the ground, and I kneel in front of him while he grabs a crown and a staff from a pillow beside him. The staff, I realise, is from the throne room where the scales resided. So is the crown. Hugan hands me the staff and then, with great gentleness, places the crown on my head. My body tingles and I look down at my hands, where the gold circlet glows brightly. Hugan's voice again booms, and I stand.

"All hail the Queen of Night, the Goddess of Balance and Power, Keilee Whitewash. Long may she reign."

The crowd repeats his words and I look over the people I now lead. A smile spreads across my face and I feel Alc come to a stand next to me, he leans over and kisses me on the temple and my smile stretches wider. I am home, with the male I love and the family I cherish. Isaac and Kelby may be missing, and there may still be threats surrounding me and my court, but I am no longer scared. For whatever arises, I will face it with my mate and my King. For the heir is no longer forgotten.

ALC

I watch as my Queen kneels before her father. Her dress flows around her, only adding to her beauty. Her eyes twinkle and the tether of our bond pulls at me. My shadows whisper to me and I smile. She is home. Wherever she may be is where I will be. My family stand proudly at the bottom of the dais and I can feel their love for her and their court. I get up and walk over to her and kiss her soft skin. She smiles up at me, causing my heart to speed. I have the rest of my life to cherish her and love her with everything I am. I will face whatever comes with my Queen beside me. For she is the Heir, and she is no longer forgotten. And she will never be again, not with me alive to remind her she is loved and cherished.